"An amazing piece of modern folklore. Allaun has crafted a story you won't want to stop reading. His gripping story made me feel like I was fighting right there alongside the coven. By weaving actual practice materials into his plot, Allaun has created a teaching-story that other practitioners are sure to glean a great deal of valuable information from. There's a real magic to creating lessons hidden beneath entertainment, and Allaun's work is a great example of exactly how this genre is meant to be written. I found myself remembering the spell sections I'd read earlier in the book without really even trying—a real feat for my distracted brain. *Whispers from the Coven* proves just how effective Allaun's skills in both magic and teaching really are."

—Brandon Weston, author of *Granny Thornapple's Book of Charms: Magic & Folklore from the Ozark Mountains*

"The underbelly of Chicago's haunted history oozes from this story. Learning sneaks in at the sides and sometimes catches you by surprise. Along with this [education], there is a satisfying sense of connectivity between the Witchcraft of different eras and locations in Christopher Allaun's latest novel."

—Lee Morgan, author of *Sounds of Infinity*

"Set in Chicago's shadows, where restless spirits abound, *Whispers from the Coven* invites us into the secret life of daring Windy City witches. Chris Allaun's enchanting tale, uniquely stitched together with historical events, urban legends, occult practices, and folk magic is a real page-turner."

—Cyndi Brannen, best-selling author of *Keeping Her Keys* and the *Entering Hekate's Magick and Mystery* series

WHISPERS FROM THE COVEN

Tales of Charms, Witchcraft & Lessons from the Spirit World

ABOUT THE AUTHOR

Chris Allaun has been studying witchcraft and paganism for over thirty years. He is an ordained minister with the Queer pagan temple, The Fellowship of the Phoenix. He is an initiate of Traditional Witchcraft and the OTO. He has spent over 20 years in the healing arts studying energy healing, massage therapy, and is a Reiki Master Teacher. Chris received his Master's Degree in Divinity from Chicago Theological Seminary.

He also teaches classes on witchcraft, spirit walking, energy healing, and magick. His goal is to bring the community together by connecting to the three worlds.

WHISPERS
from
the
COVEN

TALES OF CHARMS, WITCHCRAFT & LESSONS FROM THE SPIRIT WORLD

CHRIS ALLAUN

foreword by Devin Hunter

Chicago, IL

Paperback ISBN: 978-1-959883-68-5
Hardcover ISBN: 978-1-959883-80-7
Library of Congress Control Number on file.

Disclaimer: Crossed Crow Books, LLC does not participate in, endorse, or have any authority or responsibility concerning private business transactions between our authors and the public. Any internet references contained in this work were found to be valid during the time of publication, however, the publisher cannot guarantee that a specific reference will continue to be maintained. This book's material is not intended to diagnose, treat, cure, or prevent any disease, disorder, ailment, or any physical or psychological condition. The author, publisher, and its associates shall not be held liable for the reader's choices when approaching this book's material. The views and opinions expressed within this book are those of the author alone and do not necessarily reflect the views and opinions of the publisher.

Cover design by Wycke Malliway.
Interior by Mads Oliver.
Editing by Becca Fleming.

Published by:
Crossed Crow Books, LLC
6934 N Glenwood Ave, Suite C
Chicago, IL 60626
www.crossedcrowbooks.com

Printed in the United States of America.
IBI

This is a work of fiction based on historical events, but some dates have been changed for the purpose of storytelling. Characters are represented in fictitious scenarios based on historical events and with personalities ascribed to them by the author. Names of historical figures have been given to fictional characters, and their actions and statements do not necessarily reflect the attitudes and opinions of those historical figures.

OTHER BOOKS BY THE AUTHOR

The Black Book of Johnathan Knotbristle (Crossed Crow Books, 2023)

A Guide of Spirits: A Psychopomp's Manual For Transitioning The Dead To The Afterlife (Moon Books, 2021)

Otherworld: Ecstatic Witchcraft for the Spirits of the Land (Moon Books, 2020)

Upperworld: Shamanism and Magick of the Celestial Realms (Mandrake, 2019)

Deeper Into The Underworld: Death, Ancestors, and Magical Rites (Mandrake, 2017)

Underworld: Shamanism, Myth, and Magick (Mandrake, 2016)

CONTENTS

FOREWORD

There is something that gets lost in translation when you write works on the occult. Somehow, by attempting to explain the unexplainable we end up losing a part of the vital essence that makes the magick so potent in the first place. If you are an occultist driven by ecstatic experience and feeling, whittling the work down to digestible and repeatable steps can be soul-crushing. If you are an occultist who is naturally tuned in to the other worlds, it can be an almost impossible challenge altogether.

The art of conveying deeper magicks through the written word is challenging at best but receiving that magick through this medium is fraught with its own disadvantages, as well. As readers, often what is lost in the process of translating experience into words is so significant that we are only given a glimpse at what truly lies within our topic. This usually leaves us with more questions than answers and at times, with a false sense of security.

These problems don't seem to exist in the world of fiction and storytelling, however. We read stories as a means of transcendental exploration and pour ourselves into the trials of make-believe characters to escape reality. A good story can transport us as readers to far off places and a well-written one can be fully immersive, allowing the mind to fill in the details that would otherwise be lost in translation. There is something inherently magickal about both writing a story (fictional or otherwise) and reading one; something that pulls at the mind, body, and soul in a way that instruction alone cannot provide.

There are few authors who intuitively perceive the hedge between storytelling and metaphysical instruction, even fewer who dare to play in its foggy brilliance. Authors like Carlos Castaneda (*The Teachings of Don*

Juan), Michael Ende (*The Neverending Story*), and Robert Pirsig (*Zen and the Art of Motorcycle Maintenance*), to name a few, are all authors who have delivered deep spiritual and metaphysical teachings through contemporary storytelling. Their work explores the esoteric in ways that presents wisdom as truth, and readers are brought through acts of initiation as the characters progress along their journey. As they evolve, that piece of us that is with them evolves too, and through some grand act of contagion we are changed as a result. It is in the spirit of these authors, with an instinctual understanding of the magic found in storytelling, that Chris Allaun delivers *Whispers from the Coven*.

Unlike the other authors I mentioned, however, Chris has the unique goal of conveying specific magickal knowledge through intentional application. He blurs the lines of conventional instruction and plot to get his point across and uses real people, spirits, and events as his inspiration. He takes it even further by presenting this work to us as a journal, leaving the trappings of the hero's journey for another day, as he boldly delivers authentic magickal teachings in a way that has never been done before.

I would implore you to read each chapter twice. The first time as a curious observer who has stumbled on this book by happenstance. Let yourself have an experience as you explore the pages, as if you had truly come across them in the wild. It is from this vantage point that the spirits and magic can truly take hold in your life. During the second time through, approach the work as a student of the occult. Look for teaching hidden both gross and superficially in the text and move through the pages from a place of familiarity with the story presented therein. The spells are real, the spirits are real, the magick is real; it is merely up to you to discover their full components.

You will undoubtedly discover more on subsequent reads as a book like this has the ability to evolve with you because you are one of the characters. That, dear reader, is perhaps the most unique aspect of this book and is part of what makes it so special. Chris has constructed his magickal lessons in such a way that you cannot help but to be part of them. By flipping through these pages, you are actively engaging in a magickal act already in progress and by reading these words you have entered a hidden kingdom where reality is truly a construct.

A word of warning, however; don't be fooled into believing the magick stops when you close this book. If you are anything like me, you will find it continuing potently in your dreams and discover it occupying the spaces reserved for quiet thought. This book is both a thought-experiment and a crossroads of the spiritual and unseen. I say this not to inflate the value or to cause undue excitement in what you are about to read. Rather, I give you this warning because the work here is dynamic and persuasive; it has a lingering compulsion that is both haunting and invigorating, and not all occultists will know what to do with it. This isn't some common gem, however; *Whispers of the Coven* is a Rosetta stone that helps us discover that thing that is lost in translation, and that sort of thing sticks with you.

Chris consistently writes deep and meaningful work that continues to shape the landscape of contemporary occultism. He is always asking the tough questions and pushing boundaries, so it was no surprise that he would deliver such an unusual and timely work such as this. *Whispers of the Coven* is without question a very different kind of magickal text, but it is in that difference that we find what we will not and cannot find anywhere else.

—Devin Hunter, author of *Houseplant HortOCCULTure: Green Magic for Indoor Spaces* and *The Witch's Book of Power*

Introduction

THIS IS A BOOK OF SPELLS...

This book holds many spells of magic, power, and witchcraft. To truly understand a spell, it is better to know where it comes from, who wrote the spell, and why. Every spell has a story. If we look closely at the magic we are weaving, we can see the strands of energy that connect our hearts to the creative force of the cosmos. We can see how a spell was born and then use it for our own means.

This book of spells comes to us from a fictional Chicago coven of nine witches in 1947 who used their magic to face ghosts, monsters, and other spirits. But who are these witches? Who are the witches who wrote down their stories so they could share their magic with us?

Step into Chicago in the late 1940s. Most people see only the glitz and glamour in the bright lights of Chicago, but it is us witches who step out of these lights and into the shadows of the big city. It is the witch who dares to walk through the darkness where the lights of the city do not shine.

This is a book of magical spells, but it is also a book of magical stories. These pages contain the journal entries of the coven members and their journeys into Chicago's hidden magic. Each chapter contains the story of each witch and the spells they used to fight against the darkness...

I received a lot of great feedback for my previous title with Crossed Crow Books, *The Black Book of Johnathan Knotbristle*. I took a risk, and instead of writing a "how to" book of American Folk Witchcraft, I decided to conjure up the old ways of teaching magic...through storytelling. My teachers would sit their students down and weave stories of magic, spirits, ghosts, demons, and faeries. These stories captivated us and inspired us to practice our magical techniques and cast our spells. When it was published in 2023, I didn't know how it would be received. Would people enjoy the story? Or would they hate it because it was a non-traditional way of writing a magical book? As it turns out, many people wrote to me on social media telling me how much they loved the book and how they could see themselves in the adventures of Johnathan Knotbristle.

Would there be a sequel to *Johnathan Knotbristle*? I don't like to repeat myself. When I sat down to write *Whispers from the Coven,* I wasn't ready to create a direct sequel. I needed to do something a little different. However, I still wanted to incorporate storytelling as a teacher into this book. I grew up in Texas, where secretly—or not-so-secretly—Johnathan Knotbristle's story takes place. I wrote *Johnathan Knotbristle* with the fifteen-year-old young man in mind, just as I was a young witch living in Texas. So, I decided to write a book set where I live now…Chicago, Illinois. Oh, don't worry. Johnathan still speaks to me in spirit from time to time, and he has many more stories to tell. He is a storyteller, after all. You can't keep those ol' folk in Texas quiet fer noth'n.

Chicago, also known as the "Windy City," has a rich history of ghosts, demons, monsters, devils, and even vampires. Go on any ghost tour in Chicago, and you will learn of its haunted past. Between the people who immigrated to Chicago in the late 1800s, mobsters of the 1930s, and the first ever documented serial killer, Chicago is rich with tales of terror and the supernatural. Each of the haunted stories you will discover in this book is based on true events or recorded hauntings. I did, however, take some poetic license and change a few things, adding my own creative flair. The witches in this book are of my own creation, but the ghosts, monsters, and vampires they encounter are not.

Chicago has a deep, secret history. There are whispers from some of the old folk, people who have lived in Chicago their whole lives, who say that there is something "witchy" about Chicago. Is it the long winters of cold and darkness? Is it the genocide of the Ojibwe tribes who used to live here? Or is it the ghosts of those who were killed during prohibition by the Chicago mob? Maybe. Or maybe there is something darker that has been here for hundreds or even thousands of years. Perhaps there are ancient spirits who live deep in the subway tunnels of Chicago's "L" train. Spirits we do not understand.

I think that in any big, old city such as Chicago, you can find many people who have lived there over the years who will tell you a wealth of stories. Some stories are beautiful and inspirational, while other stories are tragic. Dreams were lost, loved ones were killed by crime, and tragic accidents happened because there were no safety laws that could have prevented the many deaths. We cannot forget about the ones who came to the big city looking for a better life, only to lose their lives to killers and monsters. Remember, the easiest way for a killer to hide is to hide in plain sight.

As you read these stories, put yourself in the shoes of the witches. They have both strengths and weaknesses, just like we do. Understand that they tried their best to do the right thing by their coven. Just like us, they learn through their successes and their failures. I ask that you see the humanity in these nine witches as they tell their stories.

And yes! The spells are real. One of the spells came to me as I was writing on my computer. One day, I was working on this manuscript, focusing on creating the spells you are about to read, and just like that—it manifested! Yes, I believe these spells work for you because of the power they hold. They are powerful because the stories you are about to read create a link between the subconscious mind, your desire, and the power to manifest your magic. Storytelling opens the gate to the creative force of the mind, the spell brings that creative force into the universe, and your desire manifests the spell on the physical plane.

Storytelling is a spell.

March 25, 1947
Day of Mars. Moon in Taurus.

I have awoken from a dream. My dream was woven with spirits, dark magic, and horrible things. A powerful dark force is coming. My coven is not ready. If that dark force were to come now, to come today, we would be in terrible danger. We must be ready. The dark is coming soon.

Allow me to introduce myself. My name is Patricia Glasspool, and I am the leader of the Lincoln Park Coven. It was my idea to give us this name because, well, we perform our rituals in a neighborhood of Chicago called Lincoln Park. The circle is of nine, including myself. We have been working together for many years. We perform acts of magic and witchcraft with the aid of the gods, the ancestors, and the spirits around us. We work in secret. There are not too many who know that we are witches. Now that the war is over, we understand that we must not create suspicion of who we are and our motives. I've been keeping up with the rumblings in politics. Everyone is suspected of being a communist. We cannot allow suspicion to be placed upon us.

I fear that the spirits are warning me tonight. There is something coming for us. Why, I do not know. At least not yet. After the dream, I performed astral work to ask the gods what I must do to prepare my circle. I was told by the gods that I must increase the power of the circle by performing a spell on the full moon. A spell to call upon the Devil himself to help us increase our magic.

The book that you are holding is our story. The story of the Lincoln Park Coven. I do not know what will happen as you turn these pages. It is my hope that you will learn of us and our magic. That you will understand that we are doing the best we can. The candle before me is flickering with no draft or wind. Spirits are present. They must be listening.

Prologue

⚡ THE DEVIL'S SPELL OF POWER ⚡

April 5, 1947
Day of Saturn. Full Moon in Libra.

After I had the terrible dream of the darkness, I contacted the other eight members of the coven and told them of my fears. I told them of the dream. As I feared, a few of the other members had a similar dream. They dreamed that the darkness was coming for us, and we were unprepared. James had the dream that several of us died. I do not know why I did not see death. Perhaps, as a leader, that is what I fear most. The death of someone I love. Perhaps I chose not to see death. Or perhaps James was able to see what I could not.

I have learned over the years that, as a coven leader, there are certain things I must understand. Each one of our coven members has certain gifts and abilities that I may not have, or perhaps their abilities are more powerful than my own. When they give me counsel, I must listen. Be discerning, yes, but I must take heed of what each member has to offer. Even those of us who are newer to witchcraft have skills that others do not have. Each of us has magic to teach the others.

Each of us agreed that we must call upon the Devil so that he may help us increase our power. The funny thing about the Devil, he works in his own ways. Some of his ways are powerful, yes, but the lessons may be terrible. On the other hand, the lessons may be beautiful as well. One never knows. This is why, as we walk upon the crooked road, we walk in fear and dread. After much conversation, the coven agreed to the spell. I forewarned each and every person that once the spell is put in motion, it will be difficult to ask the Devil to take back his magic. He can be tricky at times. Even when you beg for his mercy, he sees things that we, as humans, cannot. He sees our strengths. He sees our weaknesses…and he will do whatever he needs to grant us the power that we seek. But, as with all things, there is a cost.

THE SPELL OF POWER

Items Needed:
- One candle for each person in the circle. For our coven, it is nine in all
- An incense of myrrh, horehound, dried pomegranate seeds, and wormwood
- Dirt from a churchyard
- Dirt from a crossroads
- A small item you cherish to be given in sacrifice
- Small bowl for the sacrifice
- A skull of human, deer, or goat (replicas are fine)
- A white, red, or black candle placed upon the skull

1. Place the dirt from a churchyard in a straight line. Then, take the dirt from the crossroads and make another line, creating an "X" with the churchyard dirt and the crossroads dirt.

2. Place the skull in the center of the dirt.

3. Place the candle upon the skull. Light it and say: *"I call upon you, Devil, horned one of the crossroads. He of the cloven hoof. He of the great mystery. Liberator of humankind. Come to us as we call upon your great power. Your magic."*

4. Each person sits in the circle either on the floor or upon chairs. Light your white candle and place it around the cross of dirt and the skull. Know that this is your essence. This is the energy that you give to the Devil to transform and change. As you place your candle in front of the image of the Devil, say: *"Devil. Horned God of the witches. I give to you my essence so that you may grant me the holy power of witchcraft. Devil. Come to us. Shape us. Change us."*

5. Sit in silence and meditate on the power that the Devil will give to you.

6. Take out the cherished item that you intend to give to the Devil as a sacrifice. Think about what this item means to you and what it represents. Think about how nothing can be given without a valued sacrifice. When you are ready, place the item in a bowl and place it next to the skull.

7. The leader of the group then says: *"Devil, we come to you this night to ask that you grant us the power of witchcraft. Allow us to have mastery over the power of life and death. Of healing and cursing. Of man and animal. Of light and dark. Devil, grant us the power that we seek this night."*

8. Everyone then says: *"Grant us the power that we seek!"*

9. The leader says: *"We ask you to give us this power in fear and dread!"*

10. Everyone says: *"In fear and dread!"*

11. Once the magic is given to the Devil, you may perform the housel or simply share wine and bread, leaving some as an offering to the Devil.

12. Take the bowl of cherished offerings and place them at a crossroads.

I do not know how the magic will manifest. I do not know what the Devil has in store for us. I have been a witch for many years, and I cannot say what will happen to us next. The Devil is known as a trickster for a reason. What I do know is that the magic he teaches us will be powerful. I am both excited and filled with dread. What must we endure to receive the powers that we claim? Will what we sacrifice be worth it? According to my dream, what we sacrifice on our journey ahead will keep us safe and alive. We must be ready.

It is important that we share in our magic. After the ritual to the Devil, we drew lots to see who would take the book home with them first and journal their own stories. Once everyone has written down their magical story, we will place all of our magic together. It is my hope that we will gain the magic in enough time to stop the approaching darkness.

Patricia Glasspool

A GHOST IN LINCOLN PARK

April 20, 1947
Day of Sol. Moon in Aries.

This is Sandy Dorey. I'm not sure that we are supposed to write our last names in this book, but Patricia says that we shouldn't worry. The book will be kept safe with the coven. I suppose I am the first to write in the book. I'm not sure why she chose me. I drew the first lot, so I am guessing that my story should fill the pages first. I am sure there is a magical reason. Maybe as we all fill the pages with our stories, then we might be able to see a pattern or some logic. Some reason. Patrica said that when we write our story, we should do our best to make it a story. Like a novel or something. I'm not much of a writer, but I will do my best.

I have been with the Lincoln Park Coven for a few years now. I think I am one of the most inexperienced of the witches here. Don't get me wrong, I know a lot. I'm a fast learner. Patricia is a good teacher, and she is patient with me. I think she's patient with everyone. But, since I am the youngest of the coven, at age twenty-five, she is more patient with me than the others, I think. I joined the coven about three years ago, and I have been learning as quickly as I can. Patricia says I shouldn't worry about rushing through my witch training. "You can't rush magic," she says. In fact, she says that a lot. I just want to be as experienced as everyone else.

Patricia's dream is kind of scary. I mean, I joined the coven because I have had many experiences with ghosts, astrology, and a lot of other occult stuff. I like how she teaches us how to become more psychic. That's my favorite part of the coven. Well, that and the spells. Now, though, Patricia has this dream of someone, or something, trying to hurt us. I've learned that there's more scary stuff out there than just people. There are lots of scary things. When Patricia dreams, it always comes true. Always. She said that one of the reasons she found me and asked me to join the coven was because she dreamed about me. Patricia dreamed of my name and my age and even knew where my family was from. It's intriguing, but it can also be scary. One of these days, I want to be as psychic as Patricia. Or at least have dreams that come true like hers do. One day.

After we did the ritual to summon the power of the Devil, I took this book home and put it on the dresser. I live in Lincoln Park, not too far from Patricia. We usually have rituals at her apartment. When it's warmer in the year, we will do rituals outside, but we have to be discrete. I can't imagine what would happen if some police officer strolled up as we were chanting in the park by Lake Michigan. If we do go outside for ritual, we usually drive out of the downtown area and find a patch of woods somewhere. It's so exciting when we are able to do that. Being outside is the kind of witchcraft that makes me feel connected to nature. I remember reading a book one time that said the Puritans in Salem thought that the Devil was in the woods somewhere and the good people should stay far away from the natural world. Because it was sinful. I like the woods. Maybe because it's sinful. Or maybe because I can block out the world. Living close to downtown Chicago, there's a lot of traffic noise. So much noise. The woods hide us from the world so we can do our magic.

I work in an office not too far from my apartment in Lincoln Park. It's easy to get home. I just have to walk through the park, and I can be home in no time at all. The men at the office are saying that I shouldn't walk home alone. Maybe I shouldn't. I don't feel unsafe. One of the good things about being a witch is that you have a heightened sense of awareness. I'm aware of everything around me. Sometimes, when I'm walking home through the park alone, it's really dark. I can hear dogs barking, animals running around, and sometimes, the faint voices of other people enjoying a walk home. The path through the park is lit by lamplight, but that's not how I like to walk home. I like walking in the dark cover of the trees. It's not the same as when the coven drives out to the woods, but here in Chicago, it's the closest that we are going to get.

I walk home through that park almost every single day. I'm usually alone with my thoughts and the cold, damp April air. Yes, here in Chicago, April might as well be winter. It can snow in April, but usually it's cold and rainy. When I'm walking under those trees, I pretend that they are trying to protect me from the cold. Patricia says that trees are living beings with spirits of their own. So maybe they are. Or maybe I'm crazy and enjoy making up a good story.

Last night, something odd and mysterious happened. I was walking through the trees in the park, and I saw a man standing under the trees holding an old-fashioned lantern. It seemed like an odd thing because it would have been better if he had a flashlight to light his way. A lantern seemed old-fashioned. I have to admit I was curious as to what that strange man was doing out in the park after dark with an old lantern. I walked over to where he was standing.

He looked up at me and said, "Hello, young lady. What brings you out in the dark? A young lady should not be unescorted."

I couldn't help but smile. "'Hello' yourself. I'm coming home from work, and I am curious to know what a man would be doing walking around a park with an old lantern."

The man smiled back at me. He was dressed in an old-fashioned gray suit. "My name is Mr. Young. What is your name, young lady?"

"Sandy," I said. "Sandy Dorey."

"What a charming name, Miss Sandy Dorey."

I could tell that Mr. Young was charming. He had a handsome smile, and there was something about him that I was drawn to. Maybe that's why they call a man charming. Because you can't help being drawn to him. "What are you doing out here, anyway?"

"I'm having a wonderful stroll on a brisk April evening," Mr. Young said. He looked at me curiously. "Would you allow me to escort you through the park?"

Mr. Young seemed nice enough. I didn't see any reason to think he had any ill intentions. "I don't see why not."

Mr. Young walked next to me, holding his lantern. The light from that old lantern helped me see somewhat, but I kept thinking a flashlight would have been better. He took a deep breath, smelling the park air. "Do you know the history of this park?"

"The history?" I asked.

"Oh, my dear, this old park was at one time a cemetery," Mr. Young said. "But because the graves were so close to the shoreline of the lake, the coffins would sometimes rise. Many of the corpses would be exposed. So, they decided to move the graveyard."

What a curious thing to say. I wondered why Mr. Young wanted to tell me that. He is a mystery, indeed.

"I did not know that."

We walked for a while, and once we arrived at the Ulysses S. Grant monument, Mr. Young stopped. "This, my dear, is where I must say goodnight. Will you be alright getting the rest of the way home?"

"I'll be alright," I told him. With that, we said goodnight, and I walked the rest of the way home.

The next night, I strolled through the park as I usually do, and in the same exact spot as the night before, there stood Mr. Young with his curious lantern. He was a charming man and seemed harmless enough. I couldn't walk by without saying hello. I stepped over to where he was and greeted him. He once again asked if he could escort me through the park. This night was a bit warmer than the night before, but there was still a coldness in the air. Not the type of cold that usually comes in spring, but the kind of cold that you feel down to your bones. The kind of cold that tells you the spirits are around. Maybe Mr. Young's story about Lincoln Park once being a cemetery was starting to get to me. Patricia says I need to stop second-guessing my intuition and listen when my senses are trying to tell me something. But still, it was a nice night.

It wasn't too long before we came upon a small gray stone building surrounded by a little black fence. Mr. Young stopped and looked adoringly at the stone building. "This is a wonderful piece of history."

I was a bit confused as to what the attraction was to this little building. It was no bigger than a shed, but looking at it, it was something grand. "What is this?"

"This, my dear, is the last remembrance of the old Chicago Cemetery. This is the Couch Mausoleum," Mr. Young said. "You see, all of the other tombstones, plaques, and mausoleums were torn down or moved. But not this one."

What a strange thing to have an old little mausoleum in the middle of Lincoln Park. I've never noticed it before. Well, I suppose it was here way before it was a park. "Why didn't they move this mausoleum as well?"

"That is the great mystery." Mr. Young seemed excited about this little place. "Some say the Couch family refused to allow it to be torn down. Some say that it was too expensive to move. Others say that the spirits will not allow anyone to move the old building."

I stood there for a moment, considering what Mr. Young had told me. How odd that the city of Chicago moved all the headstones and mausoleums in the old Chicago Cemetery but left the Couch tomb.

I said goodnight to Mr. Young and made my way home. I couldn't stop thinking about this. There had to be a reason that didn't move the old tomb. Why spend money and resources moving the entire cemetery except that one small building? I'm wondering what that reason could be.

That night, I had a dream. In the dream, I was again in Lincoln Park, standing in front of the Couch Mausoleum. Then I heard a voice.

"Release me."

In the dream, the voice was haunting and seemed to be in pain. It seemed to be coming from inside the mausoleum. *"Release me,"* the voice said again.

"How?" I asked the voice.

"Release me."

Then I woke up. Is there a spirit trapped inside the mausoleum?

If a spirit needed to be freed, then I was going to need some help. I've only been with the coven for a short time. I've never released a spirit before. Truth be told, I don't have a lot of experience with spirits in general. I'm going to need someone to help me.

The next day, I called my coven mate, Kenneth. Kenneth had a lot more experience than me. Maybe not as much experience as most in the coven, but he certainly had more experience than I did. He was good with spirits.

In our coven meetings, I've seen him call up the dead and many other spirits. Patricia trains everyone in all sorts of magic, but Kenneth has a gift for calling up the spirits. More so than I do, anyway.

I could have asked the coven to help me, but our next meeting is the full moon, and that is weeks away. If there's a trapped spirit in the tomb, I wanted to help release it now.

When I first told Kenneth about the voice, he was a little uneasy. "A trapped spirit in an old mausoleum does not sound like something we should mess around with," Kenneth said to me.

"What if it's a lost spirit who needs our help?" I asked.

Kenneth looked puzzled. "Are mausoleums somewhere where spirits get trapped?"

"I don't know," I said. "Aren't you the expert on spirits?"

"Hardly," he said. "We should wait for the coven."

I wasn't convinced that we should wait for the entire coven. Then, there would be debates between all of us on what we should do. Endless debates. "We have free agency," I said. "We don't have to wait for the coven to help the spirits."

Kenneth paused for a moment to consider what I was saying. I knew he wanted to help me. I'm guessing his curiosity was piqued, as was mine. We both stayed silent for a few minutes.

Finally, Kenneth had an idea. "Before we do anything else, let's do some astral work."

"Ok. What kind of astral work?"

"We should go into a trance and astral project to the park and speak with the spirits there."

That was a good idea. I've never astral projected to a tomb before. This sounded like it would be a lot of fun.

April 23, 1947
Day of Mercury. Moon in Gemini

SPELL TO PLACE YOURSELF INTO A TRANCE

Items Needed:
No items are needed, but you may add incense, music, drumming, or anything that will help you slip into a trance. Frankincense and myrrh are good for incense. Sandalwood, as well.

1. Sit in a chair or lie down comfortably.

2. You can light your incense or play music if you'd like.

3. Begin by relaxing the entire body. Mentally tell your body to relax from your toes up to your head. Take several deep breaths as you do this.

4. Take three deep, quick breaths and one long, slow exhale. Quickly: Inhale, inhale, inhale. Slowly: Exhale. Do this several times.

5. Next, take one long inhale and one long exhale.

6. Follow this with quick inhales and exhales. Quickly inhale and quickly exhale several times. Repeat steps 4–6 until your trance is achieved.

SPELL TO ASTRAL PROJECT

Items Needed: No items needed.

1. Once you have placed yourself into a trance, you may astral project to anywhere you would like to go.

2. Close your eyes and take a few deep breaths. Understand that you are now able to leave your body in spirit.

3. Take a few more deep breaths. With your mind's eye, imagine that you are opening your eyes. Make sure you do not open your physical eyes. Only visualize yourself doing so.

4. Again, with your powers of visualization, see yourself lift your spirit arms. Now, place them back in your body.

5. See yourself lift each of your spirit legs. Place them back into your body.

6. Once you are comfortable releasing your spirit from your body, you can fly into the air or instantly astral project anywhere you want to go.

7. Visualize yourself getting up out of your body and imagine that you are flying to your destination. If you'd like, you can simply think of the place where you want to go, and you will arrive there instantly.

8. Once your astral journey is over, you can visualize yourself coming back to where your body is. Then lie down back into your body.

When Patricia taught me how to astral project, I asked her, "How do we know we are really astral projecting and not fooling ourselves with our own imagination?"

Her answer was straightforward and made sense. She said, "Energy, including the energy of our astral body, is shaped by imagination. Even if we are not actually astral projecting our whole body, only our consciousness, it really doesn't matter. It's not 'how' we get there, but rather 'did it work and did we obtain our goal?'"

This was brilliant to me. I found an old book many years ago that tried to explain astral projection, but it didn't make sense to me. But Patricia's explanation did.

As I astral projected to the Couch Mausoleum, Kenneth guided me from the physical plane. Even though I was astrally out of my body, I could still hear Kenneth's voice. I guess because a little of our consciousness is always in our body, even when we are dreaming or flying around in spirit. I'm guessing we can't completely leave our bodies because we need proper brain function to sustain us. It also helps to know that you can hear what's around you. I'd hate to have my apartment on fire and not know it!

"Are you there?" I heard Kenneth's voice say.

"Yes, I'm here outside the mausoleum." Not only could I hear Kenneth physically, but I could speak to him physically, too.

It's an odd sensation, and sometimes, my mind goes back and forth between my physical body and my astral body when I speak, but I manage to stay focused in the astral nonetheless.

"Tell me," Kenneth said, "what do you see?"

It was daytime still, and the park looked as normal as it ever did. I could see people strolling through the park. No one had a clue that I was there. "I see people. I can hear birds chirping."

"Focus on the energy of the mausoleum. What energies do you see?"

I looked around for some kind of magical barrier or some astral sigils, but I didn't see anything like that. "Nothing. I see nothing."

"Nothing?" Kenneth was surprised I didn't see anything. "Look again."

"I see nothing," I said again. As soon as I said that, I had an overwhelming feeling of dread. Like everything in my being wanted to leave this place. Then, at the doorway of the mausoleum, I saw him. Mr. Young. I saw Mr. Young guarding the doorway of the tomb. Was it him? Was Mr. Young keeping some poor, lost spirit prisoner?

Mr. Young saw me. He looked at me dead in the eye and said, "My dear girl, what are you doing here?"

I stood there speechless, not knowing what to say. What do I do?

"Be gone from this place!" Mr. Young waved his lantern at me, and I awoke from my astral projection.

Kenneth helped me up from the floor. "What happened?"

"Mr. Young," I said. "I think it's him. He's holding the spirit prisoner."

It had to be him. Why else would a strange man like Mr. Young be strolling through Lincoln Park with a lantern every night? He seemed sweet, though. I've known men to be less than desirable. Lots of men I know in Chicago are after one thing. And if that's not what they are after, then they are just trying to swindle you out of something. But Mr. Young seemed so nice. Maybe that was the scam. Maybe that odd man wants everyone to believe he's sweet when, in reality, he's an evil magician.

"Why would he be holding a spirit prisoner?" I could see that Kenneth was having a hard time believing what I was saying. "For what purpose?"

I remembered that, not too long ago, Patrica had told us that there are dark magicians who capture spirits, especially spirits of the dead, and command them to do their bidding. She said that our human psychic abilities can only take us so far and that a magician needed the aid of the spirits to become more powerful. "Maybe he wants to use the dead for power. Maybe he's trapping spirits so they can do his bidding."

"Don't you think that sounds far-fetched?" Kenneth looked at me like I should know better. Maybe he was right. Maybe I should know better, but my curiosity was getting the better of me. Besides, if a spirit is trapped by an evil magician, wouldn't it be our job as witches to free them? Kenneth saw the look on my face. Determination. I was going to free the spirit, and there wasn't any way he was going to talk me out of it.

"Sandy." Kenneth's voice became stern. "This isn't a good idea."

Kenneth didn't like to take risks. He is one of those people who likes the same routine day in and day out. Never doing anything different. Never changing. As wonderful as he is with the spirits, I wonder sometimes if his hesitation to experiment with magic and do anything new is keeping him from being more powerful. He only has a few more years in the coven than I do, but he could be one of the most powerful. He second-guesses himself too much. He holds himself back.

I was not going to give up on that poor, locked-away spirit now. Not when I knew that I had the power to help them. "Are you coming with me, or am I doing this alone?"

"You're going alone," Kenneth said. "There's no way in hell I'm going to do magic like that."

"Fine," I said sharply. "I'll just take my chances alone in a park. At night. In the dark. With spirits trying to get me."

I grinned as I saw the expression on Kenneth's face. He looked like a man stuck between a rock and a hard place. Does he help the young girl, or does he leave her to fend for herself? Kenneth didn't say anything for a long time. I could tell he was thinking about it. I'm guessing he was also thinking how he could talk me out of it. Kenneth has known me for a long time, and he knows there's no talking me out of anything. "Fine," he said at last, "I'll help you. But you have to follow my lead. You can't go doing things on your own."

I knew he would finally give in. "Agreed."

We agreed to meet late the next night. It was 2:00 a.m., so maybe it was actually early in the morning. We decided it would be better to work in the darkest hours so we wouldn't be disturbed. There weren't many people walking through Lincoln Park late at night, but still, we needed to be careful. We didn't want anyone being a busybody and distracting us from our magic. Worse, we didn't want anyone flagging down a police officer. I can't imagine what would happen if my boss found out I was a witch. He probably would think I've lost my mind and have me committed to an asylum.

We gathered the supplies that we needed and headed to the park. The night seemed darker than it usually did. When we passed the Ulysses S. Grant monument, there was something foreboding about it. Every time I pass the monument, I feel like the spirit of Grant is protecting Chicago from danger. That's the thing about statues. If there isn't already a spirit in there, then I think we create a spirit with our thoughts. You know, the more we think about Grant protecting us through that statue, the more energy builds up, and eventually, it becomes real. But that night, it looked as though Ulysses S. Grant was looking away from the park. Maybe he was. Maybe Ulysses S. Grant didn't want to have anything to do with the witchcraft that we did that night. Maybe there was a reason he turned away from us.

It's a funny thing, traipsing through the park, planning on doing witchcraft in the dead of night. Your adrenaline is going, and your senses are heightened. Kenneth and I were keenly aware of every sound our feet made on the ground.

We heard every stick that broke because of our footsteps. We heard birds moving in the trees above. But the streets around the park were silent. There wasn't a soul on the road—no one. I don't think I have ever been in Lincoln Park in the middle of the night like this. So, maybe the silence isn't so unusual. Maybe this is what Chicago is like at 2:30 a.m., or maybe the spirits are keeping quiet tonight.

When we finally arrived at the Couch Mausoleum, I felt a heaviness at the pit of my stomach.

Normally, the tomb was just a gray brick building. But that night, I felt like I was looking at an ancient haunted house. More than that, I felt like the little building was alive. Like it had its own personality. Its own thoughts, feelings, and experiences. Tonight, the mausoleum seemed to be looking at my heart. I have to ask myself, was the tomb happy to see me, or was I its enemy? I'm hoping the building knew what I was there for.

We walked around the mausoleum, looking for the door that led inside. You see, mausoleums are locked up. Maybe the family would have the key, or maybe the office of the cemetery would have a spare copy, but for this mausoleum, neither of these things was true. The Chicago Cemetery was closed long ago, and the Couch family had no one who remembered where to find the key. When we found the entrance of the little building, all was silent except for a lighted lantern that was left upon the steps of the tomb. Mr. Young was here. Was he giving us a warning?

We brought a satchel of witchcraft supplies with us. We took everything out of the bag. I could see that Kenneth was really nervous. "Are you still sure you want to do this?"

Kenneth never gives up. I was assured as I was ever going to be. "Of course. The spirit needs us."

Kenneth looked around to make sure no one was there. Even though this was the second largest city in America, at 2:45 a.m., I was confident it would be quiet and we would be left alone. "We should hurry."

"Didn't Patricia say that we can't rush magic?" I said to him, being a wise guy.

"In this case," Kenneth said nervously, "let's make an exception."

"Okay, okay!" I tried not to laugh. Boy, sometimes men sure aren't the knights in shining armor you want them to be.

Kenneth got quiet and looked around. I could tell he wasn't looking with his eyes. He was looking around with his psychic senses. He felt something. "Sandy?"

I was really curious about what he was feeling. "What is it?

"I'm feeling a spirit presence."

"Good or bad?" Shit, what was it he was feeling?

"I don't know," he said. This was not good. Was something there? Was something warning us to stay away?

I had an idea. I thought it was a good idea, but I knew that Kenneth was not going to like it. "What if we astral project inside the tomb? You know, to see it for ourselves."

Kenneth looked at me blankly, and I could see that he was trying to find a good reason not to do that. I was delightfully surprised that he agreed. "Ok, but let's do it quickly."

Standing in front of the gray door, we held hands as we closed our eyes and took a few deep breaths, easing ourselves into a trance. Both of us, at the same time, visualized ourselves stepping out of our bodies and walking into the mausoleum. It's an odd thing standing up while your spirit leaves your body.

As soon as we walked inside the tomb, we saw it: a poor, captured spirit trapped in what looked like a cage of energy. It was so small. Like a dog's cage.

The spirit inside the little cage was clothed in a tattered gray cloak. It didn't look like much of a spirit at all. Some poor, helpless figure who had been there for who knows how long. What a pathetic-looking thing.

"Be gone from here!" We heard a voice say from inside the tomb. It was Mr. Young. He quickly walked toward us, shaking his lantern. "You cannot take this spirit away from here!"

We were startled and jumped back. I have never been harmed by a spirit in the astral, but I didn't want to take that chance. The whole time, I thought that maybe Mr. Young was some evil spirit who trapped a spirit of the dead here in this place. This used to be a graveyard, after all. We had to help the poor thing. If witches are not meant to help the spirits, then what is our magic for?

Mr. Young swung his lantern at us again, and this time, it pushed us out of the mausoleum and forced our spirits back into our bodies. We both opened our eyes at the same time

"What the fuck?!" Kenneth yelled.

"We have to help the poor spirit," I pleaded with Kenneth. "It's being held prisoner."

Kenneth gathered his wits and, now more than ever, agreed to help me release the spirit.

A SPELL TO RELEASE A SPIRIT FROM BONDAGE

Items Needed:

- Three white candles
- Three black candles
- Frankincense and myrrh
- Charcoal for incense
- Incense holder
- Hexagram of Solomon on parchment or paper
- A small mirror

1. If the spirit you are releasing is in an object, place the object on the ground or a table. If the spirit is trapped inside a building or larger structure, then the spell will be performed outside of the building.

2. Place three black candles in a triangle with the apex pointing away from the object or the entrance of the building or structure.

3. Place three white candles in a triangle with the apex touching the apex of the black candle triangle. The white and black triangles should look like an hourglass.

4. Place the small mirror in the center of the black triangle of candles.

5. Place the Hexagram of Solomon in the white triangle of candles.

6. Call upon the spirits, gods, and/or ancestors you work with. You can say: *"I call upon (spirit/god/ancestor) to help me release the trapped spirit, named (name of trapped spirit). Lend us your powers of the spirit realm this night."*

7. Take a deep breath and connect to the spirit that is trapped. Visualize the spirit the best you can. Visualize your spirit helpers as well. See them giving you magical energy.

8. Imagine that the hourglass of candles works like a dropper. The white candles push the magical power of the Hexagram of Solomon into the black candles. Then, the Hexagram releases the trapped spirit. Then, the mirror reflects or pushes the spirit out of the container or building and into the triangle of white candles.

9. When you feel enough magical power built up, take your hands and push energy into the white triangle of candles, saying: *"(Name of spirit), with the power of the spirits and the power of my magic, I release you from this bondage."*

10. Visualize the energy you send as white energy. See the Hexagram of Solomon as a golden light that represents the power of the divine. Then say: *"By the power of witchcraft and the power of the spirits, you are free from your bonds!"*

11. Visualize chains or bonds around the spirit breaking. Then, see the mirror reflect or push the spirit into the white triangle.

12. Once the spirit is in the white triangle of candles, say: *"(Name of spirit), you are now free from your bonds. Go now in peace."*

Kenneth and I performed the spell just like it is written here. I had the idea of the dropper, and Kenneth helped me figure out how to create a spell with that. Kenneth is pretty good at making up spells when we need them. I'm not as good as he is, but I'm learning. We placed the two triangles of candles at the entrance of the mausoleum. The base of the black triangle was at the door, and the apex faced away from the entrance. We called upon the gods and spirits of our coven and visualized them sending us power. I could feel the power of the spirits in my body. At that moment, I felt like I was the most powerful witch in the world. In my short time with the coven, I have found that my spells work the best when I feel the power. When I'm connected, I feel like magic itself. The trick is being able to feel that way when I want to.

The magic rushed into and through me and then into the triangle of candles. I could feel the bonds of magic that trapped the spirit begin to loosen. I could also feel the power of Mr. Young working against our magic. I closed my eyes and breathed in more of the power of our spirits. Then we heard a whooshing sound. I opened my eyes, and there he was. The trapped spirit in a gray, tattered cloak stood before us in the center of the white candles. His face was unclear. I couldn't really make out a face at all. Just blackness where the face should be. Was the spirit looking at me? Did he know what had happened to him?

Kenneth and I stood there for what seemed to be forever and just looked at the spirit. No one said a word for a long time. The park was silent. There was no sound. No movement. Nothing. Just Kenneth and I trying to understand this spirit who stood in the center of the white triangle of candles. A gust of wind came up on us and blew out the candles. The gray-cloaked spirit faded into the shadows and vanished.

We heard a rustling in the mausoleum. I could have sworn I heard the sound of a squeaky door open. When we looked back at the door of the tomb, it was closed and locked just as it always was. But in front of it stood Mr. Young. He had a smug look on his face as he walked away from us, holding his lantern. Strangely, he started to whistle. It was a tune I had never heard before. The tune was dark and otherworldly. He stopped for a moment and turned to look at us one last time. "I must thank you, my dear; I could not have released the spirit without you. Well done."

And with that, Mr. Young was gone.

Kenneth and I stood looking at each other for a long time. I think we were tricked. I think. I'm not sure what had happened. Mr. Young was the evil spirit keeping the tattered cloaked spirit trapped...right? Then why would he say that? Why would he thank us for releasing the spirit? Unless...unless that was the intention all along. Shit. What did we...what did I just do?!

Without saying too much at all, Kenneth and I packed up our magical supplies and started walking home. Maybe it was all in my head, but as we walked through the park, I could feel something shift. Earlier in the night, the park felt like energy was absent. Like all the energy had left the park, and all that was left was a void. Now, instead, it felt like a thousand eyes were watching us. We were both tired after the events of the evening, but we walked through the park as fast as we could. I wanted to know what Kenneth was thinking. Was he blaming me? Did we accidentally release something? Kenneth was a hard man to read, so I didn't say anything further about it.

The further we walked through the park, the more I felt like someone was watching us. Not just one person but many people. Maybe hundreds. I was still in a mild trance from our magic, so my psychic senses were heightened. Normally, I would say I don't have a lot of psychic power. There were several witches in our coven who were more psychic than I could ever be. But right at this moment, because of the trance, I guess, or maybe because of our witchcraft, I was sensing something. Something all around us. I looked over into the darkness under a few trees, and I saw what looked to be people walking toward us. I had a sinking feeling in my stomach, and I stopped in my tracks. "Is someone over there?"

"Over where?" Kenneth asked.

"There," I pointed to the darkness to where I thought I saw people standing.

Kenneth looked over in the distance to see what I was talking about. He saw them, too. "Those aren't people." He took a breath and realized what they were. "At least not living people."

"Ghosts?" Were those people really ghosts? Were they really the spirits of the dead?

"Didn't you say that this place used to be a graveyard?" Kenneth's color drained from his face.

We looked around the park and noticed that more ghost-like apparitions were forming around us. "Yes, but they moved the corpses to other cemeteries."

Kenneth's voice was nervous and, dare I say, scared. "I don't think they moved all of them."

We raced home as fast as we could. We were witches, and Kenneth knew way more about witchcraft and ghosts than I did, and even he was nervous.

On the way home, he said that something felt off. The spirits we saw didn't feel like the ordinary ghostly haunting. Something is not right. He told me later that, usually, when a spirit comes back to a graveyard, they are peaceful unless they have unfinished business or they were victims of a crime or something. He said that these spirits were angry. Something had happened to cause them to be angry. But now the question is, why is it that no one, especially none of us witches, has seen any ghosts in Lincoln Park? That is, not until we released the gray, tattered spirit, who I'm calling "the Shadow Man."

April 26, 1947
Day of Saturn. Moon in Cancer.

I have just awoken from a dream.

In the dream, I was walking through Lincoln Park, but it must have been in the 1800s because it wasn't a park—it was a cemetery. I walked silently through the cemetery, and then I noticed that there were men taking away gravestones and dismantling the mausoleums. I walked over to the graves and watched the men work. I saw something very upsetting. The workers dug up the graves and moved coffins that looked to belong to well-to-do families. The graves that looked to belong to the poor or the forgotten were left behind. Only their grave marker was moved.

In the dream, I was in spirit, so I was able to see the spirits of the dead. They were sad, and some were crying because they knew that they would not be buried with their future relatives. But they were also sad because, now, no one would come and visit them at their graves. No one would pray for them. No one would leave flowers for them. And no one would come and talk to them. They were utterly alone.

Someone decided to leave some of the coffins behind so they would be forgotten. But the spirits did not forget. Because no one came to visit them, the spirits of the dead drifted off to sleep. Now, because we released the tattered gray spirit, the Shadow Man, and because of our witchcraft, the spirits of the forgotten dead were awoken.

In the dream, the spirits were no longer sad. Now, the spirits were angry.

I have a troubled feeling. Something is happening, and I don't know what. I don't think it's anything good. I'm wondering if the spirits are coming. Will they come for me and Kenneth because of our spell? Or will they just come for me?

I'm going to place a protection spell around my apartment just to be safe.

A SPELL FOR PROTECTION

Items Needed:
- Two short sticks of rowan
- Red thread, yarn, or string
- Protection incense: St. John's wort, frankincense, myrrh, or rosemary
- Offering for the spirits

1. Light the incense of protection and know that the smoke will call upon the spirits who wish to protect you on your path.

2. Hold both of the rowan sticks in your hands. Close your eyes and think about the spirits and gods you work with. Connect with them to the best of your ability. Then, call out to our gods, ancestors, and helper spirits. Say: *"I call to you gods, ancestors, and all spirits who help me upon my daily path. Come! Lend me your energies of magic as I work my rite of protection."*

3. Take the red string or yarn and place it in your hands. Connect to the power of protection and magic from the stars, the Earth, and below the Earth. Visualize a powerful red light of protection surrounding you and your home. Breathe the energies of the three realms into your heart. Know that your thoughts are commanding the energies to give your protection. Say: *"Powers of the Universe. Powers of witchcraft. Fill this sacred string with your protective power."*

4. Place the two rowan sticks in an equal-armed cross. As you do this, know that you are being protected by the four directions of North, South, East, and West. Then, wrap the red string around the center of the cross, binding the sticks together. As you do this, imagine the energies of the Universe protecting you. Say, *"As I bind this cross, so do I bind the energies of protection around me. Nothing shall harm me. The powers of the North, South, East, and West protect me with your magic."*

5. Use as much string as you'd like. Once the rowan cross is bound, place it in a window. If you cannot hang the cross in a window, you may place it in a sacred space.

6. Give offerings to the spirits.

7. From time to time, hold your cross and feel the energy. If you feel that it is low on energy, you may hold it in your hands and call upon the spirits of the four directions to offer you protection.

THE DEVIL OF HULL HOUSE

May 7, 1947
Day of Mercury. Moon in Sagittarius.

My name is David Lonesdale. I suppose I should write a little about myself. Patricia says that this book is meant to help other witches and witches of generations to come. She likes to say that we are the ancestors of our descendants. Well, other than nieces and nephews, I will have no descendants. I'm a homosexual man living in the Lincoln Park neighborhood of Chicago. Being a gay man in Chicago used to be a bit easier than it is now. Before the war, as long as you didn't bother anyone, then no one bothered you. We left you alone. You left us alone. But now, after the war, things are different. You see, after the war, everyone was looking for communists. People talk and make up these stories. If you are different from the good people of middle-class Christianity, then you are suspect. If you look different or act different in any way, people think you are up to something.

I'm not only gay, but I'm a gay witch. When I meet most people, I don't tell them any of these things. I know some men who marry and have kids, but then they wind up at a gay bar looking for sex. See, this is how they keep their secret. They pretend to be a loving Christian husband and devoted father. In reality, they are living a lie. I can't blame them too much. I guess what's the difference between lying about being gay and lying about being a witch? Both can get you fired from your job or evicted from your apartment, and both can give you a life of looking over your shoulder. I could have gotten married. But that's not for me. It would be too hard to hide both being gay and a witch.

Witch. I guess that's something I've been my whole life. I've been aware of spirits and other things since I was a kid. Growing up, I would just know things. I knew when my little brother was going to fall off his bike and skin his knee. I also knew when Jamie Preston, a pretty girl from school, was going to smash her car into the telephone pole. Jamie was fine and all that. I knew that, too. My mother used to know things, too. She always knew when someone was going to call or was about to visit us and come to the front door. Sometimes, I'd hear a knock on the door, and Mother would say, "Leave it be! It's just one of those missionaries." Well, Momma would be in the other room and wouldn't have been able to see who was at the door. She'd always be right, though. Every time. So, I guess I got stuff like that from her.

I have been initiated into the Lincoln Park Coven for several years now. Patricia never cared about me being gay. She said that witches would often celebrate sex. She said that sex, and even being gay, was a rebellious act against the oppression of Christianity. I think that's true. Truth be told, I think Patrica gets a kick out of having a gay man in the coven. She's a bit odd like that. Oh, that's nothing bad at all. Patricia is one of the best people I have ever known, and I am loyal to her. She took me in and taught me a lot about witchcraft. Everyone in the coven has accepted me as a gay man, and no one has batted an eye at the fact that I have sex with men. Besides, I think everyone in the coven has something odd or weird about them. Even if they are aware of it or not.

We had our Beltane ritual a few days ago. It was like any other Beltane ritual, really. You know, flowers and sexual imagery. I've heard stories about some covens having sex at their Beltane rituals, but that's nothing that we do here. That's nothing anyone in the coven is interested in. Our Beltane is about connecting to the energies of the land and the stars and doing the magic that we need for ourselves. We do healing magic, too. Sandy and Kenneth told us about the spirit that they released from the Couch Mausoleum. When they told us what happened, I got a bad feeling about it. It's not their fault. I don't think they did anything wrong. But when they told us, I looked at Patricia's face, and I could see that she was a bit worried. She didn't say anything about it, though. Wonder why.

Now, it's my turn to tell my story. A few nights ago, I was at Waldman's bar. Waldman's is a gay bar close to Michigan Avenue and Randolf. It's run by a Jewish couple. They don't seem to mind that they own a gay bar. I think they prefer it that way. No fights. Not much trouble. Once in a while, the police will come in to make sure that the men are not kissing or doing any other "inappropriate" stuff like that. The old owners never said anything, but I'm going to guess that they paid the police off. Bribes or something, I guess. It may sound like a hassle, but in every single bar in Chicago, the owners are paying off the police. This is a mob town, after all. Don't think for one minute that the mob is all gone. There's lots of shit that still goes on in the bars, the alleys, theaters, and other places. It's Chicago, after all.

As I was saying, I was at Waldman's, sitting at the bar, minding my own business. Sometimes, I like to go to Waldman's and sit at the bar and have a drink and a cigarette. Most times, I'm not there looking for a man to take home. This is a place where there are other men like me. This is one of the few places in the world where I don't have to act like anybody but myself. I even like the smell of smoke in the air. It's private. It's casual. And I like it. So I'm sitting at the bar, and this man is sitting a couple of seats down from me. The bar was a little slow that night, so there weren't that many people at the bar. Just me and this guy.

He was dressed in a nice gray suit and was smoking a cigar. Most men I know, even gay men, prefer cigarettes. They're easier to carry in your pocket and less expensive, too. That wasn't always the case. A few years ago, you mostly saw men smoking cigars or a pipe. Some men chew it. Have you ever kissed a man who was chewing tobacco? Not something that's very savory. So, he was smoking this cigar, and for some reason, I was fascinated with the glow of the cigar's ember. The man would take a puff, and the ember would glow this fiery orange color. He had his elbow on the bar and smoked this cigar like it was magic or something.

I think he noticed me watching this cigar burn, and maybe he thought I was actually watching him. He turned toward me and said, "Name's Mr. Talbott, what's yours?"

"David," I said. "Are you comfortable with telling everyone your last name?"

He smiled a grin that I found handsome. "Not everyone. Just you."

I smiled back at him. He was indeed an intriguing man. "What brings you here to Waldman's?"

"Why do you think I'm here?" he asked me in return.

This is a little game gay men play. You never know when there will be a cop in plain clothing staking out a gay bar, looking for someone to make a pass at them. I think these coppers do it intentionally. They despise us, and when we say or do something, they are revolted and use their hate as an excuse to arrest us. Most of the time, violently. Knocking us around. There are some men who speak in a code. I never did that. I do, however, wait for them to make the first move. "I'm waiting for you to tell me."

Mr. Talbott smiled again and puffed on his cigar.

Again, I found myself intrigued with the burning ember of the cigar. He leaned into me, close enough to either whisper something or kiss me. That would not be wise at a gay bar if people were watching, but part of me hoped he would kiss me.

Instead of kissing me, he said, "I was hoping to spend some time with you. Maybe away from spying eyes."

That night, we went back to my place. We kissed and had sex. The sex was good, and we talked a lot. After sex, we lay in my bed and talked about all kinds of things. I enjoyed talking to him.

He had the kind of personality that was confident, but I could tell that there was a sadness in him that he used his confidence to hide. He was interesting, though. The men I usually bring back to my apartment want quick sex and then are on their way. That's something that never bothered me. They could leave when they wanted to but with Mr. Talbott...I didn't ask him his first name. I liked it that way. Not because it was somewhat anonymous but because he seemed like a Mr. Talbott. He lit his cigar again with the matches that were sitting on the table next to my bed. Again, I was drawn to the embers of the cigar.

May 11, 1947
Day of Sol. Moon in Capricorn.

Mr. Talbott and I spent the next few nights together. He's an interesting fellow. He knows about history, art, music, and all the other typical things that gay men are interested in. He seems like a worldly man. He has a certain flare to him that I have never seen in another person. His clothes are quite ordinary. His suits have the drab colors of gray and blue, but it's his sense of humor and the way he carries himself that is enchanting. I may be one of his conquests, and this may go no further than a fling, but I wanted to see how far this would go and what adventures I might find myself in.

Last night, Mr. Talbott suggested that we should stay in his room instead of my apartment. He said it was close to his work, and he needed to be up with the sun in the morning. He did warn me, however, that he shares the house with other people.

He is living at Hull House on the Near West Side of Chicago. He rents a room there. I've never been to Hull House before, but I understand it is quite famous. It was named after a real estate developer, Charles J. Hull, in 1856. Later, after his death, it was used to help the community with a variety of services like craftsmanship and childcare.

I hadn't been to that part of town in a while, and it was nice to get out of the North Side of Chicago and see something different. I drove my car, and it was a lovely night for a drive. I parked on the street, and the two of us walked up to the front door of the magnificent building. It was red brick with wonderful pillars and large windows that stood at least six feet tall, if not more.

Just walking up the steps of Hull House, I could feel the extravagance of the 1800s. Chicago at its finest, I believe. All the homes worth their salt were built just after the Great Chicago Fire. There are a few of them that survived the fire and are older, but not many.

Mr. Talbott opened the big wooden door and let me in. A few steps in front of the door was a large Victorian staircase that led to the second floor. Mr. Talbott told me later that the bedrooms were on the second floor. To our right was a parlor and living space. There was a gorgeous fireplace with a top that looked to be made from marble. I didn't ask about it. I didn't want to be rude, after all. Two old ladies were sitting in chairs that looked to be from the late 1800s or even perhaps the turn of the century. They were dressed in clothes that I believe were from the same era as the chairs. I didn't think much of it. You see, the elderly often cling to their old clothes and their old furniture. I never understood the reasoning until we went through the Great Depression. Many people had no jobs and no way of paying for food or clothes. They depended on others for help. As Mr. Talbott tells me, Hull House was one of the places that helped the poor during that dark and dreadful time.

Mr. Talbott walked into the living area. He has a way about him every time he walks into a room. The whole room will light up with his presence. Or perhaps that's just me. Maybe I'm enamored with the handsome gentleman, and that's how I see him. He took off his hat and said, "Ellen. Enella. This is my friend, David Lonesdale."

Ellen was busy sewing something. She looked up from her chair and was not amused by Mr. Talbott's antics. "It is Ms. Starr. And that is Ms. Benedict."

Uh oh. It looks like Mr. Talbott had gotten him into a little trouble with the ladies. Ms. Benedict shook her head. "He will never learn, Ellen. Let it be."

"Nonsense!" Ms. Starr snapped. "He will one day learn respect."

Ms. Benedict gave Mr. Talbott a slight smile. "Perhaps one day."

"It's nice to meet you, ladies," I said in an attempt to change focus.

"Indeed," Ms. Starr said, "It is nice to meet you as well."

Ms. Benedict gave me a smile.

Mr. Talbott bowed to them. Not because he was being formal but because he was attempting to taunt them further. He seemed to enjoy causing a stir with the ladies. Perhaps they were relatives. Aunts, perhaps. "Well, then we must be off to my room, good night ladies."

"Do not forget to say goodnight to Ms. Addams," Ms. Starr warned.

"Indeed," Mr. Talbott took a breath and proceeded to walk across the house into the dining area, where a door led to an office. I followed him and didn't say a word. There seemed to be a bit of tension in the air. I was wondering if I should reconsider staying the night with him. Mr. Talbott knocked on the door.

"Come in," a stern voice said from inside the room.

Mr. Talbott opened the door. The door led to a small office off to the side of Hull House.

It was a little room with a desk in the middle of the office with three large windows behind the desk. At the desk sat an old woman who looked to be in her 70s or even perhaps 80s. She had a cold look on her face. "Mr. Talbott, be sure to kiss me goodnight."

Mr. Talbott slowly walked into the office and placed a small kiss on Ms. Addams's cheek.

"Will you two be needing anything further tonight?" she asked. I couldn't tell what kind of relationship they had. I'm guessing that Ms. Addams owns Hull House, and Mr. Talbott is renting a room from her. The way they spoke to each other was somber. Almost as if we were all in a dream.

"No, Ms. Addams," Mr. Talbott said.

Ms. Addams didn't say anything more. She went back to doing whatever it was she was doing in the office. I'm sure it was something important.

I followed Mr. Talbott up the old, rickety stairs to the second floor and then up another staircase even more rickety than the first. We came to his room, and the door creaked open. When I went inside, I could see that the space was bigger than a simple room but not big enough to be an apartment on its own.

The room had electricity, but as Mr. Talbott told me later, electricity was added later. In fact, he said that the third floor itself was a later addition. It was built as more housing for immigrants who had come to Chicago looking for a better life. I found it strange that Hull House was a charity for immigrants and the poor, but there wasn't anyone in the house other than Mr. Talbott, Ms. Benedict, Ms. Starr, and Ms. Addams.

Mr. Talbott laid down on the bed and gestured for me to lie down with him. We laid there together, looking up at the wooden ceiling above. I only had a brief encounter with the three ladies downstairs, but they left a lasting impression.

"Tell me about them," I said.

"Tell you about who?" Mr. Talbott asked.

"The ladies downstairs," I rolled over so that I could see Mr. Talbott's face. I wanted to see his eyes so that maybe I could read his mind. I knew I couldn't really read his mind. I was looking for an expression, a wink, or even a small flinch that would give away what he might be thinking. "Tell me about them."

"There's not much to tell." He turned over to face me and gave me a small kiss on the lips. "Let us fill our night with each other and not thoughts of old women."

I was not satisfied with that at all. Mr. Talbott was keeping something from me. Patricia says to trust the feeling in your gut. You know…that feeling in the pit of your stomach that is trying to tell you something. Patricia teaches us that your body is psychic. It knows when something is not right. I wish I was more psychic than I was. If I really could read minds, this would be much easier. I needed to find out, and I had just the spell that would help me.

TRUTH SPELL

Items Needed:

- ◆ Four white candles
- ◆ Sage, bay leaf, and sandalwood
- ◆ A picture or poppet of the target
- ◆ Four small quartz crystals

1. Place the four white candles in the four directions. Light the candle in the East and say: *"Powers of the East and the rising sun. Lend me your powers of light so that which hides in the dark will be revealed."*

2. Light the candle in the South and say: *"Powers of the South and the highest sun. Lend me your powers of passion so that the fire in the belly will burn and truth shall be revealed."*

3. Light the candle in the West and say: *"Powers of the West and the setting sun. Lend me the powers of Mimir's Well so that those who seek wisdom will gain the truth."*

4. Light the candle in the North and say: *"Powers of the North and the midnight sun. Lend me the powers of the Earth itself so that which is hidden in the mind will manifest, and all will be revealed."*

5. Hold a picture or a poppet of your target in your hands. Close your eyes and spend time thinking about your target. Send the energy of the target into the picture or poppet. Place the object at the center of the circle of candles and say: *"This is (name of target). The magic that is sent to this object is sent to (name of target)."*

6. Place one quartz crystal at each white candle with the point facing the picture or poppet. As you place each crystal, visualize a white-colored power of truth being aimed at your target.

7. Place your mixture of sage, bay leaf, and sandalwood on the charcoal. As you smell the fragrance, visualize the white light of truth surrounding your target.

8. Take the picture or poppet and place it in the smoke of the incense mixture. Visualize the white-colored power of truth filling your target.

9. Place the object in the center of your circle of candles. Place both hands over the object and summon the energy of the Universe. Imagine that this energy is the magical truth that binds all things in creation together. Allow this energy to go through your head, down into your heart, out of your hands, and onto the object. As you do this, say, *"I summon forth the power of truth. Spirits surround (name of target) with the magic of truth. The truth cannot be hidden. Truth must be revealed. Every part of your being must reveal the truth. It is only the truth that you speak. It is only the truth that you reveal."*

10. Spend some time thinking about how important the truth is and that your target will speak only the truth.

May 11, 1947
Day of Sol. Moon in Aquarius.

Today is Sunday, the day of the sun, a day of balance and illumination. The perfect day for a truth spell. When I left Mr. Talbott at Hull House, I couldn't get rid of the nagging feeling in my gut. There was something he wasn't telling me. Perhaps there were many things he was not telling me. I took the "L" train across town home. The night was cool and misty, and there were not many people on the train. Maybe it was me, but I felt like I was in a place that I wasn't supposed to be in. It wasn't the "wrong place at the wrong time" sort of thing, but more like I was out of my own space and time.

Maybe it's just because the two ladies at Hull House were odd. Or maybe it's because Mr. Talbott was being avoidant of the truth. Either way, I was going to find out.

The next day—today—I decided to do the truth spell. I was going to see Mr. Talbott again.

He said we could stay at my place, but I insisted on going back to Hull House.

There were mysteries left to be solved there, and everyone in my coven knows I like a good mystery. After I did the spell, I could feel a shift. It felt kind of like something was set in motion, or even like watching a line of dominos knock each other down, each one tumbling over the next until it ended. Enough writing for now. I will let you know what happened when I come home tomorrow.

May 12, 1947
Day of Luna. Moon in Aquarius.

I just got home from work. I ran through the events of last night over and over again in my head. So, last night, I took the "L" back to Hull House. When I walked up the steps, I could see Mr. Talbott peeking down at me from his window on the third floor.

I knocked on the door, and I was greeted by Ms. Benedict. Funny that Mr. Talbott didn't greet me at the door. He did see me walking up, after all. Ms. Benedict had the kind of smile you see when someone is forcing themselves to smile out of politeness. "Good evening. Are you here to see Mr. Talbott?"

"I am," I said.

She opened the door for me to come inside.

There was no light inside other than candlelight. I knew that the house had electricity, but maybe the ladies preferred the light of candles. The elderly can get stuck in old ways, I suppose. I walked into the front parlor, and there was Ms. Starr again, sitting and sewing something. "Good evening, Ms. Starr."

"Good evening, young man," Ms. Starr said without looking up from her sewing. "Mr. Talbott should be down shortly. You may sit down if you'd like."

I sat down in the chair next to Ms. Starr. She had an otherworldly presence about her. She seemed wise, but I got the feeling that she did not share her wisdom lightly. She sewed for a moment and looked up at me. "Sewing is an ancient folk practice, you know."

I wanted to tell her that we had learned about magical sewing in the coven, but I thought it best not to mention anything about witchcraft to her. I nodded and continued to watch her sew something on a small piece of white fabric.

"When we sew something, we are adding our own magic into a garment, a blanket, or even a piece of art."

I wasn't sure why Ms. Starr was telling me this. Maybe it was part of the truth spell. "As we sew the thread, we are adding our thoughts, feelings, and powers into something else. Each stitch adds our own personal magic into something. Sewing can be used to bring healing to someone, love magic, or even a binding. Simply focus your thoughts and feelings on your goal with each stitch."

I looked over at the fabric she was sewing. I was expecting to see something one could hang up in your home. Maybe a flower or even a "Home Sweet Home" sign. Instead, it looked to be a figure of a man with little "X" marks all over the body. This place seems to be getting stranger and stranger.

"Hello, David," Mr. Talbott called out to me from the staircase.

I said goodnight to Ms. Starr and Ms. Benedict and followed Mr. Talbott up the staircase to his room. When we got to his room, we listened to music on the record player and talked for a long while. I've only known Mr. Talbott for a short time, but the more I get to know him, the more I discover there is a sadness that he is not revealing to me. Something from his past, I think, that he is keeping to himself.

"How long have you lived in Hull House?" I asked him.

"My whole life. I've never lived anywhere else. Ms. Addams and Ms. Starr have always taken care of me," Mr. Talbot said.

"Are they your family?" I asked.

"They are like family. My mother was an immigrant when she arrived at Hull House. She was also pregnant. She died during childbirth, and Ms. Addams and Ms. Starr have taken care of me ever since."

"I'm so sorry," I said.

Mr. Talbott did not seem to grieve his mother dying. Perhaps he had already done all the grieving he was going to do and has moved on. He smiled at me and said, "No need to be sorry. I have always been safe here. The ladies have always kept me safe and away from harm."

We went to sleep, but I awoke to the sound of footsteps on the wooden floors of the second floor down below. The creaks seemed very loud, even for an old house like this.

I was curious to see who was up walking around in the middle of the night. I gently got out of bed so that Mr. Talbott would not be woken up. As I got up, I watched his face for any hint of him waking. I then crept to the door and opened it as slowly and silently as I could, closing it behind me without a sound. I slowly walked down the hall, and there stood a woman next to the big window in the hallway.

She stood there silently. She watched me walk closer to her. She was dressed in clothes that looked to be almost a hundred years old. This was a fourth woman who must live in the house. Neither Mr. Talbott nor the ladies had ever mentioned a fourth woman. How curious.

"Hello, my name is David Lonesdale."

The woman seemed kind but had a sadness about her that was similar to everyone who lived in Hull House. "I am Mrs. Hull."

Mrs. Hull? Was this the descendant of the Hull family, who were the original owners of this house? I wanted to find out more about what was going on in this house. "It's lovely to meet you, Mrs. Hull."

"You must leave this place at once!" I could hear desperation in Mrs. Hull's voice. I could see that she was trying to protect me somehow. "This place is a prison. Those who come here rarely leave."

"Prison?" I needed to find out more. "What do you mean?"

Mrs. Hull looked up at the ceiling. "Can you hear them?"

I was hesitant to ask, but I need to know. My heart started beating harder in my chest. "Hear who?"

She gazed over to the room next to us with an open door. I followed her gaze to see what she was trying to show me. I thought I saw women and children who were watching us through the door quickly hide in the shadows of the room. Without saying a word to Mrs. Hull, I slowly walked into the room. I couldn't see them well, but I was aware of the eyes of women and children in the room. They watched me with a hopeful gaze. "Who are you?"

"They are the souls of all those who have died here," Mrs. Hull said.

"Are they trapped here?" Maybe the ladies who lived in the house were more sinister than I originally thought. I turned around and faced Mrs. Hull. "Why can't they leave?"

Mrs. Hull smiled. Her expression was warm and caring. "This is a place where many of the immigrants and poor came to find a better life. They were taken in, given food and shelter, and were educated. When some of those poor people died in childbirth, from illness, or the effects of their poverty, they did not leave this place. For some, it is a sanctuary. For others, it is a place where they cannot leave."

I stood there for a moment, not knowing what to say or even what to think. Were Ms. Addams, Ms. Starr, and Ms. Benedict forcing the spirits of the dead to remain in the house? But why would they do that? What purpose would that serve?

"How can we help them?"

"I cannot help you," Mrs. Hull said. "I am the caretaker of this house and nothing more." Mrs. Hull vanished in thin air.

I couldn't believe what I was seeing. Mrs. Hull is a ghost! But she didn't look like a spirit. She looked just as physical as you or I. Evidently, this is Mrs. Millicent Hull. The wife of the builder of the house, Mr. Charles J. Hull.

I went back into the room with the spirits of the dead. I couldn't see or sense them anymore. They were gone. Gone somewhere in the magic of the house.

"What are you doing in there?" a stern voice said from behind me.

I turned around to see Ms. Addams. For a second, I didn't know what to say. I had to come up with something—and fast. "I was looking for the bathroom."

She looked at me right in the eye. She was looking for something. Maybe a sign that would tell her if I was lying to her or not. She was silent for a long moment. "Back down the hall."

"Thank you," I said. Without saying anything further, I started walking down the hall toward the bathroom.

"Be careful," Ms. Addams said, "when you look for shadows, you may find darkness."

I quickly made my way to the bathroom and then back up to Mr. Talbott's room on the third floor. He was still sound asleep and had no idea I had even left.

This was good. The fewer people who suspected that I was up to something, the better. I got back into bed with Mr. Talbott and looked up at the ceiling. I needed to help those poor spirits escape this place. I just needed to figure out how I was going to do it.

May 13, 1947
Day of Mars. Moon in Pisces.

The next day, I said goodbye to Mr. Talbott and was on my way. I did not see the ladies in the house at all. Perhaps they had other business to attend to that morning. It was probably for the best. Ms. Addams was already suspicious of my intentions, and I did not want to give any further excuses to suspect me of something. I was curious to know what kind of power Ms. Addams and the other ladies had over the spirits of the dead who were trapped in Hull House. Were they witches? Did they have a magical power to keep the dead captive in that old house? I needed to find out more information about the house.

I spoke with one of the members of our coven, James Bower, and I told him my story. He said that Hull House has an interesting reputation. He said that people who lived in that neighborhood had reported strange things like ghosts, demons, and things like that. I wonder how true those stories are. He also said that because most of the people who passed through the doors of that house over the years were either poor or immigrants, the stories may have been told simply because those people were believed to be "riffraff." James said the best thing to do would be to go back to that area of town and speak with some of the old-timers there. The people who had been there over the years and who knew what was going on in that house.

That afternoon, I went back to South Halsted Street, the location of Hull House. I was determined to find some answers. I walked around the neighborhood looking for something or someone who knew about that house. But how do you go up to a stranger and say, "Hi, what do you know about ghosts and Hull House?" They would either laugh at me or think I'm crazy. Maybe both. I spent an hour walking around the neighborhood. I had no idea where I was going or what I was looking for. There had to be something.

Finally, I decided I would have to start asking questions if I wanted any of the answers I was looking for. I found a little grocery store, and I decided to ask someone inside some questions. When I walked in, there was no one shopping. The only person inside was the man working behind the counter. I guess I could start with him. The man looked to be in his 40s, I think. It was hard to tell his age exactly because he looked like he had the kind of life where he had to work hard for everything he's gotten.

A tough life, I suppose. Not the kind of life that's filled with street crime and drugs, but the kind where you work your whole life to make money and support your family and have almost nothing to show for it.

I walked up to the counter, and I asked the man, "Excuse me. My name is David Lonesdale. Would you happen to know anything about the history of Hull House?"

The man raised his eyebrow and pulled his head back. You see? I knew if I asked about that house, they'd think I was nuts. "Are you going to buy anything, mister?"

Shit. He was going to go that route. "Sure, can I have a pack of Lucky Strikes, please?"

The man behind the counter turned around and took a pack of Lucky Strike cigarettes off of a shelf that was close by. He plopped them on the counter between us. "That'll be twenty cents."

I fished out two dimes from my pants pocket and laid the coins on the counter. "Do you know anything about the history of Hull House?"

"No," the man behind the counter said.

"Ok. Thank you." I felt like I was never going to find the answers that I was looking for. I took the Lucky Strikes and put them in my pocket. I started walking toward the door. I suppose I can keep looking for someone to help me find what I'm looking for.

I opened the door to the little store when the man behind the counter said, "There's two women down the street who talk to ghosts. The Honeybourne sisters. They're Spiritualists. Maybe they would be able to help you."

Spiritualist? Now, that was something that might be helpful to me.

"Their home is a couple blocks west down the street. Red brick building. You can't miss it. They help people see their dead loved ones. For a fee, of course."

"Of course," I said in agreement. "Thank you."

I left the little store and walked down a few blocks, keeping my eye out for a red brick building. The building wasn't hard to find at all. The only brick building on the street. There was a big sign with painted lettering that said "Honeybourne." I guess this was the place. I walked to the big wooden front door and knocked. After a moment, the door opened, and out stepped a woman dressed in a pink and white dress. "How can I help you?"

"I would like to speak to someone who knows the history of Hull House," I said.

The woman paused and then said, "We cannot help you."

"I have money," I said.

The woman nodded and then opened the door for me. "Follow me."

I followed the woman into the house. It was decorated with furniture that seemed to be almost fifty years old, but it looked well-kept. Maybe the sisters inherited everything from relatives. She showed me into the parlor, where there was a large, circular wooden table draped in a black cloth. She pulled out one of the wooden chairs for me, and I sat down. "Would you like tea?"

"Yes, I would," I said.

There was a nearby wooden tray with a teapot and four porcelain teacups. She placed one teacup in front of me and then two other cups on the table as well. "Betty! We have a visitor."

Another woman dressed almost identical to the woman who met me at the door walked into the parlor. "My name is Sophia, and this is my sister, Betty."

"How do you do?" Betty asked.

"Well, thank you," I answered.

Sophia looked to be the oldest of the two sisters, but from what I'm guessing, not by much. "You have money?"

"Yes." I took a wad of cash out of my pocket and placed it on the table. I had no idea how much was there, but there was a five-dollar bill on the top of the pile, so it looked like I had the money they needed.

Sophia placed her hand over the bills and slid them towards her. "How can we help you?"

"I'm looking for information about the Hull House," I said. "Any information would be helpful, really."

The Honeybourne sisters looked at each other as if they were secretly speaking with each other with their minds. I could tell that they knew something but were hesitant to say anything. I wondered why. Did the residents at Hull House have so much sway over the community that they were afraid to talk? Finally, after a long silence, Sophia said, "Hull House has a rich history of community service. They helped so many people in need. Jane Addams is a saint."

"Do you know her?" I asked.

"Everyone around here knows her," Betty answered. "She's quite famous."

I could see that there was so much they were not telling me. "I know you are a Spiritualist. Can you tell me about the ghosts at Hull House?"

"Every house has ghosts of the dead," Sophia said. "But Hull House is different. There's something about that house that is different. Powerful."

"What do you mean?" I asked her.

"It's as if the house was built to be a spiritual gateway for the dead." Sophia's answer was foreboding. "The house was built in 1856 by Charles J. Hull. He built it for his wife, Millicent, but she would only live there a short time. She died in 1860, and it is said that she still walks the house each night."

That was definitely the Mrs. Hull I saw last night.

Betty sipped her tea. She placed her teacup on the table. "The house was then given to a relative of Hull's named Helen Culver. Helen was a friend of Jane Addams and a supporter of her work. She allowed Ms. Addams to stay in Hull House so that she could work with the people who were in need."

"Ms. Addams does sound like a saint," I said.

"There's more," Sophia said. "In 1913, an immigrant woman gave birth to a monstrous child. Some say it was deformed, and others say it was the Devil himself born to the world. The mother died in childbirth. The child of the Devil's first act upon Earth was to kill his own mother."

Betty took another sip of her tea. "Someone left the devil child on the steps of Hull House. Jane Addams, being who she was, could not turn the thing away. Little did she know it was the Devil in disguise. She kept the child hidden in the house. Word quickly spread that Jane Addams was keeping a devil baby protected within her walls. The rumors flew through the countryside. People came for miles, wanting to catch a glimpse of the Devil. But Jane Addams would not allow it. She kept him safe upstairs. It was said that well-to-do people would come for miles to see the child. They would even offer Hull House a lot of money to see the Devil. But Jane Addams kept the child away. Some say that they could see the devil child looking down on them from the third-floor window."

Betty said something that got my attention. "You said 'being who she was.' What do you mean?"

"Child," Sophia looked me dead in the eyes as she spoke. "Jane Addams has been dead since 1935."

Dead? I just spoke to Ms. Addams yesterday. Suddenly, it hit me. I spoke with the ghost of Jane Addams yesterday. Holy shit! I couldn't believe it! Of course, I had thought I was speaking to real, living, physical people, but I wasn't! I was speaking to spirits of the dead. What is troubling me, though, is how they were able to appear so physically real. They didn't look like any apparitions I'd ever seen. The few times we conjured the dead in the coven, I usually couldn't see them. If I ever did see them, they looked like fog or even smoke. Now that I recall speaking with the residents of Hull House, I realize I never touched any of them. I never shook their hand or anything like that. I'm wondering if the spirits did something to my mind to make me think I was seeing them in the flesh. I should ask the coven about that.

If Ms. Addams was dead, then who was keeping the other spirits captive, and what did Mr. Talbott have to do with any of this? I needed to know more.

"I saw spirits of the dead in Hull House. We have to help them."

Sophia took another sip from her tea and looked over at Betty. She took one more sip of tea. "We don't disturb the spirits at Hull House."

"But they need our help," I said. "There's also a man who lives on the third floor. I think the spirits are controlling him in some way."

Betty echoed her sister. "We don't disturb the spirits at Hull House."

"I have money." I put down more bills on the table. There's one thing I know about Spiritualists: they are a business, and to make a business work, you need money.

Sophia placed her hands on the bills and brought the money to her. "We cannot guarantee that you will receive the answers you are looking for."

SPELL TO INVOKE A SPIRIT OF THE DEAD

Items Needed:
- One white candle
- Incense of wormwood, mugwort, and myrrh
- Charcoal
- Incense burner

1. Make sure that the room is completely dark. Draw the curtains and turn off the light.

2. As you light the white candle, think of the spirit of the dead you wish to invoke.

3. Sit down in a chair and close your eyes. Visualize the spirit you wish to invoke. If you do not know what they look like, you can "tune in" to their presence with your heart. If there are other people in the room with you, they should also visualize the spirit.

4. Call aloud the name of the spirit. If you do not know their name, you may say, "Unknown spirit" or "You who wish to be heard."

5. Visualize the spirit of the dead standing behind you. Next, visualize the spirit stepping into your body. Their legs connect with your legs, their torso with your torso, their arms with your arms, their head with your head, then their mind to your mind.

6. The invocation may be full or partial, meaning you may choose to fully invoke the spirit of the dead into your body, or you may wish to invoke a small amount of energy into you. If you choose the latter, make sure that you invoke enough energy to communicate clearly.

7. When you are ready, allow the spirit to speak through you. Remember, you have full control. You can end the session at any time.

8. To end the session, visualize the spirit detaching from your body and leaving.

9. Give them thanks and offerings. Offerings can be incense, candles, or food.

It only took a moment for the sisters to darken the room. They took a large white candle off of a nearby shelf and lit it with a match. Betty closed the black curtains, and Sophia sat in a big chair in the corner of the room. Betty lit a piece of charcoal and placed it on a small dish. She took a little container down from the shelf that had herbs inside.

She took a pinch and placed it on the lit charcoal. There seemed to be a sort of void in the room. It was the feeling you get right before you conjure a great work of magic.

All three of us were silent. We were waiting for the dead.

"We call to you, spirits of Hull House," Sophia said in a voice that seemed a bit dramatic to me. Maybe this was all part of her Spiritualist schtick. "Spirits of Hull House, come to us. Come to my body and tell us your story."

"Come to us, spirits," Betty said, closing her eyes as well.

Sophia took a deep breath, and then she opened her eyes, *"Who are you? Why have you summoned me?"*

"Are you a spirit who dwells in Hull House?" Betty asked.

"The spirits of Hull House are not allowed to leave," Sophia said in a voice that was not her own. *"I am Marta. I am one of the watchers of Hull House. There are those of us who make sure secrets stay hidden."*

I was anxious to know what those secrets were. "What is happening at Hull House?"

"The spirits there cannot leave," Marta said through Sophia.

"Are they trapped?" I asked. "Is Ms. Addams keeping them trapped there?"

Sophia looked into my eyes. Those eyes were not the eyes of Sophia. They were of someone else. Someone with a strong power. *"The spirits of Hull House cannot leave."*

"How can we help them?" I asked.

"The spirits of Hull House cannot leave!" Marta said more sternly.

Without warning, Sophia took a deep breath, and the spirit of Marta was gone. Betty quickly got up from the table to give her more tea. She gathered herself and said, "You should not disturb the spirits of Hull House."

The Honeybourne sisters did not give me much to go on, but I'm convinced I need to help those spirits. When I was at Hull House, I could feel a lot of suffering. I believe it is the suffering of the spirits trapped in Hull House.

As a witch, I have the power and the magic to make things right in that house. If I don't do anything, I feel like I would be letting down the spirit world. Also, there's Mr. Talbott...I like him a lot. He's been kind to me. Watching him with those phantom ladies, I can see that they have some control over him. They are keeping him in that house against his will. I wonder what their purpose is with him. I need to go back to Hull House one more time and make things right.

May 13, 1947
Day of Mercury. Moon in Pisces.

When I left the Honeybourne sisters, I went to see two of my coven mates, Kenneth and Mary. Between the three of us, we came up with the perfect spell. I decided to see Mr. Talbott at Hull House that night. I told him I wanted to see him…which is true, but I was primarily going over to Hull House to help the spirits trapped there move on. I believe the only way to do that is to cut the magical bonds that Ms. Addams has over the spirits and Mr. Talbott. To do that…I needed to banish the ghost of Ms. Addams.

I packed up the items I needed for the spell in a small overnight bag. Whatever I needed to do, I needed to do it in secret. Not even Mr. Talbott could know. The funny thing about being under someone's magical control is that you're spellbound to *not* destroy the spell that binds you; therefore, you'll do anything to keep the magic intact. Even if it harms you.

I went to Hull House, and sure enough, Ms. Starr and Ms. Benedict were sitting in the front parlor, sewing their strange designs into a white fabric as they did night after night. Ms. Addams was in her office as she was every time I visited.

Again, the only lights in the house were those lights from the candles placed around the house. I wondered if the ladies had any idea of what I was planning. Were they psychic as well? Did they have a plan to stop me? Hopefully not. If I'm discovered, I'm not sure I'll get the opportunity to do the spell a second time.

Mr. Talbott came down the stairs to greet me, just like he had the previous nights, and I followed him up the rickety old staircase to the third floor. We sat on his bed and talked for a while, and I finally asked him, "Do you know the legend of the Devil Baby of Hull House?"

Mr. Talbott laughed and said, "My dear man. You don't believe in stories told by the superstitious, do you?"

I shrugged and said, "I've seen some strange things over the years."

Mr. Talbott kissed my head. He smiled like a knowing parent. "Don't worry your handsome head over nonsense. Besides, if there were a devil in this house, I would know about it."

Maybe, I thought. Unless the ghost of Ms. Addams was keeping it away somewhere secret in the house.

A SPELL TO TRAP A SPIRIT

Items Needed:
- A small wooden box
- Two small hand mirrors or pieces of square glass
- The Seal of Solomon (you may buy this or draw it on paper)
- Sweet-smelling herbs of your choice
- A few drops of whiskey or some other alcohol
- A quartz crystal
- Small padlock for box

1. Take the wooden box and glue one small mirror (or square glass) on the inside bottom of the box and one small mirror on the inside of the top of the box. The two mirrors should be facing each other when the box is closed.

2. You may buy a Seal of Solomon, or you can draw one on paper.

3. Glue the Seal of Solomon at the center of the bottom mirror.

4. Place sweet-smelling herbs of your choice inside the box. You can use lavender, rose, jasmine, or any other herbs that smell sweet. A teaspoon of two or three of the herbs will work well. The energy and fragrance of the herbs will draw the spirit to the trap.

5. Take the whiskey or other alcohol and sprinkle some on top of the herbs.

6. When you are ready to trap the spirit, place the box, lid open, in the center of your ritual space. Then say: *"I summon the spirit of (name of*

spirit). Come and be enticed by the fragrance of sweet herb. Take the offering of alcohol. These offerings are for you. Replenish yourself, (name of spirit)." Repeat this until you see or feel that the spirit is in the room with you.

7. The offerings of herbs and alcohol will entice the spirit to the box (spirits love offerings of alcohol), and the quartz crystal will mesmerize or enchant them into going inside the box. Once inside the box, the Seal of Solomon will magically trap the spirit inside.

8. Quickly close the box and lock it with a small padlock.

9. Keep the spirit trap safely out of the sight of others.

10. If you wish to release the spirit, open the box and take out the crystal and Seal of Solomon. Say: *"Go now in peace, (name of spirit). Do not cause harm to anyone as you leave. Be in peace."*

I waited until around 3:00 a.m. to gently leave the bed where Mr. Talbott slept soundly. It was like he was dead to the world. Carrying my satchel, I crept downstairs to the main parlor on the first floor as silently as I could. That was the place where I saw the trapped spirits, so I'm guessing this is where most of the power of the house would be. I placed the satchel on the ground and took out the spirit trap I had made with Kenneth and Mary. I opened up and called out to the spirit of Jane Addams. I called out to her three times, and on the third call, Ms. Addams appeared before me. She looked at me with curiosity. She had no idea that I had the power to summon her spirit.

Ms. Addams could smell the herbs and the alcohol. She walked closer to the spirit trap and looked inside. She became fixated on the crystal. She didn't know that the Seal of Solomon was secretly placed underneath. She was drawn in closer and closer. Then, with a big *WOOOSH,* she was sucked inside!

I ran to the spirit trap, slammed the lid closed, and snapped on the padlock, magically sealing the box.

"What did you do?!" Ms. Starr screamed as she ran down the hallway.

"Release her at once!" The ghost of Ms. Benedict appeared in the parlor with me. She ran over to the spirit trap, but I could see that she couldn't touch it. She did not have the power to release Ms. Addams.

Ms. Starr walked into the parlor and stood with Ms. Benedict. Both of them looked down at the spirit trap. All of a sudden, Hull House changed. The beautiful Victorian house lit by candle faded away, and in its place was a house filled with electric lights and modern furniture. The glamour of Hull House was gone. My magic worked. Jane Addams could no longer keep her hold on the spirits of the house. The parlor became full with the departed spirits of immigrants and the poor. They all looked so sad to me. Why were they not happy with being released from the power of Jane Addams?

One of the spirits looked at me and said, "She's gone. She can no longer protect us."

Another one of the spirits said, "We must go. This place is no longer a safe refuge for us."

With that, the dead residents of Hull House vanished.

Creak. Creak. Creak. Creak.

The sound of someone coming down the staircase was loud. Down the stairs slowly walked Mr. Talbott. He gave me a smile and said, "My handsome man. I knew you would come through for me."

"What do you mean?" I was confused as to what was happening.

Mr. Talbott took out a nail file and began filing his nails. When he finally came down the staircase and into the parlor, I could see him filing black claws. "You see, Ms. Addams and the ladies have been keeping me their prisoner for thirty years. Oh, yes, I can leave when I wish, but I was trapped on the Earth plane and always summoned back to my prison on the third floor."

I didn't know what to say. I could see the skin of Mr. Talbott's face slowly turning into what looked like scales. I could see fangs where his teeth used to be. He kicked off his shoes, and hooves were in the place of his feet. "I'm free. Thanks to you."

I couldn't believe it. Mr. Talbott was the Devil of Hull House! Jane Addams was not keeping the spirits of the dead prisoner…she was keeping this creature prisoner!

Mr. Talbott gave me one last grin. I watched him walk out the front door and down the sidewalk, singing "Chicago, (That Toddlin' Town)" by Fred Fisher to himself.

I released Jane Addams from the spirit trap. She appeared in front of me and gave me a solemn look, "Now, see what you have done…"

THE VAMPIRE OF ROSEHILL CEMETERY

May 27, 1947
Day of Mars. Moon in Virgo.

My name is Margaret Foyle. It's my turn with this magical book. I read the previous entries of my coven mates, and I have to say, it's quite fascinating. I think Patricia was right to have us cast that spell to call the Devil to help us become more powerful. I think David and Sandy have learned a lot. There were mistakes made, but Patricia says that the best way to learn magic is to "fuck it up" and then clean up the mess. Well, I'm hoping I don't "fuck it up." Maybe. Who knows? I think the best thing to do is to take things as they come and do my best.

I've been with the coven since its start. That was many years ago now. Some of the men in the coven like to boast how powerful they are and how long they've been a witch, and *yadda, yadda, yadda.* I didn't join the coven to acquire power, per se. I joined because I've known I was a witch since I was a child, and when I found the coven, it was a godsend.

I mean, covens are hard to find, even in Chicago. I suppose witches find each other by word-of-mouth and things like that, but covens are scarce. I think a lot of it has to do with people not wanting others to know that they are witches. Nobody would burn us at the stake or anything, but Christianity has power in the United States. More power than I'd like, to be honest.

I suppose my story, my entry into this magical tome, starts with a dream. A couple of nights ago, I had a dream that a woman crept into my bedroom through the window.

This was an odd thing because my apartment is on the sixth floor, and we don't have a fire escape by my window. The fire escape is down the hallway on the other side of the building. There's no way that someone could climb up six floors!

In the dream, the woman climbed into bed with me. She was dressed in a Victorian-style gown. She looked very sad, and she looked into my eyes. She didn't say a word.

After a few moments, she got out of bed and left my room through the window again. When I woke up, I didn't think much of it because, well, you know, it was a dream. The next night, I dreamed once again that the same woman came into my bedroom through my window and lay in my bed next to me. Again, she didn't say a word, and she just looked at me.

It was as if she was trying to tell me something without speaking. After a minute or two, she left out of the bedroom window just as quickly as she came.

On the third night, she came in again and lay next to me. In the dream, I asked, "Who are you?'

She didn't say anything for a long time. She was about to say something, but then she hesitated for a moment. It was almost as if she was scared to speak to me. Finally, she said, "Etta Young."

I suddenly woke from my dream. I think Etta Young was trying to tell me something.

Later that day, I met with Sandy for coffee, and I told her about my dream. Well! Sandy told me that she remembered an urban legend about the Vampire of Rosehill. As the story goes, the Young Family was a prominent family here in Chicago. Well, in 1873, there was a tuberculosis outbreak, and many people in the Young family died, including poor Etta.

Here's where it gets odd. After Etta died, the family kept getting sicker and sicker. It was believed that Etta was coming back from the grave and attacking her own family members.

If this is real, then it's really exciting. I didn't know vampires were real. Well, I didn't know witches were real either, so I suppose there's a lot that I still need to learn.

I wanted to know more about Etta Young. Was she a vampire, or was I picking up some residual psychic energy? Was Etta reaching out to me from the grave? So many questions.

I wanted to speak with her again, but I didn't want to wait until she came to me in my dream. Sandy had a great idea for a spell.

A SPELL TO RE-ENTER A DREAM

Items Needed:
- Charcoal
- Incense burner
- Incense of lavender, sage, and star anise
- A white candle

1. Take the three herbs of lavender, sage, and star anise and grind them into a powder while saying: *"Herbs of dreams, herbs of spirit, and herbs of psychic connection, bring me back to my dream."*

2. Light the white candle and say: *"Spirits of the dream world, open your doors so that I may come into your realm. Bring me back to my dream."*

3. Place the powdered herb mixture on a lighted charcoal and say: *"Guardians of the gates of dreams, open your gates to me. I ask to use my dream as an astral portal so that I may speak with the spirits who wish to speak with me."*

4. You may lie down or sit in a chair. Close your eyes and take a few deep breaths. Allow your body to relax and put the day's concerns away for now.

5. Visualize your dream as much as you can remember. See as clearly as you can the place you were when you had the dream. Visualize the people and/or animals there.

6. Next, visualize yourself rising out of your body and stepping into the dream.

7. Take a moment to visualize your surroundings in the dream world as clearly as you can.

8. When you are ready, you may speak with the people and/or animals in the dream. If you only dreamed of light or objects, you may speak with them, too. Sometimes, spirits come to us in dreams as people, animals, light, or objects.

9. When you are done speaking with the spirits, give your goodbyes and thanks and leave an offering for them once you awaken.

It was easier than I thought to re-enter my dream with Etta Young. I saw myself back in my bedroom, and there, sitting on my bed, was Etta. She looked somewhat sad and stoic. The expression on her face was disconcerting to me. It looked almost as if she was daydreaming or in a world of her own. It was as if she was there but not there at the same time.

I sat down beside Etta. I wanted to understand why she came to me in my dream. "Is your name Etta?"

She didn't say anything for a second or two and then looked me in the eye. "Etta?"

"Yes," I said. "Is that your name? Etta?"

"Etta," she said once more. "Yes, I believe my name is Etta."

I wanted to place my hand on her shoulder. Maybe offer her some comfort. But if I did, would she attack me? Would she leave out the window again? "Etta, why have you come to me?"

Etta looked at me with sad eyes. She didn't say anything at all this time.

"Etta, do you need my help? Are you a vampire? What do you want?"

"What do I want?"

"Yes, Etta. What do you want? Why did you come to speak with me?"

Etta's eyes went from lifeless to full of rage. She lunged at me, and I could see the blood dripping from her eyes and mouth. I was startled, and I quickly jumped off the bed. "Etta, what do you want from me!?"

"I want you to release me!" Etta screamed like an animal caught in a bear trap, and then, like the nights before, she quickly went out of my bedroom window. She was gone once more.

I stood there in my dream for a second, trying to understand what was happening. There was a vampire who came into my dreams and needed my help. The coven will never believe this!

May 29, 1947
Day of Jupiter. Moon in Libra.

The day after I spoke with Etta in my dream, I decided that I may be in over my head, so I asked Patricia what I should do. I had experience, yes, but there were members of the coven who had more experience than me. Maybe someone else should help Etta.

Patricia said that the spirits led Etta to me for a reason, and it was my responsibility to "take care of it." I wasn't sure I was the witch that was needed. We really didn't know much at all about vampires, but Patricia said that the spell we cast had asked the Devil to teach us how to be more powerful, and maybe this was part of that spell. She said that if I really needed help, then I should ask.

The next day, I decided to go to Rosehill Cemetery and speak with someone in the office. Maybe someone knew about the Rosehill Vampire, and they could help me. I'm not even sure what help I really needed. All I knew was that I needed to get more help. The office isn't very big at all. There were only a couple of rooms, and I could tell that they were also very small. The office was quiet when I walked in. A cute little old lady was sitting behind the desk.

"Hello," I said.

"Hello," the old lady greeted me in return.

"I was wondering if you could help me. I'm looking for someone who knows the history of Rosehill."

The old lady smiled at me. I could see that it gave her joy that someone was interested in this old place. "Well, Rosehill is a very old cemetery. She's seen many famous people, not-so-famous people, and many tragedies, as well."

Tragedies. That's exactly what I wanted to know. "What kind of tragedies?"

"Oh, miss," the old lady said, "Chicago is an old city. We've had everything from organized crime to vice presidents buried here."

"What about the unburied?"

The old lady pulled her glasses down toward her nose and gave a look that said she wasn't interested in any troublemakers. "Excuse me, miss?"

Well, here we go. There was no beating around the bush. "There's a legend about the Vampire of Rosehill. Do you know of it?"

"I know of folklore and urban legends, yes. All cemeteries have ghost stories, miss."

I got the impression that the old lady knew something. "Yes, but this is no ordinary ghost story, is it?"

"Etta Young was the daughter of a well-to-do man in Chicago," the old lady said. "She died very young from tuberculosis and was buried here at Rosehill. Soon after, other members of her family began to die. Upon their deaths, they were found to be bleeding from the nose and mouth. In the last century, that was the sure sign of a vampire. I believe Etta's father lost his mind. He hired a vampire hunter who exhumed her body and burned her lungs. The hunter believed that was the only way to kill the vampire."

"Burning the lungs?" What a strange thing to do. "No stake through the heart?"

The old lady smiled. "I'm not a vampire hunter, so I can't say why he did what he did."

"But if Etta's lungs were burned, then how can she still be…"

The old lady lifted her eyebrow, "Still be what?"

"This may sound odd," I said, "but I dreamed of Etta. She came to me in a dream."

The old lady smiled. I could tell she knew more than she was letting on. "You know, they used to say in the old country that vampires come to you in your dreams. That's how they get you. When you are asleep. Vulnerable. When you don't even know you are dreaming. That's when it's too late."

"How can I find her grave?" I asked. I figured that if the old lady was giving me this much information, then what's the harm in asking for more?

"That's easy," the old lady said, "Etta is buried right next to Mary Sheldon."

"Who's Mary Sheldon?"

The old lady smiled again. "Poor Mary Sheldon was poisoned by her own husband. They say that if you look closely, you can see Mary's face in her grave marker."

Hmm. That was interesting, indeed. Why would they bury Etta Young right next to the grave of Mary Sheldon? Did Chicago like burying all the young victims together?

"The cemetery closes at 4:00 p.m.," the old lady warned. "Make sure you are done by then. We wouldn't want you to get trapped here, would we?"

I left the Rosehill office and decided to come back later that night. But first, I needed to find Mary Sheldon's gravestone. Once I did that, Etta Young would be the grave right next to it. I wanted to find it while the sun was still out because once it got dark, I may not be able to find it. Rosehill is a really big cemetery. I'm not sure how big, but you could easily get lost in it. Lots of people do. The cemetery is beautiful, with many trees giving plenty of shade. There's a mausoleum that holds some of the wealthiest men in Chicago—if not all of America. If you have ever been to Rosehill Cemetery, it feels like it's something out of a dream. The thing about dreams, though, they often turn into nightmares.

That night, I walked around the outside of the cemetery, looking for an easy way in. The front gate of the cemetery was enormous. It's never a good idea to sneak into a cemetery from the front. Too many people who can't mind their own business looking for people like me who can't mind our own business. I walked around the side and eventually found a part of the fence that was not very high at all. I was able to enter Rosehill without much of a struggle. The cemetery was darker than I thought it was going to be. Maybe because all the trees hid the street lights. Or maybe because after dark, the shadows of the spirits walked freely.

It took a long while to walk from the back of the cemetery to where Mary Sheldon's grave was, but it was easy enough to find. There, just like the old woman said, was Etta Young's grave next to it. I still think it's odd that a vampire and a victim of poison are buried next to each other.

I heard rustling noises coming from the shadows.

What the hell was that?! I heard someone moving in the yew bushes. I quickly jumped back and ran behind a tree. Was it one of the people who worked at Rosehill? A caretaker, perhaps? Whoever it was had heavy boots and a heavy walk.

THUD. THUD. THUD. THUD.

I stayed hidden behind a big oak tree. Rosehill was dark as hell. I don't think anyone saw me. I watched a man in a long black coat walk over to the grave of Etta Young. He had what looked like a briefcase or something like that. He placed the case on the ground and opened it up. He took out a strange-looking metal tool. "Etta Young, I call to you. Etta Young."

Who was this? A witch? A magician?

"Etta Young! I summon you forth from beyond the grave!" The man took out a flashlight and shined it around the gravesite. Maybe he didn't want to be surprised if a vampire jumped out at him.

I was intrigued by what he was doing. Was he summoning a vampire out of the grave? I didn't know you could do such a thing. I bent over further so I could get a better look at what he was doing, then, *dammit!* I fell into a yew bush.

The man stopped his summoning and walked over to me. He reached out his hand to help me off the ground. "What on earth are you doing out here at night?"

"I could ask you the same," I said, trying to get to my feet.

The man walked back over to Etta's grave. "Vampires, my dear miss."

I found it odd that he had no hesitation to tell me what he was doing. He didn't try to disguise it in any way. He put his tools back in his satchel. I tried to see what was in the bag, but it was too dark, and he was too quick to hide them from my sight. "Why are you out here trying to summon vampires?"

"To kill them," he said. "Forgive me. You must find this all strange. Let me introduce myself. My name is Dr. Charles Dyer."

"Margaret Foyle," I said, extending my hand again.

"You see, Miss Foyle, there is an outbreak of vampire deaths all over this area, and it is my job to destroy them."

Vampire deaths? I haven't heard anything about anyone dying from the bite of a vampire. Is that something that would be in the paper? Or would their deaths be hidden so as not to cause panic?

I have to admit, Dr. Dyer is a handsome man. There's something about him that I find compelling. He's attractive, yes, but not more so than any other man that one may run into on the street. It wasn't that he was outrageously beautiful. It was that he had a way of carrying himself, a charm about him, which I find most interesting. Something about his eyes, perhaps. Or perhaps I was simply intrigued that he was hunting vampires in the middle of a graveyard on the North Side of Chicago.

Dr. Dyer picked up his satchel. "We must be going. May I walk you out?"

I walked with Dr. Dyer down the dark paths of the cemetery. He told me all about vampire lore. He told me that vampires were nothing like Bela Lugosi in *Dracula*. Vampires were not the beautiful creatures who lured you into their beds so that they might bite your neck. He said that they are found in most cultures around the world. It's not that they need blood per se, but the life force that is in the blood. He told me that vampires do not roam the night in their physical body. Their bodies remain in the grave as their astral form looks for suitable victims whose life force they want to steal. As Dr. Dyer explains it, when you die, you shed your physical body, and then you shed your astral body. Sometimes, if the spirit does not want to move on, it can remain earthbound, using the astral body to move about. But...just as the physical body breaks down after death, the astral body will eventually break down as well. This is called the "second death." In order for the spirit to use the astral body on Earth and prevent it from breaking down, it must have the energy to sustain the astral self. The spirit must feed on the life force of humans or animals. Human life force is better.

I said goodnight to Dr. Dyer, and he gave me his telephone number. I confessed to him that I was intrigued by hunting vampires. That seemed to please him a great deal because when I said that, he smiled and became excited by the prospect of having a hunting partner. I wanted to confess to him that I was also attracted to him. Before I said so, I came to my senses. It would have been very humiliating if I'd done that, and thankfully, I kept it to myself. We parted ways, and I took the "L" home to my apartment in Lincoln Park.

The whole way home, I could not help but think of poor Etta. What a tragedy that a young woman would lose her life to tuberculosis at such a young age. I wonder if, upon death, she decided that she was not ready to die and that she wanted to remain on Earth. As the story is told, Etta went back to her family and took several more people's lives with her. Did she plan for them to die, or was she simply feeding herself to stay "alive"? Perhaps she wanted her family to join her in her death. Etta has been dead for many decades. Why is she coming back now?

May 30, 1947
Day of Venus. Moon in Libra.

It's a little after 2:00 a.m., and I have just woken up from another dream. In the dream, Etta came into my window just like she did the other nights. She crawled into bed with me again and looked at me with a vacant stare. According to the vampire lore that Dr. Dyer told me, Etta would be looking to feed on my life force. But that's not what she did. Not at all. I wouldn't say I'm very psychic, but my senses were telling me that Etta didn't want to feed on me or hurt me. She needed me for something. I think she wants me to help her. In the dream, she just kept looking at me with this expression on her face, like part of her needed me, but part of her wouldn't or couldn't tell me what she needed.

A strange thing happened in the dream. I knew I was dreaming. So, I guess I was doing what they call "lucid" dreaming. I wanted to find out more about what Etta was doing in my bedroom night after night. "Etta, why are you here?"

Just like before, Etta didn't say anything for a long while and just looked at me. "Help."

"Etta, how can I help you?"

"Help," she said again.

This was frustrating. I didn't know how I could help her. What could I do? Was she asking me to get rid of Dr. Dyer so he wouldn't destroy her? Was this her attempt to stay alive, even still? "Etta, how can I help you?"

"He's here." Etta sensed that someone was near. For a moment, she became aware of her surroundings and quickly went back out the bedroom window.

I sat there in bed, wondering who was "here." What is happening?

In the doorway of my bedroom stood Dr. Dyer. He looked even more handsome than he did in the cemetery. He took off his black coat and dropped it on the floor. I wanted to ask him how he got into my apartment, but at that moment, in the dream, I didn't care. He took off his clothes and got into my bed with me. We kissed. He held me. I wanted to have sex with him, but I couldn't bring myself to ask him. He drew me closer to him and kissed me again. Then I woke up. I lay there in my bed, awake and alone. Was that all a dream? Or did Dr. Dyer have the power to enter someone's dream?

May 30, 1947
Day of Venus. Moon in Libra.

It's late at night, and I must write about the events of the day. The entire day, I could not stop thinking about Dr. Dyer. I wanted him to call me... and he did, with a little help from witchcraft.

SPELL TO INFLUENCE SOMEONE'S THOUGHTS

Items Needed: No items needed.

1. Take a deep breath and clear your thoughts of all distractions. Take another deep breath and connect to the energies of the Earth and the stars. Breathe in the power.

2. Think of your intended target. Visualize them in every way. If you are having trouble visualizing them, you can say their name a few times. Connect with the energies of your target.

3. As you maintain the connection to your target, think of what thoughts you want them to have. Visualize your target thinking, feeling, or doing what you want them to.

4. Continue to breathe in the energies of the Earth and stars until you feel your body filled with power.

5. Imagine that your thoughts are empowered by the energies. Take another deep breath in, and on the exhale, send the thoughts and energies to your target.

6. One last time, visualize them thinking, feeling, or doing what you want them to do.

Not long after I did this little spell, Dr. Dyer called me on the telephone. He said he wanted to see me again and would love to tell me more about vampires. I have to admit, my heart fluttered like a schoolgirl's. It's strange, but I normally don't act like a schoolgirl when it comes to men. Magic, yes! But men, no. I'm wondering if I'm attracted to him because he is magical in some way. He has to be magical to conjure vampires, I suppose.

He asked me to a café where we had a small dinner, and he told me about his life as a doctor and how he became a vampire hunter.

He told me that in his line of work, many things happen to people that science just can't explain. He assured me that he was a true scientist through and through, but he was also a religious man, and he believed that the Devil was raging a war on Earth. I didn't tell him that I'm a witch and that witches don't see the Devil as "Satan" or the evil-doer that Christians make him out to be. I've read the Bible from cover to cover, and it seems to me that the wrath of Yahweh is more vengeful than the Devil could ever be. I mean, the Devil questioned God and gave the fruit to Eve so that humans could become intelligent creatures and have a will of their own. That doesn't seem evil, does it?

After dinner, we strolled through Lincoln Park. Yes, I read Sandy's story at the beginning of this book about how she accidentally released the "Shadow Man," as she calls him. I have to admit that while we were walking through the park, I was keeping my guard up just in case Shadow Man made an appearance. I wasn't too worried about it, though, because I was on the arm of a genuine vampire hunter. I don't think I've ever felt more safe in my life.

When we got to the lagoon in Lincoln Park, Dr. Dyer told me the story about Suicide Bridge. Apparently, in 1893, the city of Chicago started to build a bridge over the lagoon that was almost seventy-five feet high. It was completed in 1894. That's when the deaths started. As soon as the bridge opened, people would walk to the highest part of the bridge and kill themselves. Some would jump into the cold lagoon in the winter, others would shoot themselves, and those who survived the jump would often drown in the foot-deep waters. There were so many deaths that the city closed the bridge in 1919.

Here's where the story gets interesting. Dr. Dyer—I guess I should call him Charles by now—Charles told me that the tormented souls who committed suicide at that bride often became vampires. What a horrible thing. To want to end your life and then your spirit roams the Earth, looking for blood or some kind of life force to sustain it. Charles says that he has destroyed many vampires that killed themselves off of Suicide Bridge.

As we walked through the park, I slowly became aware of the many spirits of the dead that roamed that area at night. I didn't see any spirits, but I could feel them. I knew that they were there. Maybe it was Charles' story. I think perhaps my mind was so enthralled with the story that my psychic awareness was opened, and I was unintentionally "tuned" into the dead. That often happens to me when I'm listening to old records or reading a book about real-life people who have died. One of the blessings of being a witch, I suppose. Walking through the park was lovely and romantic, but at the same time, I could feel the spirits of the dead watching us. I couldn't hear any voices. I'm still learning how to "see" spirits. I can see them on occasion, but mostly, I feel them with my heart. Well, sometimes in the pit of my stomach, too.

Patricia says that my ability to see spirits will strengthen in time. But do I want to see spirits all the time? When I do learn that skill, I hope I'll be able to turn it off and on as I want to.

May 31, 1947
Day of Saturn. Moon in Libra.

It's 3:00 a.m., and I have woken up from another dream.

Just like the nights before, I dreamed that I was lying in my bed, and Etta came into my room. She crawled into my bed, and this time, she looked at me like she was a long-lost child who found their way home. Again, I knew I was dreaming, and I wanted to find out why Etta had been visiting me for three consecutive nights. "Etta, why are you here? Why do you visit me night after night?"

Etta leaned in closer to me. She seemed to be fascinated with me. Like she had never seen anyone like me before. "Your life force is strong."

"My life force?" Was Etta here to feed on me?

Etta smiled innocently and kept her gaze in my eyes. "Your blood has power."

"What do you mean, Etta?"

"Your witchcraft makes your blood strong."

Etta and I laid on the bed for what seemed like forever, looking at each other's eyes. I was prepared to defend myself against the vampire Etta if I needed to. She never tried to harm me. She looked at me with almost, dare I say, love in her eyes. Like I was her relative or friend. Then, after a while, Etta popped up from the bed.

"He's here."

Just like the night before, Etta fled out of the window and back into the night.

Charles was standing in the doorway again, just like he was the night before. He took off his black coat and all of his clothes and got into bed with me. He kissed me softly, and I could feel myself melting into him. I wanted him. He kissed me harder the second time and pulled me close. We had sex. I have to say, this was the most amazing sex I have ever had. It was physical, it was raw, but it was also beautiful. I felt like my heart was in his heart, and his heart was in mine. We were together. There were times when I forgot who I was, and all I knew was that Charles was engulfing me with his body. In the coven, we talk about achieving a trance state of ecstasy through various techniques, and with Charles, I was truly in an ecstatic trance state. I have never felt ecstasy like this before. I fell asleep, and when I woke up, Charles was not there. Was he here at all? Was it really just a dream?

June 1, 1947
Day of Sol. Moon in Scorpio.

I got up out of bed, and I decided I wanted to see Charles. I felt as though I should tell him about my dream. He would think I was silly and impulsive. I can't tell him my dream. I called him, and we met for breakfast at a café in Lincoln Park. The neighborhood was busy. It was warming up. Chicago has long winters that can last until June. When the weather warms up, everyone loves to come outside. If you walk the lakefront, you are sure to see lots of people enjoying the warm breeze and the beautiful lake. At the café, I found myself closing my eyes and enjoying the warm sunlight on my skin.

I decided to tell him about my dream. He might think I'm crazy. He might think I've lost my mind. The more I thought about it, the more I thought that I needed to tell him everything. For some strange reason, I couldn't help but feel safe with him, and I believed that I could say anything to him. When he arrived at the café, I told him about my dream with Etta. I told him how she would come to see me and was trying to tell me something. I told him how she would visit me in my dreams night after night. Such an odd feeling. The longer I was with him, the more comfortable I was telling him my dream. The more I spoke with him, the more I was falling for him.

I must admit, I was hoping he would tell me that he was feeling the same way about me. But instead, all he could talk about was how Etta was a vampire who wanted to drain me of my blood and life force and that we needed to destroy her. I told him that in the dream, she didn't want to harm me. I told him that instead, I think she was trying to give me a message. What message, I did not know. My intuition was telling me that there was something more to Etta.

"We need to destroy the vampire!" Charles seemed excited about this.

Charles gave no indication that he was feeling the same way I was. "Charles, do you have…how do you feel about me?"

Charles didn't say anything for what felt like the longest time. In fact, he looked downright confused. "How do I feel about you? What do you mean?" Was he purposefully being obtuse?!

"I mean, I believe I am falling for you, Charles." I should have been more coy and…well…all those things we do when we pretend that we're uninterested in the man we're falling for. Mother used to say that men think aggressive women are tramps. Maybe I should have listened to her, but at that moment, I didn't care about that.

Charles looked at me with sympathetic eyes. He was finally understanding what I was trying to say. "My dearest Margaret. I may have given you the wrong impression. I have enjoyed our time together, but my intentions are to hunt and destroy the vampire. I cannot afford the time spent on relationships and marriage."

Those words hit me like a hammer on the head. Have I misread him? Did I have a desire for him that he did not have for me? I must confess that he only came to my room in my dreams. I sat at the café table, trying not to look pitiful or upset. I couldn't decide if I was broken-hearted or pissed off. I think I was both.

Charles paid for our meal, and he said, "Tonight, we must destroy the vampire for your sake. If we do not, I'm afraid, dear lady, you will be doomed. Your dreams may seem innocent, but vampires are cunning, nasty business."

Charles was right. Even though my heart fluttered when he was around and I was having sexual dreams about him, the vampire is more of an important matter. I couldn't be too angry with Charles. He did want to help me, after all. I agreed to meet him at Rosehill Cemetery after dark at the grave of Etta Young. He told me to prepare for a long night. Well, if nothing else, at least I will learn how to magically destroy a vampire.

But first, I'm going to cast one more spell.

A SPELL TO ENSNARE THE ONE YOU LOVE

Items Needed:
- Two wax dolls in red or white (or unsculpted wax)
- Three red candles
- Three needles
- Two stemmed roses with thorns
- Red fabric or handkerchief

1. Melt wax in a pan and fashion two dolls, or obtain two pre-made wax dolls. One doll represents you, and one represents your target. The color of the wax may be white or red.

2. Once you have created or obtained your dolls, consecrate them to you and your target. Take the doll that represents you and say: *"This doll I name (your name). This is my body, spirit, mind, and soul."* Hold this doll in your hands and spend some time thinking about how this doll is you.

3. Take the second doll and think about all the attributes of your intended target. Say: *"This doll is (target's name). This is my love. It is them in body, spirit, mind, and soul."* Hold this doll in your hands and spend some time thinking about how this doll is your target. Visualize them as clearly as you can.

4. Take the three red candles and place them in a triangle with the apex pointing in the direction of your target. Light the first candle and say: *"I call to the spirits of the heavens. Come to my intended love and make them love me with the power of the stars."* Light the second candle and say: *"I call to the ancestral spirits. Spirits of the dead. Come to my intended love and make*

them love me with the power of the Otherworld." Light the third candle and say: *"I call the spirits of this world. Spirits of the Earth. Come to my intended love and make them love me with the power of the Earth."*

5. Next, hold the wax doll that represents your target and think of them again as clearly as you can. Know with all of your being that this is them. Take the first needle and heat the end with the candle flame. Pierce the head of the doll and say, *"(Name of target), you cannot stop thinking of me. You will not know peace of mind until you are mine and I am yours, bound together in love."*

6. Take the second needle and heat the end over the candle flame. Pierce the genital area of the doll and say: *"(Name of target), you want to join your body to mine. You want to have sex with me today and every day. You will not know satisfaction until you are mine and I am yours, bound together in love."*

7. Take the third needle and heat the end over the candle flame. Pierce the heart of the doll and say: *"(Name of target), you want to join your heart with mine. You love me above all things. You will know only sadness until you are mine, and I am yours, bound together in love."*

8. Make sure the needles are halfway inside the doll. Then, take the flame and heat the exposed ends of the needles inside the doll of your target. You can also soften the wax of the doll that represents you. Next, take the doll representing you and place it onto the exposed needles of the target doll, saying: *"(Name of target), you are connected to my mind, heart, and body. We are bound together in love."* Place both dolls together in the center of the three candles.

9. Take the rose petals off the rose and hold them in your hand. Visualize an energy of magic and love surrounding you and your target. Place the petals around the dolls and think of all the ways that you and your target will be together bound in love.

10. Take the thorned rose stems and place them in an "X" shape over the dolls. As you do this, visualize you and your target bound together

in love. Say: *"(Name of target), you and I are bound together in love. Let no person or spirit undo the magic I do here tonight."*

11. Sit with thoughts of love for as long as you'd like. Then, take the red fabric or handkerchief and wrap the dolls together. Place them in a box or someplace where no one will disturb them.

June 2, 1947
Day of Luna. Moon in Scorpio.

The events of last night were like a waking dream. Something out of a vision you may not have asked for but was sent to you by the spirits. I'm awake, but I'm not awake. I can feel my heartbeat in my chest, but I feel like I may have died last night. As I write this, I know it sounds silly. In witchcraft, each ending is like a death. With each death comes new life and new powers.

Powers of magic that can heal and harm. Boon and bane. Create or destroy. This is the way of things. The way of the Universe. I'm not sure where to start on this tale, so I suppose I will start with what I remember the beginning to be.

I met Charles at Rosehill Cemetery just as we had planned the day before. From his car, he took out a shovel as well as his satchel. We found a place along the cemetery fence where we could easily get inside and take the long walk to the grave of Etta Young. We walked in silence for a while. I was wondering if my love spell had started working yet and would glance every so often to Charles to see if there were any signs of love coming from him. He didn't say much as we walked the winding paths of the graveyard.

Finally, we found Etta's grave. The feeling in the air was a combination of magic and sadness. Maybe that was just me and the things I was feeling. I wasn't certain that Etta was the terror that Charles made her out to be, but he was the vampire hunter, so I guess that he knew more about these things than I did.

Charles put the satchel of tools on the ground and took out everything we needed for tonight's magic. He took out candles, a hawthorn wand, and a sickle. He placed the shovel on the ground and began his ritual.

SPELL TO DESTROY A VAMPIRE

Items Needed:

- Three white candles
- Incense burner and charcoal
- Incense of wormwood and mugwort
- Hawthorn wand (oak, rowan, or any wood that commands spirits can work as well)
- A sickle consecrated to the Old Gods

1. Place three white candles in a triangle in your ritual space. If you are able to perform the ritual in the cemetery, place the candles over the grave of the suspected vampire.

2. In the center of the candles, place your incense burner with charcoal. Place the mixture of wormwood and mugwort onto the burner.

3. Take out your sickle and place it to the side, preferably out of the sight of the vampire spirit.

4. Conjure the powers of the Old Gods: *"I call to the Old Gods, you were the first. You, who created God himself, the first gods among many. Old Gods, forgotten by time, we call to you this night. We seek your power to guide us and help us destroy the spirits who wish to destroy us."*

5. Conjure protective angels: *"I call to you, Michael, the right hand of God, prosecutor of evil. We seek your flaming sword tonight so we can destroy the spirits who wish to destroy us. Help us maintain balance upon the world so we may live in peace."*

6. Next, summon the spirit of the vampire with these words: *"Spirit of the vampire (name of vampyre), we summon you into our magical triangle. By the power of the Old Gods and the archangel Michael, we command you to manifest before us!"* Say these words while visualizing the vampire appearing before you. Keep saying this conjuration until the vampire appears.

7. If the vampire spirit does not appear, say: *"The Old Gods and the archangel Michael command you to appear before us!"* Visualize ancient gods and Michael using their ancient magic to compel the vampire to manifest.

8. Once the vampire manifests in the magical triangle of candles, say: *"Spirit of the vampyre (vampyre name), you are magically compelled to stay within the magical triangle by the power of the Old Gods and Michael. You are imprisoned and bound with our magic. There is no escape for you. You are an abomination to mankind. A predator who kills without mercy or glory. Who harms men, women, and children. Who should not be on this, the physical plane. Who cannot pass on through the veil of death into the afterlife. You are an abomination. A spirit who is alive but dead. Who is dead but alive. We must maintain the order and balance of the Universe with your destruction."*

9. Take out the consecrated sickle and, without stepping into the triangle of candles, stab the heart of the spirit as hard as you can. Visualize the vampire spirit vaporizing and disappearing forever.

10. Then, take the sickle and energetically draw a white pentacle where the spirit once was so that the spirit is forever sealed from ever returning to the physical plane.

11. To close the ceremony, say: *"We thank you, archangel Michael, for your power here tonight. Peace be with you on your journey. We thank the Old Gods for your power here tonight. Go now to your ancient realm. Peace be with you on your journey."*

When Charles started to perform the ritual, I felt uneasy. Something did not feel right to me. I understood that Charles wanted to destroy a menacing vampire, but Etta did not harm me. I think she was trying to tell me something.

I could see that she feared Charles, but it makes sense that a vampire would fear a vampire hunter. During the ritual, I could see that Charles commanded great power over the spirits. It came to me as he was conjuring the spirit that the magic of vampire hunters, witches, and cunning people were similar. We just use different terminology and perhaps different spirits who help us during our rituals.

It wasn't long before Etta appeared within the magical triangle of candles. She looked at me with great sadness. Something was wrong! What…what was going on? Etta appeared in my mind. It felt almost as if I was daydreaming or creating a fantasy in my head. But it wasn't a daydream. It was Etta manifesting in my consciousness.

In my mind, Etta seemed more aware than she had been before. She looked desperate. In my thoughts, she said, *"Beware of Dr. Dyer!"*

In this trance-like state, I could speak with her as well. "Why?"

"He's not who you think he is."

"Who is he, then?" I asked

Etta gave one last desperate warning. *"He is the leader of a vampire—"*

Etta disappeared.

I regained my focus within the physical world and saw that Charles had finished stabbing Etta's spirit with the sickle. She was gone.

Charles finished the ceremony and placed the sickle down on the ground.

"What was Etta trying to tell me, Charles?" I asked. I sensed that the answer he was going to give me was one of dread.

"Poor, poor Etta," Charles began. "The daughter of a wealthy businessman. You see, during that time, girls were nothing like the girls today. They were subservient to all men and did as they were told. Changing her into a vampire was easy. The power I received every time she killed one of her family members was like a beautiful tonic."

I didn't quite understand what Charles was telling me.

"For years, Etta—and vampires like her—would drain their prey of life, and I received their essence. I created the vampires of Chicago, after all. They are my children—or slaves, depending on your point of view."

"Children? Slaves?" My heart was beating a mile a minute.

"Etta betrayed me," Charles explained, "she knew I had my eyes on you. She was warning you. But she only had so much agency of her own. She wanted to warn you that I wanted you next. Etta had to be destroyed for betraying me."

No! This can't be. Dr. Charles Dyer, my Charles, was a vampire leader, or witch, or whatever the hell he is!

"I thought it would have been much harder to turn a witch into a vampire, but with your love spell binding us together, you made it much easier than I thought it was going to be."

He tricked me. Charles wanted the added power of a witch to help him drain the life force from people for his own benefit.

I ran away from the cemetery as fast as I could. I didn't know what to do. I couldn't think. I got on the "L" and made my way home as fast as I could.

There's no way he could capture and control me. No way. Right? My coven will protect me. We can all join our magic together, and Charles will not have the power to control me.

I'm sitting here in my apartment, writing down everything that I could remember about last night. I'm glad I'm writing it down. Maybe I can read it again. Someday. The memories of last night are fading from my thoughts. I need to tell the coven what happened before it's too late. The sun is up now. I need to go to bed. I need to go to sleep. I need to dream.

MOULIN VERT

June 6, 1947
Day of Venus. Moon in Capricorn.

This is James Bower. I've been with the Lincoln Park Coven since the beginning. Back then, there were only a few of us. Patricia brought us together. She taught us everything we know and made sure that we always knew what we were doing. I got into witchcraft quite by accident. You see, I wanted to be a Ceremonial Magician. I used to read things by Aleister Crowly. I read his book, *Magic in Theory and Practice,* when I was younger. I wanted to be initiated into the O.T.O. in the beginning. I used to frequent the Occult Bookstore and was hoping to run into other Ceremonial Magicians. You might say I was a novice with magic. But, as often as I could, I'd go to the bookstore hoping to meet a magician who could introduce me to the O.T.O. Weeks went by, and nothing ever came of it. The few people I talked to were nice and all, but I never met anyone who really knew the O.T.O. Maybe they didn't want me. Maybe the spirits had other things planned.

One night, I had a dream. In the dream, I was given a spell to increase my magical power and call out to the magical folks I was supposed to be with to learn from them.

A SPELL TO INCREASE YOUR MAGICAL POWER

Items Needed:
- A white candle
- Incense of frankincense, rue, and rosemary
- Charcoal
- Four quartz crystal points
- A black bowl filled with water

1. On the night of a full moon, prepare your ritual space. Perform a banishing or room cleansing of some kind. You can use a fumigation or perform the Lesser Banishing Ritual of the Pentagram.

2. You will sit on the floor and place a white candle, a black bowl of water, the incense holder, and incense in front of you. Then, place the four quartz crystal points facing you in the four compass directions of East, South, West, and North.

3. State your intention for more power by saying: *"I call to the great mystery, the unknowable Universe. Grant me the power of magic. Increase my powers so I may serve the gods in the New Aeon."*

4. Light the white candle and say: *"Spirits of the terrestrial, the subterrestrial, and the celestial, I call to you this night. Bring to me those who will show me the mysteries of magic and bring me closer to the light."*

5. Light your charcoal and place the incense mixture on top of it. As you smell the scent, think of yourself in the future as a powerful magician. See yourself being taught the mysteries of magic. See yourself wielding great power and as a master of the Universe, serving the good of all things. Now say: *"Great beings of the Universe, grant me the power I seek. Show me a great teacher. Show me the path of magic and healing. Grant me the magic I seek so I may help all beings usher in the New Aeon."*

6. Next, look into the black bowl of water. This is your scrying bowl. Gaze into the scrying bowl to see the face of your future. Look for the faces of those who will lead the way to the path of magic. If you do not see images, visualize your future magical self in the black bowl of water.

7. Now, take a deep breath and inhale the energy and magic of your future self into your body. Continue to take deep breaths and inhale your magical future self into your body until you feel yourself containing all the essence of your future self. Have a deep "knowing" that your future magic is with you at this moment.

8. Give thanks to all the spirits you have called.

9. Banish any residual energies from your ritual room.

After I cast that spell, it wasn't too long before I met Patricia, and we began speaking of the world of magic and witchcraft. I wanted to be a Ceremonial Magician, but the way Patricia spoke of witchcraft made it sound like something I could use. I figured magic was still magic, no matter how you packaged it. I listened to my gut, and my gut was telling me that the spirits had led me to Patricia, and she was the teacher and guide I was looking for.

Well, that was quite a few years ago. I suppose you could say that the spell I cast that full moon was successful because I have been practicing magic and witchcraft for many years now, and I have had many adventures, I guess you could say. I would agree with Patricia when she says that the coven's magic has become stagnant over the years. We have been performing the same spells over and over again. We went from learning magical techniques and experimenting with new magic to the same ol' full moon rituals and the same ol' sabbat rituals. It's always good to perform magic with the coven, but I must confess that I was getting a bit bored. I wanted more. Hell, I always want to learn more magic. I was glad that Patricia had the dream, and we did the spell to conjure the Devil so the Witch Father could help us increase our magic. Part of me is looking forward to my adventure, and part of me is keeping an eye out for trouble.

That brings me to the Green Mill Lounge.

Last night, I was sitting in my apartment. I spend a lot of my time alone, except when I'm with the coven. I like my time alone. After work, I may stop at the market to get something to make for supper, and then I come home. After I eat, I'll read or sometimes re-read my books on magic. I like magical techniques that manipulate energy and astral projection. Those two things are my favorite. Well, I was sitting in my apartment, and I had an unusual thought. I should go to the Green Mill.

The Green Mill is an old cocktail lounge in Chicago's Uptown neighborhood. There are several theaters not far from the lounge. I have to admit, I'd never been to the Green Mill before, so I thought it was quite odd that my mind manifested that desire. I was going to ignore it at first, but then I wondered if maybe the thought in my head was part of the spell that we cast. I stopped for a moment and remembered that I had agreed with Patricia that our magic had gotten stale. I put on my hat and decided to catch a cab to the Green Mill.

The Green Mill. When I got out of the cab, I looked up at the flashing sign that read "Green Mill Cocktail Lounge" in green neon surrounded by white light bulbs, just like the signs you see at theaters. I opened the door, and I was greeted with jazz music. Not any old jazz music, but the kind of jazz that makes you forget all your troubles. It takes you away to a place of glitz, glamour, and booze. It was crowded. Real crowded. Everyone was drinking and laughing and having a good time. Men were dressed in their suits and the women, jeez, the women all looked like they were from the pictures. Everyone was beautiful. I have to admit, I'm not used to seeing sights like this. I suppose I spend too much time alone with my magic books. But, let me say, this place has magic all its own.

I looked for a place to sit. All the tables were taken, but maybe I could find a stool at the bar. As I walked down the long bar, I kept getting shoved here and there by people trying to make their way through.

"Sorry, mister," a beautiful woman said.

"Hey, watch it, bub!" a man would say, all the while shoving me.

I found a seat at the part of the bar that curves around. This was a good place to be. I could see the whole lounge. I could see everything.

The loud band stopped all of a sudden. Everyone stopped talking and laughing to see what was about to happen on stage. The spotlight went up and out came...her. The jazz singer came out on stage, and she was a vision. She was beautiful, but she had the kind of beauty that transcended this world. If I were to imagine what a goddess might look like, it would be her. She began singing this song. I wish I knew the name of it, but she began singing this song, and it was like she was singing to my soul.

I looked around, and all the men were hanging on every word she sang. Every note. Every breath she took. Even the men who were with women.

Hell, even the women took notice. She sang song after song. I sat there with my drink and just listened.

After a while, she finished her song and came down from the stage. Someone handed her a martini, and she began laughing with a crowd of people. I wished I was with that group of people, but I didn't know them, and they didn't know me. Hell, I decided to go down there and give it a go. I could at least tell her my appreciation for her music, and that would be that. I was nervous as hell as I made my way through the people waiting to say hello to her; the same thing I wanted to do. I made my way through the crowd and found myself standing next to her. I think she saw me there out of the corner of her eye. She took a sip of her drink, turned toward me, and said, "I've never seen you here before."

"No, ma'am," I said. I don't think I've ever been this timid talking to a woman before.

She smiled at me and said, "Name's Beth Willows. What's your name, mister?"

"James Bower," I said.

"Well, James, have a drink with me, won't you?"

I stood there in a stupor for a time. I couldn't believe this beautiful woman, this goddess, wanted to have a drink with me. "Anything you'd like."

She led me to a corner booth that was near the stage. It seemed to me that this was her booth. In a crowded place like this, there were no empty tables. She was that kind of woman. The kind of woman who had her own table at a jazz club. We sat at the table, and a girl came over to take our drink order.

Beth looked around the room and seemed to be savoring the crowd. "This your first time here, James?"

"Yes, I decided to come here on a whim."

The girl brought us our drinks, and another band got on stage and began playing up-tempo jazz.

"Tell me about yourself, James," Beth said. I could tell she was used to having men say and do whatever she wanted.

I told her how I lived in Lincoln Park and about the kind of work I did. Nothing impressive. I was afraid that if I talked too much, she might get bored. I didn't tell her I was a witch. Couldn't do that. I could see that she wasn't the kind of woman who was into magic, spirits, and devils.

"Who's your friend, Beth?" a man wearing a sharp suit said. The man looked to be Italian. He also looked to be in charge.

"This is my new friend, James," Beth said.

The man extended his hand to me, all the while keeping his eyes on Beth. "Name's Jack. I run this joint."

"Nice to meet you, Jack," I said. When I shook his hand, I could feel his energy. I could sense that he was up to no good. I got this feeling in my heart. A feeling of darkness.

Jack gave me a devilish look. "Keep an eye on old Beth here. You don't want her to get you into trouble."

Beth didn't say anything. I had the feeling that she knew he was no good, and saying anything would only make matters worse. She stayed silent until Jack walked away and started to talk to the other patrons at other tables.

"Wanna get outta here, James?" Beth said.

"Sure, where to?"

Beth suddenly looked sad. I felt a shadow over her. "Anywhere."

We got up from the table and made our way out of the lounge. Beth was behind me as I made my way through the place. I opened the door and went outside to the street. When I turned around, Beth was no longer behind me. She was gone. I went back inside and walked back toward the stage, and there she was, back at her booth, talking with a group of people. It felt strange to me. But maybe she'd changed her mind.

June 7, 1947
Day of Saturn. Moon in Aquarius.

The next day, I couldn't get Beth out of my thoughts. I did think it was strange that she wanted to leave the Green Mill only to go back to talk with friends, though. Still, my day was filled with thoughts of her. She was a resident singer at the lounge, so I was sure that she would be there again tonight. She seemed to like me. Maybe I was lying to myself. I'm just an ordinary guy, and women like that probably wanted a guy who was something. As much as I tried, I couldn't stop thinking about her. I don't lose control over women, but I could see myself being happy to lose control over her.

Just like the night before, I took a cab to the Green Mill. Just like the night before, the lounge was filled with sharply dressed men and women drinking and carrying on. The jazz band played a fast-tempo song. Some couples were dancing while others drank their cares away. Beth's booth was empty. Was she not singing tonight? Am I an idiot for thinking a beautiful woman like her could like a schlub like me? Then the band began playing a slower song, and she came out on stage. Beth walked out and began singing a sultry song. Maybe it was an ordinary song, but the way she sang it…was sultry. It was slow. It was hypnotizing.

When she finished her song, she sat in her booth. She saw me staring at her and waved me over. I sat down with her at her booth. "What happened to you last night?"

Beth scooted closer to me and said, "Oh, James, you're a good guy. There are things in this place you wouldn't understand."

I knew places like this were associated with the mob. In the 20s and 30s, the mob owned Chicago. Nowadays, the old drunks at bars like to say that the mob still owns the bars in Chicago. Not just some of them. All of them. "Forgive me for being bold, but if it's the mob you are worried abo—"

"James!" Jack said, seemingly excited to see me. "You're still associating with this broad?"

Jack seemed like a man who could be dangerous. Normally, I'd have something to say to a man like him, but my gut told me to keep my mouth shut. "Beth is one of those broads who get you into trouble."

"Jack…" Beth was getting quite upset. "If you didn't run your mouth all the time, then we wouldn't be in this situation, would we?"

Jack grabbed Beth by the arm, pulling her toward him. "You just shut your pretty little mouth…"

I quickly stood up to punch Jack in the mouth when the doors to the Green Mill were kicked open. "This is a raid! Everyone with your hands up!"

Five police officers shoved their way through the crowd of patrons. The band stopped playing, and everyone was hushed.

No one said a word. The officers looked quite angry and had machine guns. I had never seen machine guns before except in the pictures. They shoved their way to Beth's table. They were looking for Jack.

"Fellas, Fellas…" Jack put his hands in the air. It seemed as though Jack was used to police raids at the lounge. "We can work this out. What do you need? Money? We have an agreement. My boss won't be happy if you break our agreement."

The police officers pointed their machine guns at Jack, but he didn't look frightened at all. Not one bit. "Fellas, if you take me in, my boys will have me out in less than an hour. Let's do us all a favor and just take the money you want."

BAM! BAM! BAM! BAM! BAM! BAM! BAM! BAM! BAM! BAM! BAM! BAM! BAM! BAM! BAM!

Bullets were being shot everywhere! The police officers were shooting their machine guns. Jack fell to the floor. I quickly took Beth's arm and forced her under the table with me. This was the only thing I could think of for protection. Everyone was screaming!

BAM! BAM! BAM! BAM! BAM! BAM! BAM! BAM! BAM! BAM! BAM! BAM! BAM! BAM! BAM!

More shooting. Holy fuck, I had never been so scared in my life. From under the table, I could see people falling to the ground. I was frozen stiff under that table. I held on to Beth's arm as tightly as I could. I didn't want to let her go. She forced herself free from my grip, and she stood up to run out of the lounge.

BAM! BAM! BAM! BAM! BAM! BAM! BAM! BAM! BAM! BAM! BAM! BAM! BAM! BAM! BAM!

Beth was shot. She tumbled to the ground. There were so many bodies on the ground. The Green Mill was shot up to hell. The walls had so many bullet holes in them they didn't look like walls anymore. It was a lounge of death. I crawled to the next table. Then the next, then the next. I watched the police officers walk out of the lounge with their machine guns. They were not police officers. This was a mob hit, and I was lucky to be alive!

After a while, I figured it was safe to go outside.

I tried to remain calm as I had to walk over dead bodies that were bloodied with bullet holes. I opened the door, and when I got outside, I vomited. I couldn't believe what just happened. Beth was dead. They were all dead. I calmed down enough to notice a cop car coming my way. I ran out into the street and flagged them down. The police officers must have known something was wrong by how I was yelling "Stop! Help!" in the street.

The police car pulled over, and an officer stepped out of the car.

"They're all dead!" I yelled. "All of them! Shot!"

The police officer took out his gun and slowly went to the front door. I followed him inside. The shooters were gone, so I knew it was safe to go back inside. With his gun drawn, the officer crept through the door. I was staying behind him just in case. When we got inside, the band was playing. People were alive. People were drinking and laughing. It was as if nothing had ever happened. Beth stepped on stage to sing again. Jack was staring at Beth from the same table he usually was. The shooting never happened. It never happened.

The police officer looked very angry at me. "Wise guy, huh?!"

"I don't understand…" What in the hell was going on? What had just happened? What was it that I just experienced?

"Next time," the police officer said, "call a cab home and don't bother us."

June 8, 1947
Day of Sol. Moon in Aquarius.

The whole next day, I kept replaying what happened in my mind. Was the shooting some kind of dream or hallucination? Or have I lost my damn mind? Were the spirits playing tricks on me? I had no idea what was going on. I need to go back to the Green Mill again tonight. Maybe I was hallucinating, but that hallucination nearly got me killed. I needed help, so I decided to call Margaret. Maybe she could help me. She has experience with dreams, magic, and vampires. Maybe she had some ideas.

I went over to her apartment, and it was a strange sight. The place was dim. She had put in new curtains. They were a dark shade of something. Brown, or maybe burgundy.

It was hard to tell because it was so dark. She had a few candles lit. It was warm in her place. The windows had been covered by those thick, dark curtains.

June in Chicago was usually temperate. The occasional cool breeze might come in off the lake. I hope she plans to open the curtains by July, or it'll be unbearable inside this place.

Margaret looked pale and thinner than usual. She's always been thin, but it looked as though she hadn't eaten in days. "Margaret, how are you feeling?"

Margaret lit a cigarette. "I'm perfect. Why do you ask?"

"You look a bit tired," I said. Normally, I'd never say something like that to a woman, but Margaret is my coven mate, and we all have a close bond. Like a magical family.

Margaret took another puff of her cigarette. "I've been seeing a gentleman friend. His name is Dr. Dyer. He's been keeping me up at night."

"Is that so?" I read Margaret's entry in the book, so I knew what she was talking about. I pretended not to know because I wasn't used to Margaret being so forward like that. We are like family, yes, but we don't talk about sex with each other. Especially the women with the men.

We have to maintain some standard of decorum. I'm sure Margaret would have understood that I've already read what she wrote. It seems that she is being influenced by Dr. Dyer. I don't want to believe it. Maybe if I could get her to do magic…if I could get her to create a spell for me. Maybe she'll come back to her senses. Come back to herself.

"So what is it you need today, James?"

I told her the story about what happened the night before. Margaret was good and thought up magical spells. I really liked the spell she gave me.

A TAROT SPELL FOR INSIGHT

Items needed
- Tarot cards
- Two purple or white candles
- Incense of mugwort, sage, and rosemary

1. Think of the insights that you need. Shuffle the tarot cards and draw a card as you think of the wisdom you need. Place your card on a table or sacred space.

2. Light the charcoal, and place the incense mixture in your hands while thinking of the wisdom and magic that you need. Place the mixture on the charcoal and let the scent bring you thoughts of magic.

3. Place the two candles on either side of the card. As you light the candles, say: *"We call to the spirits to open a portal into the astral plane for us. Give us the guidance that we seek. Open the door of insight and wisdom. Tell us the story of magic so that we may help others as well as ourselves."*

4. Memorize every detail of the card that is on the table. Open your heart and call out to the spirits. Know with all your being that the spirits will show you what you need to know.

5. Close your eyes. Bring to mind the tarot card. See the card as a doorway. Step into the portal and allow yourself to be taken to the part of the astral plane that is exactly like the card.

6. Once you are inside the card, look around. Take note of what looks like the card and everything in this place that the physical card was unable to show you.

7. Everything in the card is a spirit. The people, animals, plants, clouds, and objects are all sentient beings. Using your intuition, go to the person, animal, or item that calls to you.

8. Ask the spirit what it is you wish to understand. Remember, spirits can communicate with words, visions, pictures, sensations, and feelings. Be open to what the spirit has to tell you.

9. When you are ready, thank the spirits for their wisdom and come back to your physical body.

10. Leave offerings for the spirits.

Margaret helped me with this spell. She walked me through it. She had a little magical rattle, and she continued to rattle it so that I could keep my trance state. I never have problems staying in trance, but with the smell of the incense and the rattling, I was quickly placed into such a deep trance that I almost forgot the reason I was in the astral plane in the first place.

I wanted to know what was going on at the Green Mill. What secrets were they hiding? The tarot card I drew was the Seven of Swords. This card showed a man stealing several swords. I visualized this card as a portal. I stepped into the tarot card picture. Suddenly, I found myself in a camp of some kind. Maybe it was a medieval military camp. There was a large tent surrounded by smaller tents. I could tell it was late at night because everyone was sleeping. Then I saw him. A man sneaking around the camp, stealing soldiers' swords. My first instinct was to yell, "Stop, thief!" but this spirit was *supposed* to be stealing the swords. I walked up to the thieving spirit, and I asked him my question. "I'm so sorry to disturb you. My name is James Bower, and I humbly ask for your assistance."

The thief put down the swords and looked at me, trying to figure out who I was and what I was up to. "You trust the words of a thief?"

"I understand that the spirits have their own way of doing things, and I am not one to judge those beings I do not understand," I said. I remembered to always be respectful of the spirits, no matter how weird or dark some of them might be.

The thief looked at me devilishly. "You are a wise man. What help could I be to you?"

"I wish to understand what is happening at the Green Mill," I told him.

The thief took one of the swords that he had stolen and placed it in my hands. "Look into the blade of this sword and find the answers you seek."

I did what the thief asked and gazed upon the metal of the sword. This was a scrying technique I had never seen before. Suddenly, my consciousness left my body, and I was standing in the Green Mill. I was but a shadow watching a memory of that place. I saw Jack sitting in a booth sitting with another man. I could see sunlight coming in from the windows in front of the lounge, and the place was almost empty. I slowly walked up to the booth to hear what Jack was saying.

Jack took a big gulp of his whiskey. He had a serious look in his eyes. "Bugs Moran has become a real thorn in my boss' side. It's time to do something about it."

The other man was smoking a cigarette. He flipped the ash in an ashtray. "And what does your boss want us to do about it?"

Jack had a smirk on his face. From what little I knew of Jack, I could see that he had power and always got his way. "I need you to take care of Bugs and his gang."

The other man took a drag from his cigarette. "A man like Bugs ain't no easy target. It'll cost you."

"The boss will pay up," Jack said.

"So when do you want it done?" the other man asked.

"Tomorrow."

"Tomorrow?" The other man was surprised. "Tomorrow is Valentine's Day."

Jack lit a cigarette for himself. "Then think of it as a love letter to the boss."

Suddenly, I appeared in a garage. There were six mobsters inside. Cops burst in and told them to drop their weapons and turn around. The mobsters did what they were told.

BAM! BAM! BAM! BAM! BAM! BAM! BAM! BAM! BAM! BAM! BAM! BAM! BAM! BAM! BAM!

Shots from machine guns blew up the garage, killing all six men. These were not cops. These were rival gang members sent to execute Bugs Moran and his men.

A dark feeling hit my spirit. These dead mobsters wanted revenge. Their spirits wanted revenge.

A bowling alley. There he was. Jack was bowling with friends. Three men came up behind him and shot his brains out. His blood splattered on a calendar that said February 15, 1936.

Then I woke up from the vision.

It was strange. The spirits…the ghosts. I assumed that maybe they had died inside the Green Mill. Maybe some of them did, but many of them did not. The police officers I saw shooting up the club were the murdered men of the St. Valentine's Day Massacre, back to give Jack a taste of his own medicine. But that means…Jack, the St. Valentine's Day Massacre, Bugs Moran…of course, this is Jack McGurn, "Machine Gun Jack" himself! They came back to enact revenge, doing to him what he had done to them. But Jack himself didn't die in the lounge. He was murdered in a bowling alley, for God's sake. What about Beth? I still didn't quite understand her story. I need to find out what the hell is going on with that place.

After I woke up from the vision, I wanted Margaret to help me with the Green Mill. Maybe we could free the spirits or something like that. "Margaret, I need you to help me. I don't think I can do it on my own."

"Fuck 'em," Margaret spouted.

Wait. What? Margaret is usually willing to do magical things like this. She's usually one of the first ones ready to do magic. There have been many times that Margaret and I have gone off on our own to do magical rituals and spells and things like that. This was odd behavior for her. "Why do you say that?"

"Aren't you sick and tired of helping spirits and never getting what you really want?" Margaret didn't sound like herself. She sounded...I don't know. Not like her.

"What do you mean? I love working with spirits and doing magic."

"You mean *the coven's* magic," she said with a bit of spite in her voice. "It's always what the coven wants to do. Do you ever just want to say 'fuck it' and do what you need?"

"I do what I 'need' all the time," I said. "The coven is a guide, not the rule."

"Suit yourself," she said. "I'm going to do what I want to do."

I left Margaret's place feeling off. I was grateful for the spell and it worked well, but she is not okay. Maybe I should spend more time with her, but my thoughts were still on those people at the Green Mill.

I spent the rest of the day wondering what I was going to say and what I was going to do for those spirits. They had to be spirits, right? The thing that was bothering me all day, though, was that I'd worked with spirits many times before, and never once had they manifested so physically. As if they were alive and in the flesh like you or me. I didn't get it at all. I went straight from Margaret's apartment to see Patricia. Patricia always says that we can just "drop by" anytime. So I went to my teacher and mentor, and maybe she could help me with the spirits.

Patricia was always brewing a tea of some sort. Today, it was a nice sage tea with blackberry leaves. Yes, she would make coffee if someone asked for it, but her place always had the wonderful scent of brewing herbal tea. Over tea, I told Patricia the story of the Green Mill. "What do you think I should do?"

"I think you should trust that the spirits led you there for a reason," Patricia said.

"To free them? To help them? To do what?" I wanted more than just a cryptic answer.

Patricia took a sip from her tea. "Remember the ritual we did to ask the Devil to help us gain more magical power? The gods will put us in situations so we can learn from our experiences. I can tell you what I would do as myself, Patricia, but it's better if you learn what *you* would do. I have my own experiences and talents, and so do you. What I would do may not be what is needed in this situation. The spirits led you there, not me. And if I just told you what to do, would you really learn, or would you simply be hanging on my coattails?"

I figured that Patrica would say something like that. I'm not surprised. Patricia is fond of getting all of us in the coven to figure things out on our own. Sometimes I just want her to give us the answers and stop being so damn cryptic all the time. I know she's right. She's always right about these things. "You all need to learn how to figure magic out for yourselves. Otherwise, I've failed as a teacher," she would say. Well, I guess I'll just have to figure this out on my own.

Before I left, I wanted to say something to Patricia, "I'm worried about Margaret."

She put down her tea and exhaled. "I've been sensing something."

"What have you been sensing?"

"Something is blocking me," she said. "I've tried to call her, but she doesn't pick up the phone. She knows it's me calling."

"What are we going to do?"

Patricia looked worried. "I'm not sure."

I left Patrica's apartment feeling concerned for Margaret, yet at the same time, I felt empowered. I felt reassured by Patricia that the spirits had enough confidence in me to let me handle the Green Mill in my own way. "Even mistakes in magic teach us how to become more powerful," Patricia would often say.

Once the sun went down, I took the "L" back to the Green Mill. Just like the other nights, as soon as I opened the door, the place was busy and loud with patrons. People were laughing, drinking, and listening to the band on stage.

Of course, there she was, Beth, singing an enchanting song on stage. The men were hypnotized not only by her beauty and grace but also by the way she enchanted them with her song.

I sat in her booth and waited for her to come over. Once her song was done, she slowly made her way to the booth, stopping here and there to say hello to the gentlemen and even the ladies who wanted a small piece of her time. Beth sat next to me and ordered a martini from the waitress.

I was done playing her little game. "Beth, come clean. What the hell is going on? I saw you get shot. Hell, I saw everybody get shot, and then a minute later, it's like it never happened. What gives?"

Beth lit a cigarette and took a sip of her drink. "These people, these souls, they don't know what's happening to them. Night after night, most of them think we only just arrived. From their point of view, we've only been here hours when, in reality, we've been here for years."

"A psychic echo," I explained. "When a traumatic event happens and leaves an energetic imprint or recording on a place, and night after night, the event replays itself."

"You are assuming the people here are just an echo of what happened to us," Beth said. "No, these spirits are real. Doomed to repeat our deaths, night after night."

I sat there for a moment and ordered a drink. I needed something to calm my nerves. What the hell was I going to do?

The waitress came with my drink, and I drank it in one swoop. It went down strong, but it's what I needed.

Jack McGurn came to the table just like he did every night. This time, instead of harassing Beth, he came to talk to me. "So, this is the witch who can get us outta this?"

"Maybe," Beth said. "I was hoping for a witch or a psychic who knew what they were doing."

That was rude. "Hey, I know what I'm…"

She was probably right. I didn't know what I was doing, but I guess I was here to figure something out.

Jack McGurn was impatient. I could tell he wanted me, or frankly, anyone who had magical powers, to help them. "Listen, do what you need to do. Just get us outta here."

Jack was a piece of shit. A low-life mob guy who killed people for money and then laughed about it. He deserved to suffer. I wasn't afraid of Jack like the others were. "And why should I help you?"

Jack laughed. Even his laugh was fucking evil. "Because helping me helps this dame."

Fuck. He was right. I couldn't pick who could go and who had to stay. Maybe someone with more experience with this could do that, but I certainly didn't know how. I'd have to help everyone, including Jack.

The front door was kicked open. Men dressed like police officers carrying machine guns burst into the lounge and started firing.

BAM! BAM! BAM! BAM! BAM! BAM! BAM! BAM! BAM! BAM! BAM! BAM! BAM! BAM! BAM!

Bullets sprayed everywhere. Glasses shattered, and people ran, screaming. Bullets knocked people down, leaving puddles of blood everywhere. Even though I had already witnessed this before and knew now that this was a ghostly scene of the spirits' revenge, it was very real to these poor, trapped spirits, and it felt real enough to me. Maybe the bullets wouldn't kill me, but I sure as hell wasn't going to take that chance. "Come on! We gotta get out of here!"

"Follow me!" Beth took me by the arm, and we dashed to the bar. The bartender lifted a trap door, revealing stairs that led to the basement. Beth kept running through the basement and into tunnels that led under the streets of Chicago.

"Where the hell are we?" I asked as I followed her down the dark tunnels.

"These tunnels were an underground escape route for Capone and his gang," Beth said as we made our way through the darkness. "They came in handy during police raids."

I felt a hand on my shoulder. "What's that?!"

I turned around, and there stood a woman dressed in 1920s clothes. Her throat was cut. Out of the shadow walked a man who had bullet holes in his chest. Then, a woman came from another shadow with purple hand prints on her neck. Then another person, then another, and another. All spirits of the murdered dead. I had no words. These poor souls were people who were killed and their bodies "taken care of."

Beth saw the horror on my face. She took my hand and tried to lead me away, but I was too stunned to move. "These are the victims of Capone's men. Some of them are Jack's handy work."

"What do they want?" I asked.

For the first time, Beth had a sorrowful look on her face. "The same thing we all want. To be free of this place."

My mind was spiraling. What spell did I know that could help these people, these spirits? What could I possibly do that would help them? I had to stop to center and ground myself for a moment. I needed to gather my energies and my wits. I wouldn't be able to help anyone if I couldn't calm down. I needed to think straight. "There has to be a source. A center that is keeping the spirits from moving on."

Now that I had my wits about me, I could focus. The Green Mill was just like any other haunted house, right? People who were murdered here maybe had unfinished business or…they wanted justice for their deaths. And who was the kingpin behind all this? Yes, Al Capone was the boss, but he put Jack McGurn in charge of the Green Mill. It was Jack who gave the orders for these people to be killed. It was Jack who hired the men to kill Bugs Moran and his men on St. Valentine's Day. I fucking had it! The spirits of the dead wanted justice, and it all focused on one man. Jack McGurn.

CLAP. CLAP. CLAP. CLAP.

"You finally figured it out," Jack stepped out of one of the shadows. He'd been following us the whole time. "If you get rid of me, then everyone gets to live in the hereafter. Maybe heaven, maybe somewhere nice. As for me, I'm not going to someplace nice."

"Why won't you let the spirits go, Jack?" I asked.

"Let them go?" Jack laughed. "I ain't keeping shit here. You think I know or even give a fuck about these spirits? All I know is that I may be dead, but I'm still in charge. A party night after night. Sure, it's interrupted by those assholes with machine guns. But we resume our drinking and women. James, ever fuck a ghost? It's not bad, really. Some say it's even better than when they were alive. I don't keep these worthless fucks here. They want justice, but I'm already dead."

"Fuck you, Jack," I said. What a piece of shit.

Jack held out a gun and pointed it right at me. He was a ghost holding what I assumed to be a phantom gun. I wasn't sure if the gun was real or not. Shit, I didn't want to take any chances of Jack killing me, too.

I could hear the clicking of the gun. Jack looked at me right in the eye. "I'm wondering what would happen if I pulled this trigger. Would you die and join the rest of us, or would it pass right through you? I guess there's only one way to find out."

"Jack, no!" Beth screamed out.

At that moment, in that second, I knew I could very well die. The only thing that ran through my mind was the word *survive!* No one was going to help me. I was on my own, and I was a witch.

I'm a powerful witch who is connected to all things in the Universe and protected by the Devil himself. I am he, and he is me. Survive. My internal survival instinct overpowered my fear. Then, without thinking, without hesitation, I pushed my hands toward Jack and screamed, *"Enough!"* A wave of energy shot through my arms, pushing the spirit of Jack McGurn across the room.

He was knocked down, but he would soon come to his senses. I couldn't wait any longer. I had to banish his spirit. Forever.

SPELL TO BANISH A WAYWARD GHOST

Items Needed:

- ◆ Ritual dagger
- ◆ Triangle of Art

1. This spell is to be used only when all other methods of convincing the ghost to move on have failed. This spell is for those ghosts who terrorize others and cause physical, mental, emotional, and spiritual harm.

2. Call upon the deity that you work with and honor. This must be a deity that you have worked with and have a relationship with. Calling a deity you don't know will work, but it will not have the same desired results.

3. Place the Triangle of Art on the floor with the apex facing away from you.

4. Ask the deity to surround you with protective energy, spirits, and ancestors.

5. Call upon your ancestors. Ask your ancestors to call upon the ancestors of the wayward ghost. Your ancestors act as spirit guides for you and may be called upon to find other ancestors in the afterlife.

6. Summon the wayward ghost into the Triangle of Art by saying, *"By the power of (deity), I command the spirit of (wayward ghost's name) to appear before me in this magical Triangle of Art. By the powers of the gods, angelic beings, and spirit helpers are you bound within this Triangle of Art."*

7. Once the spirit is bound in the triangle, take out your ritual dagger. Hold the dagger with both hands and point the dagger toward the heavens. Take a deep breath, and as you inhale, visualize white celestial light from the center of the Universe filling up the blade with powerful magical energy.

8. Point the blade to the wayward ghost. Take a deep breath and visualize the white light shooting out of the blade like a canon

vaporizing the astral body of the ghost. As you shoot the beam of white light, very aggressively shout: *"Banish!!"*

9. The pure spirit of the ghost will remain. Ask the spirit's ancestors to take the spirit to the afterlife for healing. Open a portal to the afterlife and visualize the ancestors taking the spirit where it will find healing.

10. Give offerings to the deity and your spirits and ancestors.

I needed to banish Jack's spirit, but I didn't have my ritual tools with me. You would hope that after years of being in the coven, I would learn to have small portable magical tools with me when I was going to someplace terrorized by spirits. "Beth, I need something to make a large triangle."

Beth quickly looked around the tunnels and found three thin wooden boards leaning against the walls of the tunnels. "What about this?"

Boards. Perfect. "Hand them to me!"

I put the three boards into a triangle around Jack. Usually, a Triangle of Art has Hebrew god names or the names of angels written on each side, creating a magical barrier that contains the spirit. When evoking a friendly spirit, it helps them manifest on the physical plane, but when evoking hostile spirits, it keeps them bound within the triangle. As I placed the boards into a triangle, I called out to the archangel Michael. "Archangel Michael. The Right Hand of God. Defender of all that is good. I ask that you use your angelic power and bind Jack McGurn into this magical triangle."

Jack was coming back to his senses. He stood up and tried to take a step toward Beth and me, but he was stopped by the Triangle of Art. "What is this?"

"You're trapped, Jack," I said. I have to admit I was feeling in control and powerful. It was nice to turn the tables on Jack for a change. "The Triangle of Art and the power of Michael bind you."

"Listen, without me, these people would roam the Earth like lost souls," Jack said. "If it wasn't for me, they would be lost forever."

I called my protective deities, spirits, and ancestors to help me with the banishing ritual. It was time to send the pure essence of Jack's spirit back to his ancestors. Once I saw my own ancestors appear, I asked them to bring me the ancestors of Jack McGurn. It wasn't too long before

Jack's ancestors surrounded the makeshift Triangle of Art with Jack stuck inside. The spirits looked both angered and sad. Maybe they were sad that one of their own descendants caused so much heartache and pain.

One of Jack's ancestral spirits said, "Jack, come back with us of your own free will, and you will avoid the second death."

The second death is something most people, other than witches and magicians, know nothing about. When the physical body dies, the etheric body soon dies as well, leaving the astral, mental, and spiritual bodies. The dead person is able to use their astral bodies in the afterlife or even haunt the physical plane. The second death is when the spirit of the deceased evolves spiritually enough to where they no longer need their astral body, and it is shed, leaving the pure spirit of the person. This is the spirit or essence of the person that is reincarnated life after life. However, this ritual can force the second death on someone whether they are willing to evolve or not. What happens to the spirit when this happens is between them, their ancestors, and their god.

"I like it here," Jack said. "These people need me."

Out of the shadows walked more spirits of the dead. Each one had signs of violence against them. There were some with gunshot wounds. Others had their heads bashed in, and others had stab wounds. These spirits walked close to Jack. They pushed their way through Jack's ancestors. One of the dead said, "You trapped us here."

The spirit of a woman who had her throat cut said, "None of us deserved to die. Yet by your hand, you murdered us. For what? Power? Money?"

The spirit of a man who had bullet holes in his body said, "With each death, this place became a prison for us. A spiritual trap that none could escape from."

"I protected you!" Jack screamed.

"You imprisoned us," another spirit said.

"Prepare for the second death," Jack's ancestors said.

I didn't have my ritual dagger, but I didn't necessarily need it. I could draw energy from the Universe and direct it with just my index finger. I closed my eyes and focused on the power of the Universe. I took a deep breath, and as I inhaled, I visualized white energy from the most powerful part of the Universe coming into my body through my crown energy center and into my heart energy center. The spirits all stepped aside as they saw me draw in the light. I took another deep breath, and as I exhaled, I yelled out, *"Banish!"* I sent the beam of light to Jack, and his astral body was vaporized. Only the spirit essence of him remained in the triangle.

I removed one of the boards that made the Triangle of Art, and his ancestors took the spirit of Jack, and then they were gone. They took him to the afterlife, where his spirit would start all over again. Maybe he would do better in his next life. I'm not sure what's going to happen to his spirit. I know there's no hell or anything like that. Maybe he has to work on his karma in the next life, or maybe he will be reincarnated as a bug. Either way, Jack was gone. He could do no more harm to these poor souls.

Beth took my hand. "We are free. Thank you."

I could see the spirits of the dead whom Jack and his boys had murdered slowly fade away. I hope they find peace and healing in the afterlife.

Beth still had my hand, and I could feel her energy begin to fade. "Beth, how did you find me? How were you able to find me so that I could help you?"

She kissed me on the cheek and said, "Sometimes, it's better the devil that you know…"

And with that, she was gone.

My head was spinning all over the place. I was exhausted and full of energy at the same time. I was able to free these trapped spirits. I was feeling…hell, I really don't know how I was feeling. Just that I did a good thing and that I had learned more about spirits in just a few nights than I had in several years of study. I guess it's true what Patricia says—you can only learn so much from books. The real power is in the experiences that you have as a witch.

I found my way back to the stairs that led up to the secret trap door behind the bar at the Green Mill. I climbed the stairs, opened the trap door, and walked back into the lounge. I looked around, and it was the oddest thing.

There was no party, no loud people were drinking and laughing. There wasn't even a jazz band. The bartender looked at me with what I could only interpret as shock. There were maybe ten people in the whole place. I didn't say a word as I walked out from behind the bar. I was just about to leave when I saw a picture of Beth singing on the stage of the Green Mill with her band.

"Bartender, who's in this picture?"

"Oh, that's Beth Willows," the bartender answered. "She was a jazz singer here back in the 20s and 30s."

"Whatever happened to her?"

"I don't know," he said. "She just went missing one day. I wonder about her sometimes. I hope she's okay."

"I think she's okay," I said. Then, I walked out of the Green Mill Lounge.

THE LIPSTICK KILLER

June 17, 1947
Day of Mars. Moon in Gemini.

My name is Linda. I don't want to give out my last name. Well, maybe not right now. You see, I work in a very conservative office, and if they got wind I was doing witchcraft, they'd either fire me or who knows what. Just "Linda" is fine for now. Maybe one day, I'll write more about my personal life in this book. Yes, I know that this is a secret book, and no one except current and maybe future members of the coven will ever see it. A girl can't be too careful. I can say this at least: I live in an apartment building in Lakeview here in Chicago with a roommate named Frances. Well, I suppose I shouldn't tell you her name either because then you would know who I am.

Frances and I have known each other for a few years. We are close to the same age, and when we became roommates, we quickly became the best of friends.

She's from Indiana, and I'm from southern Illinois. Both of us came from small farming towns and moved to Chicago for…well, adventure, I suppose. I left home for Chicago as soon as I could. I knew it would have more to offer than corn and chickens. I wanted culture, art, and maybe even to find someone to love who wasn't a farmer. I found the Lincoln Park Coven some years back.

I met Patricia in a tea parlor. She was reading tarot cards for a friend, and I was curious to know what she was doing. Patricia had a mystique about her. She had a feel to her that no one back then had. I guess no one now has her energy, either.

I asked her to tell me about the cards, and that conversation over tea led to my interest in the occult and witchcraft.

I must admit that when Patricia spoke to the coven about her dream—you know, the one where she found out that some great "evil" was coming for us—I was concerned, yes, but I was not convinced that we should call upon the Father of witches himself to put us in scenarios that would teach us to be more powerful as witches. The Master, that's what we sometimes call the Horned One, or the Devil, has his own ways of doing things. He teaches by throwing you into the fire, and you have to figure it out, or...or I don't know. Suffer? I wasn't too keen on the spell that we cast.

I trust everyone in the coven. I trust Patricia, but I'm not sure I trust myself. If I'm in real danger, will I be able to handle it?

The most horrible thing happened about two weeks ago. A six-year-old girl named Suzanne Degnan was kidnapped from her own bedroom. Soon after, there was a ransom note asking for $20,000 for her to be returned home safely.

That did not come to pass. The body of that poor little girl was found in the sewer drains not far from her house. All of Chicago is in an uproar. The papers keep running headlines scaring people. I guess scary headlines sell papers.

They have no clues and no leads. The only thing they have is a ransom note.

I have a friend who is a Chicago police detective. Well, he's a little bit more than a friend, but I'll write more on that later. Anyway, he says they weren't able to find prints, nothing. No way to know who this monster is. He's still out there.

This whole thing is creeping me out.

I have to protect myself. Yes, I saw the protection spell that is at the beginning of this book. That's a fine spell. But I have a spell that I like for protection.

There is this occult shop here called the Occult Bookstore. It's been here for years. Since 1918, I think. There was this woman who used to shop there at the same time I used to shop there. I used to joke that she somehow "knew" when I was going to be there. After we ran into each other a few times, we became friendly, and she shared a powerful protection spell with me.

THE PROTECTION OF THE DEAD SPELL

Items Needed:
- Graveyard dirt
- Three white votive candles in glass votive holders
- Dittany of Crete
- Charcoal and incense burner

1. Go to a graveyard. Using your intuition, find the grave of a spirit that will allow you to take some of the dirt. Tell the spirit that you wish to ask them for protection, and in return, you will give them offerings of food and water. If you sense that the spirit is in agreement, you may gather the dirt. If not, find another grave and speak to the spirit once again.

2. Once you have gathered the graveyard dirt, place three coins as payment into the hole where you gathered the dirt.

3. Take the dirt home and create a line of graveyard dirt behind the front door of your home on the inside of the door.

4. Place three candles on the dirt. Before you light the first candle, think of the Underworld spirits who guard the gates of the dead. Light the candle and say: *"Great gatekeeper of the Underworld, I ask that you open the gates of the Underworld so that the spirit I conjure may come to me for protection this night."*

5. Before you light the second candle, think of the Great Goddess Hecate, she who leads the dead to and from the Underworld. Light the second candle and say: *"Great Goddess Hecate, Keeper of the three keys of the three worlds. She who is Mother to the unwanted dead. I ask you this night to escort the spirit of the dead to our world so they may protect me this night."*

6. Light your incense of dittany of Crete to draw the spirit of the dead to you.

7. Before you light the third candle, think of the spirit whom you asked at the cemetery to come to you for protection. Light the third candle and say: *"Spirit (name of spirit if known), come to me from the afterlife and*

protect my home and all who dwell within. In return, tomorrow, I will give you food and drink as an offering."

8. Spend some time connecting to the spirit of the dead and know that they will use their powers to protect you from all harm. Once you feel the spirit is present, you may put out the incense.

9. In the morning, leave a bowl of food and a glass of water as an offering. You may do this spell on occasion or every night if you wish.

June 18, 1947
Day of Mercury. Moon in Gemini.

I performed the spell exactly how I wrote it down last night. Frances knows I'm a witch, and she is fine with it. She isn't a religious person at all, and I think she thinks that witchcraft is more like a hobby than anything else. I'm fine that she thinks that. I'm grateful that she isn't a crazy religious person who would scream "Satan!" every time I cast a spell at home. She's just as worried about the killer as I am. She told me last night that even though she doesn't believe in God and the Devil, my spell made her feel a little better, knowing that maybe there are things she doesn't understand that are protecting us. I trust the magic of the spirits, but I'm no dummy. I'm still sleeping with one eye open.

I've been dating this Chicago police detective named Patrick. I'm not sure he would appreciate me writing about him in my coven's book of witchcraft, so I'm going to trust that whoever reads this keeps it a secret. Patrick and I have been seeing each other for quite a few months. Not quite a year. He's a swell guy. Hardworking. It seems as though he's always working on a case. If you guessed that he works homicide, then you will have guessed right. He usually doesn't tell me about his jobs. But this one. The murder of that little six-year-old girl has got him in such a way. I can't describe it. If I didn't know better, I would say he's scared. Maybe not scared for himself. I think he's scared for our community and probably scared for me. I'll be fine. I have witchcraft on my side.

I would really like to help Patrick solve this case. He knows I'm a witch, too. He keeps joking with me and says that I better not turn into the mean ol' Witch of the West. It's funny what people think of when we say the word "witch." They always think of the *Wizard of Oz*, as that is their only reference.

I'm glad that Patrick is charmed by me being a witch. I once asked him why it doesn't bother him, and he said that in his line of work, he's seen so much death and the worst of humanity, so a little thing like casting spells is nothing in comparison. He says if I can do some good in the world with magic, then maybe it's a good thing that people just don't understand. I like to think he's right.

June 19, 1947
Day of Jupiter. Moon in Cancer.

I can't believe what is happening. Last night, at around two in the morning, Frances and I were awakened by flashing police lights. We both bolted out of bed and ran for the windows. Luckily, June was one of the warmer months in Chicago, so we could open up the big bedroom window and see what was going on. There must have been ten police cars a couple of blocks away from our apartment. My witch's senses were telling me that Patrick was down there with those policemen. Something terrible had happened, and I just knew it!

I told Frances to stay in the apartment, and I put on some clothes as fast as I could and hurried down the street. Now, no one, especially women, was allowed at a crime scene, but knowing Patrick was there, I might have some special privileges. Maybe, maybe not. I just had to see what was going on.

As I ran down the street, my heart was pounding in my chest. There was something telling me that I just had to go. I just had to find out what was going on.

When I arrived at the scene, I tried to sneak by a couple of police officers who were standing near the doorway of the apartment building.

"Not so fast!" a police officer said.

"Just where do you think you're going?" the other officer asked in a stern voice.

"Dames aren't allowed at crime scenes," the first officer said.

I normally don't do things like this, but I figured I could use my feminine charms, and maybe he might let me pass. "Officer, I just wanted to see Detective (last name omitted)."

"Scram!" the second officer said. "We said dames ain't allowed!"

I decided that my charms were not good enough for these officers, and I had to find another way into the building.

I walked around the back side of the building. Maybe there was a backdoor that I could use to get inside. I walked around through the alley, and I found the back entranceway. Strange. The doorknob had been broken by a large rock or something. I don't think the police have gotten back here yet.

A SPELL TO BE UNSEEN

Items Needed: No items needed.

1. Find yourself a hidden place where you will not be seen.

2. Breathe in the energies of the stars and hold them in your body. Breathe in the energies from under the Earth and hold them in your body. Breathe in the energies of the land and hold them in your body.

3. Take in another breath and send all of the energies to your heart and then your hands.

4. Visualize your hands glowing with the powers of the witch.

5. Place your hands on the top of your head. Take another breath. On the exhale, move your hands from the top of your head to the bottom of your feet. As you do this, imagine magical smoke or mist coming from your hands and encasing your whole body, making you invisible. You cannot be seen by anyone.

6. Maintain the visualization as you pass by those whom you wish not to see you.

7. When you are ready to be seen, take a breath, and on the exhale, blow away the smoke or mist and know that you can be seen once again.

This spell to be unseen is quite an easy spell to cast. I've used it before on many occasions to slip by those I wish not to notice me. After I cast the spell, I walked up the staircase and walked right past several police officers who were standing nearby. Even though I had used an "unseen spell," a noise too loud could easily break the glamour and reveal myself to them. I already got yelled at once. I wasn't ready to get scolded again for not minding my own business.

It wasn't too hard to find the apartment that was the scene of the crime. I walked past another police officer and went into the apartment where everyone was standing. Patrick looked up from whatever it was he was doing and saw me. He saw through my glamour. Maybe because we have a strong connection, or maybe I wasn't focusing enough. Either way, he saw me.

"Linda, you shouldn't be here," Patrick said.

"I needed to see what was going on over here," I said. "This is my neighborhood, and I have the right to know."

Patrick was aggressive and grabbed my arm. That was strange behavior for him. He's never once laid a hand on me. "Linda, get the hell out of here!"

I jerked back, breaking free from his grip. What the hell had gotten into him? I quickly turned around, and that's when I saw it. A scarlet red pool of blood made a little river from the bedroom of the apartment into the living room. Everyone watched as I followed the trail of blood into the bedroom.

For some strange reason, no one said a word as I walked into the bedroom. No one said anything, and no one tried to stop me. I slowly walked into the bedroom and saw that there was so much blood coming from the bed.

I walked closer and saw that a middle-aged woman had been stabbed several times. Above the headboard on the white wall was a message written in red lipstick. It said:

FOR HEAVEN'S SAKE CATCH ME BEFORE I KILL MORE.
I CANNOT CONTROL MYSELF.

Patrick walked me home and told me to lock the doors. There was a killer on the loose. He was still out there somewhere in the night. On one hand, I was in shock, but on the other, I wanted to do something about it. That poor, poor woman. Her name was Josephine Ross. She was only forty-three years old. She never married. She never had children. Now, she would have life unlived. Some monster took her life from her, and he is still out there.

Patrick told me to tell no one about what I saw. He needed to catch the killer, and he didn't want the papers to get wind of this and spill the beans. He says that sometimes there are copycat killers who will mess up their crime investigation. Who in the hell would copy such a terrible crime?

As difficult as it is to fathom, Patrick says that the crazies are out there, and we need to keep this under wraps. I'm not sure I could tell someone else what I saw. I can't bring myself to tell Frances. She's a sensitive girl. I think a big heart makes one sensitive. For now, I'll tell her that there was a terrible crime and that it was far too terrible to talk about. I don't want to worry her any more than she already is.

June 20, 1947
Day of Venus. Moon in Cancer.

I couldn't bring myself to go to work today. I couldn't stop thinking about the poor woman who was murdered last night. The killer is on the loose. I couldn't stop thinking about it. All day long. Nothing but blood and death and killers who were not caught.

The papers were not allowed inside the bedroom where the scene of the crime was. But like papers do, they certainly found out who the woman was and everything one needed to know about Miss Josephine Ross, including her age, where she grew up, and her job. A woman just lost her life, and the papers were treating her like a sideshow freak. The papers were saying that the murder of Josephine Ross was the same killer of that six-year-old girl who was found dismembered in the sewers. Were they connected, or did Chicago have two killers on the loose? Patrick likes to remind me that Chicago is a big city, and there are things out there that are so terrible, and no one knows about it.

I have to find the killer. I have to. Patricia told the coven once that witches were often sought out to catch thieves. Maybe the power of the witch can be used to catch a killer.

I needed to cast a spell. A spell that would compel the killer to reveal themselves. I can't remain silent when I know I have the power to help bring the guilty to justice.

I think I know just the spell.

A SPELL TO REVEAL THE GUILTY

Items Needed:
- White wax to form a doll
- Incense of High John the Conqueror root, lemongrass, and devil's shoestring
- Mortar and pestle
- Charcoal
- One black candle and one white candle

1. Create your doll out of white wax. While you are melting wax on the stove in a pan, pray to the gods of justice to reveal the perpetrator. You may pray to Athena, Thor, Ma'at, or Shiva, but you may pray to your personal gods as well.

2. Once the wax is melted, begin fashioning your doll while saying: *"(God of justice), I come to you in search of the truth. Reveal to me who has done (the crime or misdeed). May the spirits not rest until all is revealed!"*

3. Next, create your incense blend with a mortar and pestle. As you add High John the Conqueror root, think of justice being served, and say: *"You will reveal yourself to me. You who have done (the crime or misdeed), you cannot hide from the gods of justice."*

4. Add the devil's shoestring and say: *"You will be ensnared in my witchcraft. You cannot escape the magic of the gods."*

5. Add the lemongrass and say: *"With the power of the spirits and the gods, we will be cleansed of your wrongdoing!"*

6. Place the black candle on the right side of the wax doll and the white on the left side. As you light these candles, visualize the energy of justice surrounding the perpetrator. You may visualize a white light if you wish.

7. Take the incense blend and place some on the charcoal. Make sure there is lots of smoke. Wave the incense around the wax doll until there is a thick smoke.

8. Now, place your hands together side by side. Take a breath and visualize the perpetrator revealing themselves to you. As you exhale, spread your hands apart as if you are parting the veil of secrecy and blow the smoke away. The magic will reveal who the perpetrator is.

9. Say: *"You are found! You are caught! Justice is served!"*

10. Give offerings to the spirits and gods.

June 21, 1947
Day of Saturn. Moon in Leo.

Today is the summer solstice, the longest day of the year. Today is a day of healing and joy, and yet I am the most terrified I have ever been in my life. I don't think I'll be going to the summer solstice ritual tonight with the rest of the coven. I can't. I just can't.

I have to write down everything that happened last night. I don't want to write this down, but I must. If not for my sake, then maybe for the coven or perhaps someone from a future generation. My writing may sound strange. I haven't stopped shaking all day. I have to gather my senses. At least long enough so I can write this entry in this magical book.

I cast the spell to reveal Josephine's killer. I had to know. The spell was done carefully to the letter. Not one step was skipped. This spell has been used many times before. Many times. But this time, the spell worked differently. Perhaps the spell worked better than it was meant to. Right now, I really don't know what is "meant" to be or what is "fated."

Last night, after I cast the spell to reveal the guilty, I also decided to cast the spell calling the spirits to protect me in my home. With a murder on the loose, I needed all the protection I could get. Frances was going to be out with her fellow. All night. She sometimes would spend the whole night with him. Her boyfriend owned a small home on the Far West Side of Chicago. She was supposed to spend the whole night there. The whole night.

I fell asleep last night at about 10:30 p.m. or so. I didn't know. I mean, I just didn't know. I didn't know that Frances and her fellow got drunk at some bar and got into a fight. They've gotten into fights before, but last night, Frances wanted her fellow to take her home. I didn't know. I just didn't know. Well, he dropped her off and drove home. Frances climbed up the stairs and opened the door to our apartment. I didn't know until this morning that, when she opened the door, she accidentally knocked over the magical candles and messed up the barrier line of graveyard dirt. The candles went out, and there was an opening where the line of dirt should have been. We were exposed. We were vulnerable. Frances came to bed. We live in a one-bedroom apartment. We have two twin beds in the bedroom that we share. I heard her come in, but in my dreamy state of mind, I didn't think about the protection spell. I just didn't think.

It must have been around 2:00 or 3:00 a.m. I'm not quite sure. A noise woke me up from a sound sleep.

POP!

I heard the sound of someone breaking the lock on our front door.

Creak. Creak. Creak. Creak.

Footsteps.

I opened my eyes. I need to get up! I need to see who was in our apartment. I need to see who that is.

No.

Wait.

I can't.

No.

I can't move.

I can't move.

I have sleep paralysis.

I fucking can't move!

Someone walked into our bedroom. I could hear the creaking of the hardwood floors as someone put their weight on each foot. The person sounded heavy. A man? Maybe. I couldn't see. I couldn't move my head to see who was there. Having sleep paralysis is the most frightening thing. I was wide awake, but I couldn't move my body or open my eyelids. But I knew that I could astrally open my eyes. Maybe I could see. Maybe I could do something. I can't move.

The figure walked to Frances' bed. Her bed was closer to the bedroom door. The figure stood over the bed. I think he was just looking at Frances. What the hell was he doing? Was he admiring her? Was he going to attack her?

A knife.

The streetlight coming in through our window shimmered on the steel blade.

Thrust.

Thrust.

Thrust.

A stream of scarlet red fell from the bed to the floor.

My heartbeat was pounding so hard and so fast that I thought I might have a heart attack.

Fucking let me move! Gods! Devils! Someone, let me move!

A scream.

Frances screamed. It was the most blood-curdling sound I have ever heard. Like a wild animal giving its most primal scream, hoping someone would hear her. Hoping I would hear her. Frances started punching and slapping the figure as hard as she could.

Thwack! Thwack! Thwack!

The figure fought her. I could see that the figure was a man. A man who had stabbed Frances. A man who had killed just the night before. A killer in my bedroom, and I was powerless to do anything.

Frances hit the man hard in the face. He stumbled back and looked into her eyes. Only the face looking back at Frances was not of the man. It was Margaret Foyle. My coven mate. The friend who was losing herself to the powers of the vampire.

What's happening?

I called out to her with my mind, "Margaret!"

The specter of Margeret was inside the man. She was possessing him. I didn't know vampires could do that. I didn't know.

Margaret controlled the man's body. He took two fingers, dipped them into Frances' blood, and placed them in his mouth. Margaret smiled at me.

I could do nothing. I was paralyzed.

Frances screamed again. She gathered what little strength she had and got out of her bed. Blood dripped down her belly and thighs. She was headed for the front door.

BANG! BANG!

Margaret shot her. My friend. My roommate was dead.

Margaret put the gun back into the man's pocket. Margaret faded away. He took a deep breath and looked like he had just awakened from a nightmare. A dream that he could never fully awaken from. He was awake, but Margaret was still there.

Somewhere. I could sense it. I could feel my coven mate somewhere deep inside that man.

He walked over to the nightstand. Frances' red lipstick was sitting on top. He took the lipstick. He removed the lid and wrote on the white wall above France's headboard.

FOR HEAVEN'S SAKE CATCH ME BEFORE I KILL MORE. I CANNOT CONTROL MYSELF.

Frances is dead. It was Margaret who killed her. She was somehow inside a man's body. I think she was possessing him. Like a demon. Or maybe even like a god.

I know one thing, though. The man who killed Frances didn't do it on his own. It was Margaret. Was this man an unwilling participant in these horrible murders?

I'm in shock, I think. One of my own coven members is a killer. My head is spinning. I need to find out more.

June 22, 1947
Day of Sol. Moon in Leo.

I told the coven what I saw. I had sleep paralysis, and I couldn't move. I could open my astral eyes and see what was happening. I saw a man enter our home and kill my friend Frances. I saw the spirit of Margaret inside the man's body. Everyone in the coven was aghast. They were horrified, and rightly so. Our worst fears were realized. Margaret was no longer the sweet, innocent girl who came to our coven seeking friendship and a community of witches. Of like-minded people. She is gone.

Patricia told us that in old vampire lore, vampires could use their magic to control the living. Essentially turning them into a vampire themself. Margaret is not dead. She didn't get bitten by a vampire and turned into a monster. She is a living human being who is under the control of a powerful vampire. Patricia said that she had heard of living vampires who can astral project their spirits into unwilling human hosts and control them. She said this happens because the possessed has weak energy, a weak aura.

I asked Patricia if we could get Margaret back. Bring her back to the coven. But she said that Margaret was gone. She said she used her psychic ability to contact her. She said Margaret met her with rage. Patricia said that Margeret was gone. Only a monster was left. I asked her about the man. The man Margaret's spirit was possessing. She said that the only hope for him was to do an exorcism.

And because I was the one who saw Margaret's spirit, it was better if it was performed by me.

June 26, 1947
Day of Jupiter. Moon in Libra.

The last few days, I have felt like I have been walking in a dream. A nightmare, really. I go to work. I come home. I eat. Actually, I force myself to eat. I can't sleep in the bedroom anymore. The manager of the apartment building tried to clean the lipstick off the bedroom wall, but you can still faintly see it. He said I shouldn't have to ever see that again, so he had a painter come in that very day and paint the walls in the bedroom. Their walls are sky blue now. I can't sleep in that room. The landlord said I could break my lease, but I can't think of that right now. I'm sleeping on the couch. I lock the door every night. And every night, I put a chair under the doorknob so no one can get in.

Patrick had a police car stationed in front of my house every night. That helped a little bit. At least I knew there was someone there. Patrick said it was for my protection, but I wondered if the officer was also there because Patrick was hoping he could catch a killer.

Earlier today, this afternoon, a man fitting the description I gave to the police was seen trying to break into a woman's apartment down the street. A neighbor saw him and called the police. From what Patrick told me, the police were nearby and came running. The man saw the police officer and shot at him. The officer shot back, and the man ran. He didn't get too far because a neighbor on the floor above saw the man running and dropped a flower pot right on his head. He was knocked out cold.

The man's name is William Heirens. They brought him in and immediately pinned the killings, as well as the murder of the six-year-old girl, on him. Patrick said that he was in prison all day, and the cops beat a confession out of him. He confessed. But who was it that confessed? Was it William, or was it Margaret?

Patrick called me at home and told me they caught the killer and I should come by the station and make sure it was the same guy. He said they got a confession, but it would hold better in court if I could identify the murderer since I was the one who saw him. This was my chance. I packed the Spell of Exorcism and everything I needed to perform it. I just needed a few minutes alone with William.

I was very nervous when I arrived at the police station. I found Patrick, and he took me to identify the killer. Yes, it was him. I will never forget his face. Never.

I needed Patrick to help me without him knowing what he was helping me with. "Patrick, I need to speak with him alone."

Patrick looked at me with both fear and a protective gaze. "Not in your life. What are you? Crazy?"

"Maybe," I said.

"That's against every police protocol in the book!"

"Patrick, do you trust me?" I asked.

Patrick gave me a little smile. He knew I had gone through so much. I knew he just wanted to protect me. "You know I do."

"Then do this for me," I said. I knew I could use his sympathies for what I had been through to get him to do what I wanted. "Then let me in the room. He'll be handcuffed, right? And you will be right outside. I need to do this. I need to speak with him so I can move on."

Patrick took a breath. I could see that this was the last thing he wanted me to do, but if it meant me finding some peace, then he would be willing to do it.

"Okay. Ten minutes. No more. And I'll be right outside the door." He leaned into me and whispered in my ear. "This wouldn't have anything to do with you doing witchcraft, would it?"

"Okay," I said. "Ten minutes."

I sat in a room with a table in front of me. Patrick brought in William and handcuffed him to the table. He wasn't going anywhere. He was my prisoner.

I looked at him for a moment and took a breath. I had to do this quickly. "William, are you there?"

William began looking me dead in the eye. "Oh, Linda, Linda, Linda…"

Fuck, that was Margaret. It wasn't a dream. It wasn't something I made up because I was scared.

It was real.

"Have you come to help William?" Margaret asked. "He's mine, you see?"

"Margaret, he does you no good if he's in prison," I said.

"But he does," Margaret said. "I can drain his life force until every bit of his life is mine."

"Let him go."

"Is your witchcraft powerful enough to force me out?"

"I don't know. Let's see." My purse was sitting on the floor, under the table, out of sight. I picked it up, put it on the table, and took out the magical items I needed to perform the exorcism.

THE SPELL OF EXORCISM

Items Needed:
- Pentacle of Solomon necklace
- Two small bowls
- Small container of water
- Small container of salt
- Frankincense
- Charcoal and burner

1. Place the Pentacle of Solomon around your neck. This will keep any spirits out of your body.

2. Pour some water into one of the bowls. Draw a Pentacle of Spirit over the water, saying: *"Out of thee all that is impure. May only the essence of the Great Goddess remain."* Then, pour some salt into one of the bowls. Draw a Pentacle of Spirit over the salt and say: *"Out of thee all that is impure. May only the essence of the Great Goddess remain."* Combine the salt into the

water bowl and say: *"Water and salt combined, the blood of the Great Goddess. This water is now consecrated."*

3. Light the charcoal brick and place frankincense on top of it. Draw a Pentacle of Spirit over it and say: *"Fire and Air combined. The breath of the Great Father. This incense is now consecrated."*

4. Take the incense and walk around the room, visualizing all spirits who do not belong leaving. Say: *"By the power of Hecate. By the power of witchcraft. I banish all unwanted spirits."* Then, take the incense and fumigate the possessed person and say: *"By the power of Hecate. Titan. Keeper of the keys to all worlds. Your grip on this person is weakened."*

5. Take the salt water, sprinkle it in the four directions, and say: *"By the power of Hecate, only the angelic beings may be here this night. By the power of the dark mother, may they remain to aid me in my witchcraft."*

6. Visualize the archangel Michael. The Right Hand of God. Keeper of the flaming sword. Call him into your body. Visualize him entering your body as you say: *"I call to you, Michael. The Right Hand of God. You who is the enforcer of justice. I invoke you into my body so we can free this person from spirit possession."*

7. Once Michael is in your body, allow him to speak with the possessing spirit in his own voice and say: *"Spirit, do you leave upon your own free will?"*

8. If the spirit leaves of its own free will, you may skip down to Step 10. If it does not, continue to the next step.

9. Visualize the spirit inside the possessed person. Allow Michael to take your hand and grab the possessing spirit. Using your hands, Michael will hold on to the spirit with an unbreakable angelic hold. Visualize him stepping out of your body, still holding the spirit.

10. Visualize Michael holding the spirit. He's now out of your body, and you can now cut the astral cord that connects the spirit to the person. You may use a sacred dagger or simply your finger to cut the cord.

11. Then, visualize Michael taking the spirit away to a faraway realm such as the Abyss, the Underworld, or an astral prison.

12. Send white healing light to the person who was possessed. Then, visualize the Hexagram of Solomon in gold implanted inside the person's mind. This will keep the person from being possessed again.

13. Close by thanking Hecate, Michael, and any other spirits who may have helped you in your exorcism.

As I started fumigating the small room, Margaret laughed. Her laughter sounded terrible. "You have no power over me. I have both powers of the witch and the vampire."

I continued the fumigation and then sprinkled the salt water. I called upon the angelic being to help me in my magic. I could feel the room vibrating with angelic magic. I couldn't see the angelic spirits, but I could feel them.

"Linda." Margaret leaned closer to me. "Don't you want unspeakable power? Aren't you tired of the god-forsaken coven always trying to tell you what to do and how to do it?"

I didn't answer her. She was a vampire. Everything she said was bullshit. I visualized the archangel Michael before me. I imagined him stepping into me and wearing my physical body as clothes. He stepped into my legs. His heart joined with my heart. He placed his arms inside my arms like he was putting on a shirt. He placed his head in my head. His eyes saw with my eyes. My voice was his voice.

"Oh, look, a fucking angel," Margaret snarled. "I'm not going anywhere, Michael."

Michael looked deep into William's body and found where Margaret had attached her vampire spirit around his heart. She was growing in size, and Michael had to act now. "Margaret, do you leave this body freely?"

"Fuck off, Michael!" she yelled.

Michael reached inside William's body and grabbed onto Margaret's vampire spirit. As he pulled, she unraveled and released his heart. He held her tightly. I could see Margaret's spirit writhing around, trying to break free, but Michael, God's warrior, had the strength of seven stars. She wasn't going anywhere.

"What are you going to do with her spirit?" I asked Michael.

"She's alive. She still breathes." Michael was strong, but he was compassionate. "I cannot take her to the Abyss."

"Can you save her?" I asked. "Can you take the vampire energy away from her?"

"She made her choice," Michael said. "I will take her vampire spirit and seal her back into her own body. Never again will she be able to possess anyone."

Then Michael and Margaret were gone.

William opened his eyes and looked at me. "No, no, no, no, no!"

I rushed over to him and sent him healing white light and a visualization of the Hexagram of Solomon in his mind. He was free from possession, but the damage was already done.

"I didn't do it!" William screamed. "It wasn't me!"

He's right. He didn't do it. He was the victim of a powerful vampire spirit who made him kill so that the vampire could feed on the life force and energy of fear from her victims. But now, William had to pay for what he did not do.

"I'm sorry, William." I wished there was something I could do to help him, but at least now he was free from the grip of a vampire.

"I didn't do it! I'm innocent!" William kept saying over and over again.

Patrick heard William yelling and quickly opened the door to the interrogation room. He uncuffed William from the table, placed his hands behind his back, and forced the cuffs on him again.

"I didn't do it! I'm innocent! I didn't do it! I'm Innocent! I didn't do it! I'm innocent!"

ETERNAL SILENCE AT GRACELAND CEMETERY

July 9, 1947
Day of Mercury. Moon in Pisces.

My name is Kenneth Ruthan. I don't know if I have much to say or talk about. I am entrusted with this magical book for now. Each of us has to take turns writing down our spells and experiences. I don't have much to talk about. So, for now, I'm going to use these pages to tell you where I am and my thoughts. Maybe a spell will come out of me, or maybe nothing will happen. I can only say I will do my best to write what I can.

I have been with the coven for five years. Everyone in the coven likes to joke that ghosts and death are my specialty. I don't know if that's true, but I will admit that I have a fondness for death. Death is a friend of mine. Death is the silent companion that does not judge us for our successes or failures but takes us when our time has come. Death does not care who we are in life, nor does death care who we are when we cross over the veil to the afterlife. Death is a silent companion and yet, at certain times, speaks to our souls when we are ready for change. I believe the essence of death is change.

When you are ready for something new, the old thing dies. Our childhood dies so that we can become adults. Our old selves die when we are ready to mature and evolve. Nothing is new forever. Even the idea of "newness" dies eventually. Then, when it is our turn to die, our friend Death will come for us. Will Death be compassionate when we die from our lives as we know them now? Perhaps.

Perhaps Death does not care either way, and it is us who place judgments on the things of death, change, growth, and all things that take us away from our familiar selves.

I would like to speak about Margaret Foyle. I met Margaret when she first joined the coven a few years ago. She is beautiful in a special way. I don't mean that she is not traditionally beautiful. I mean that she has a spark of life that makes her more beautiful than she already is. We spent time together both inside and out of the coven. There have been many times where she and I have spent time together. She's one of the coven members who likes to tease me and say that I'm in love with death. I work well with the spirits of the dead. I respect them, and because of this, they are fond of working with me.

I can admit this now. I love her. I think I've loved her since the day we met. I should have said something to her, but a girl with her spirit wouldn't be interested in a man like me. Even still, if I had the courage to tell her of my feelings for her, it wouldn't matter. Margaret was taken by the vampire spirit, and I know that I may never see or speak to her again—at least, not as I once knew her. I know she wanted to help the vampire, Etta Young, but it went terribly wrong. I see that Margaret has cast a love spell on Dr. Dyer. One must be very careful when casting love spells. They never go as you planned, and you must accept the consequences of that spell. When she cast the spell, she didn't know that Dr. Dyer was a vampire himself. Dare I say he's a vampire master, and he is still out there somewhere in the city of Chicago.

The coven has talked a lot about this. It seemed that Dr. Dyer was a vampire himself, and Etta was trying to warn Margaret, but Etta was under Dyer's control. She could not or would not reveal his true nature. He charmed her, or rather, he enchanted her to fall in love with him, and she cast a spell to force him to love her. Love spells always bind the target to the witch who casts such a spell. Margaret fell into Dr. Dyer's snare. Her spell only made her more bound to him than he could have hoped.

Soon after the spell, all of us in the coven noticed that Margaret began to change. She didn't want to connect with the coven for full moon rituals. She would help us with our magic from time to time, but she never came to coven rituals. I believe this is because she knew that Patricia would have discovered what was going on with her. She was becoming a vampire.

Not all vampires are the undead who feed on the blood and life force of their victims. Living people can become vampires as well. There's something that is called a "psychic vampire." This is usually a person who intentionally or unintentionally drains someone's life force from them. One sign of a psychic vampire is feeling drained, tired, and low energy every time you are around them. There are many people who are psychic vampires who don't realize what they are. I think most psychic vampires are those people who have learned to siphon energy from people unintentionally. These people usually have unhealthy boundaries and need a lot of attention.

There are other living vampires as well. There are living vampires who wish to use the life force of others for their own power. They wish to gain as much magical power from others as they possibly can. These creatures do not wish to help or heal others. They only wish to have power over others. I feel that these people are disconnected from the ebb and flow of the Universe and have no connection to the love of humanity. In my opinion, if you are not connected to the community in some way, then what is the point of magic anyway?

I read Linda's account of how Margaret was able to possess a man and murder two women. She truly is lost to us now. I have been thinking about this every day since Linda told the coven. Patricia has instructed us to place protective spells around our homes. We cannot take the chance of Margaret taking our life force. I fear, though, that she may use her connection to the coven against us. I pray to Hecate that this does not happen.

In my sorrow, I have been spending many afternoons at Graceland Cemetery on the Northside of Chicago. Many famous people are buried here. The cemetery itself seems like it could be its own necropolis. A city of the dead. I have heard many stories over the years about how Graceland is haunted. Most people see cemeteries as places for the dead and the dead alone, but I have found them to be healing and restorative. There is a kind of peace that I find here that I have never found anywhere else in the city of Chicago.

I can clear my thoughts as I walk the endless paths here in Graceland Cemetery. I find that the dead do not judge the actions of the living. They do not care what you have done in your past and they do not care how much money you have. The dead are our connection to the spirit world. Right now, I need help from the spirits. Not magical help. I don't need anything right now. I need them to help me work through my sorrow of losing my friend, Margaret.

I have learned to speak with the dead in my own way. I find the dead are more comforting than the living.

A SPELL TO CONNECT WITH THE DEAD

Items Needed:

- A cemetery or graveyard

1. Open your heart, send out a call to the spirits of the dead, and ask who would like to speak with you today.

2. Place yourself into a light trance and begin walking through the cemetery.

3. Keeping your mind and heart open, tune in to the spirits around you and the spirits who would like to speak with you.

4. Using your intuition, sense which direction the spirit is calling you toward. Walk in that direction and keep walking until you find the grave of the spirit who would like to speak with you.

5. Place your hands on the grave itself or the grave marker. Close your eyes and visualize yourself in the cemetery. This is the astral plane. Visualize the spirit standing or sitting next to you.

6. Just as with any new conversation, introduce yourself and allow the spirit to introduce themselves.

7. Have a conversation with the spirit, get to know them, and allow them to get to know you.

8. When you are finished, thank the spirit and leave an offering of coins, tobacco, alcohol poured on the ground, food, or water.

I have met many spirits of the dead this way. Some of them I speak with every time I come to Graceland and others I may speak with once or twice. Just as with the living, there are some people you have a connection and bond with while others you do not. I try not to judge what kind of relationship I have with the spirits of the dead. I try to let the relationship evolve naturally. Most of my visits to the graveyard are peaceful and soothing. But something happened today.

I was sitting near one of the graves, speaking with a charming spirit, when I saw a little girl run by in the distance. I didn't think too much about this until I saw her run by again. I wondered where the little girl's mother was. My curiosity was getting the better of me, so I thought I should investigate. I walked toward the little girl, and I could hear her laughing and having a wonderful time. "Little girl, what is your name?"

The little girl stopped laughing and giggling and looked up at me. "Inez," she said. "Inez Clarke."

Inez looked to be a charming little girl full of laughter and happiness. "Well, Inez, where is your mother? Little girls should not be playing in the cemetery by themselves."

"I have no mother," she laughed.

How strange, I thought. "No mother? Then where is your father?"

"I have no father either, silly," she said, giggling once more.

"No parents?" I wondered if this child was playing a make-believe game or simply trying to play a joke on me. "Who takes care of you?"

As it often does in Chicago, the weather was quickly changing. Dark rain clouds were rolling in. There was a sudden drop in temperature, and it was surely going to rain. From the look of those clouds, it might be a thunderstorm. One does not want to be caught out in a lightning storm. "Inez, let us go find shelter. We need to take you to your caretaker before the lightning starts."

Inez's smile quickly turned to a look of dread. She turned the other way and began running as fast as she could. Instead of laughing, she was now screaming.

"Inez, come back!" I ran after her, but she was much faster than I had anticipated. Although I must admit, I was not wearing the proper shoes to be running through the graveyard.

CRACK!

Lightning struck nearby.

Inez screamed again.

"Inez, where are you going?!" I yelled.

"We have to hurry!" Inez ran to the front of the cemetery. She ran toward a large bronze sculpture and then was lost from my sight. I followed her to the bronze sculpture, thinking she might be hiding in front of it, but she was nowhere to be found. What I saw was a tall, ghostly statue of a figure wearing a cloak. It looked like the Grim Reaper or even the Angel of Death.

The bronze had turned a bluish-green color. I couldn't tell if it was supposed to be a man or a woman. The cloak they wore was ghastly, and their face was pitch black. This strange statue was clearly more than just a sculpture marking a grave. I could feel that it housed a spirit of some kind. I felt like the spirit who dwelled inside this statue was a guardian. What was it guarding, though?

CRACK!

Lightning struck again nearby. At that moment, I had forgotten that I was looking for the little girl, Inez. I was mesmerized…no, as I gazed upon the face of the statue, I was placed in a hypnotic trance. I have placed myself in a trance on many occasions, but this was a different kind of trance. It was almost as if I was being forced to focus on the statue against my will. For a moment, I couldn't tell the difference between myself and the statue. It was as if we were one and the same being.

It began to rain. It was a summer rain, so the water rushing down my head was refreshing. I should have run for shelter, but I could not. That's not correct. I didn't want to leave the statue. I was connected to it, and the statue was connected to me. Then, there was a voice in my head. "I am the keeper of the ways. I am the guardian of the gates. Keeper of the last mystery."

The statue was speaking to my mind with some kind of telepathy. "My name is Kenneth Ruthan. What is your name?"

The statue responded, "Here, I am called the Eternal Silence. Yet, others call me Death. My task is to guard the gates and protect all who dwell within my realm."

"Are you a spirit, angel, or god?" I asked.

"I am the shepherd and the lamb. I am the beast and the blade. I am the wolf, and I am the moon."

The energy I felt coming from the statue was something I had never felt before. I had conjured many spirits and gods, and this didn't quite feel like any of those things.

CRACK!

The lightning struck again. I wanted to touch the statue. To feel the spirit being that dwelt within, but I got a clear message in my mind. *No.* Not yet. I said goodbye to the being and quickly ran through the cemetery, looking for something to cover myself. Inez was nowhere to be found. Perhaps her mother had taken her home, away from this heavy rain. I must come back to this statue tomorrow.

July 10, 1947
Day of Jupiter. Moon in Aries.

The next day, I went back to the Graceland Cemetery and returned to the statue named Eternal Silence. When I approached the statue, it seemed as though the spirit was sleeping. Or maybe I felt that way because the statue's eyes are eternally closed.

I walked along the path of the cemetery, trying to remember exactly where it was. Graceland is a very large cemetery, after all. One could become lost very easily if one was not careful and observant of their surroundings. I found the statue of the Eternal Silence. I decided I needed to know more about this spirit.

A SCRYING SPELL TO KNOW

Items Needed:
- ◆ A scrying mirror, bowl, or dark surface
- ◆ A candle

1. Place a scrying mirror, bowl, or dark surface in front of you.

2. Place yourself into a trance using the technique of your choice.

3. Gaze into the dark surface. Allow your eyes to soften and become unfocused. Look deep into the surface as if you can see several feet into it. It may help to pretend you are looking at the bottom of a dark pool.

4. Allow images, feelings, and thoughts to come to your mind. You may or may not see images on the dark surface. Sometimes, the images or a thought will appear in your mind, seemingly at random. This works as well.

5. Once you have an image, use the dark surface as a portal and astrally project yourself into the scene. You may ask the people, animals, or objects questions and have a conversation with them.

6. If you see images in your head, close your eyes and know that the dark surface is a portal that takes you into the astral realm.

7. When you are finished, thank all the spirits and leave an offering for them.

I was glad to have found the hooded statue once more. I was sure to remember that one always approaches all spirits with grace and humility. In the Lincoln Park Coven, we know that all spirits deserve our respect. We do not pass judgment on spiritual beings, especially if we know nothing about them.

We must be kind and courteous no matter what. One never wants to anger a spirit who could be a strong spiritual ally.

I slowly walked up to the hooded statue. I opened my heart and sent a beam of energy to the heart of the Eternal Silence. "Hello. Greetings. I have returned."

"Hello," Eternal Silence said. "I sense that you are looking for more answers."

"Yes," I replied. "May I use magic to understand you better?"

"Proceed," the Eternal Silence said.

I used the Scrying to Know spell on the statue. The statue has a dark face, so it wasn't very difficult to use the spell. I suppose one could use the spell on anything really, however, a dark surface is easier. This is what I saw in my vision:

I saw a man named Dexter Graves leading a group of thirteen families to Chicago from Ohio in the year 1831. Just thirteen years later, he died and was buried in the Lincoln Park Cemetery, and was later relocated to Graceland when that cemetery was permanently closed. His son, Henry Graves, left a substantial amount of money to build the hooded statue upon his death. I saw Dexter Graves as a man who cared deeply for his community and loved Chicago. I saw his ancestral spirit still in the astral realm of Chicago, trying his best to protect the people of the city. The statue called the Eternal Silence was created seventy-five years after the death of Dexter Graves.

The man who created the statue was named Lorado Taft. I saw the spirit of Dexter Graves influencing Taft in spirit. There was magic at work here. Graves so loved the city of Chicago that he connected to the mind, spirit, and body of Taft to create the Eternal Silence. A great statue that could house a guardian of Graceland Cemetery.

Then I awoke from my scrying spell.

"Did you see all that you wanted to see?" the spirit of the statue asked.

I saw many things, but I wanted to know more. "Yes, thank you, but there is more I would like to understand."

"As you connected to me for understanding, I connected to you," the spirit of the statue said. "You are a good man, and you wish to help others. I will give you the answers that you seek."

I didn't know that the spirit had connected to me. This was a good reminder that when you work with any spirit, they get to know you as you get to know them. This is why it's always important to be honest with your intentions and your true self. Spirits have a way of knowing the energies that reveal things about us.

"Leave an offering at my feet," the spirit said, "and I will help you."

I took out a small offering of fruit and a few coins. I laid the offerings at the feet of the statue.

"Place your hand upon me and look with your psychic abilities," the spirit of the statue said to me. I wasn't sure what the spirit was trying to tell me. I placed my hands on the statue and suddenly felt energy enter my body. I think the spirit, which I now understand wishes to be called "Silence," gave me a power or perhaps a deeper understanding of psychometry. Here is the spell that Silence placed in my mind.

A SPELL OF PSYCHOMETRY

Items Needed:
- Any object you wish to know more about

1. Place your hand on the object or hold the object in your hands.

2. Take a few deep breaths. Allow any distracting thoughts to disappear as you breathe.

3. Take a few more breaths and allow yourself to go into a light trance.

4. Visualize your aura around you opening up to receive the energies of the object. Visualize your crown, third eye, and heart energy centers

opening like the petals of a flower. Know that you are opening up your psychic centers to receive the energetic impressions of the object.

5. Send a beam of energy from your heart to the object.

6. Allow your mind to remain empty of thoughts and distractions. Allow any pictures, thoughts, or feelings to come to you. Sometimes, you may see people or scenes, or you may have a feeling that will assist you in answering questions or clarifying the situation.

As I held my hands upon Silence, I was shown that they are a piece of death. I understand that sounds strange, but as I held my hands on the statue of Silence, I saw the day they were placed in Graceland Cemetery. On that day, the Angel of Death came to the cemetery and gave the statue an angelic blessing. The Angel of Death created a spirit, a thought form that would gain consciousness and become "alive." I then saw how, year after year, Silence became a spirit guardian. Not just to the Graves family but to the entire Graceland Cemetery. I saw how people would come, day after day, to see the Eternal Silence statue, and some would leave little offerings. Most of these offerings were coins. One day, a little girl was passing by with her mother, and she wanted to give Silence an offering of her small stuffed bear. I think most parents would have thought that was a silly thing to do, but the little girl's mother agreed that would be the right thing to do.

I saw days and days go by for Silence. Silence happily guarded the cemetery and kept people from doing any harm to the tombs and graves under their care. I could see how, in the astral plane, Silence could see the thoughts of those entering the cemetery intending to cause mischief. Silence would then energetically enter their mind and change their thoughts.

"This is not a good place to play games."
"No, you don't want to cause harm here."
"You want to leave this sacred place."

It's interesting how a spirit can enter our thoughts if they choose to. This is why it's so important to know who you really are and what you think. That way, you will be able to know when a spirit or even a witch is trying to influence your thoughts with magic.

I saw the days when Silence used their astral vision to reach out of Graceland Cemetery and watch the comings and goings of the city of Chicago. At first, they watched people in the nearby neighborhood. Then, they would send their gaze downtown. I felt a sense of both pride and sadness from Silence. Pride in guarding the cemetery and sadness because they could never leave this place.

As I stood there connecting to Silence, a vision intruded upon my thoughts. There was a dark force that was moving, or rather, slithering, into the cemetery. It was living in the shadows. Graceland has many shadows from the many trees and tombs that are spread throughout the grounds. When the shadows of the leaves danced in the breeze, the dark force took the opportunity to move about. Unnoticed by humans. But Silence could see the darkness move. They were showing me what they saw.

"What is this?" I asked Silence.

"There is a darkness that has been here for many days," Silence said.

"What is this darkness?"

Silence seemed sad again for a moment. "This spirit was released from bondage, and it has come here to Graceland."

The Shadow Man. When Silence said that to me, my heart sank to my stomach. I stood there trying to gather my thoughts, and I must admit, my wits about me. Sandy and I were tricked into releasing a dark spirit from the Couch Mausoleum in Lincoln Park a few months ago. I had hoped that we would never see that spirit again, yet here it is. I wondered if I should tell Sandy right away, but Silence told me that I should have a better understanding of the Shadow Man before I went off and did something I would regret. We were already tricked once. I needed to get more information before I involved Sandy in this.

I released my psychic connection from Silence and thanked them for the magic that they taught me. I was grateful. Silence told me that I needed to learn more about the Shadow Man. "Why can't you use your magic and banish the Shadow Man?"

"This spirit is more powerful than any I have encountered before," Silence said. "It will need more magic than I have to send the spirit away."

I backed away from Silence and looked around the cemetery. There was no one there at the moment, so I had the entire cemetery to myself. There were gray clouds that floated by and would hide the sun from time to time. There will be more shadows today than usual. But how will I begin learning about the Shadow Man? I had no idea how to do that. One of the things that we learned in our coven is that the best experience is just doing the magic. Patricia can't teach us everything we need to know. She freely admits that she knows what she knows, but there are many forms of magic that she is learning with the rest of the coven. I guess I'll be on my own with this.

I had an idea. Maybe the spirits of the dead could help me. When I work with the dead, I do it on the astral plane. I close my eyes, connect with their energy, and visualize what they look like or what I think they look like from how their energy feels to me. It would take too much time to go from grave to grave looking for a spirit who may be able to help me. I needed to speak with the dead, who were able to help me. So, I thought if I could combine the Spell to Connect with the Dead with scrying and psychometry, then maybe I would be able to see the spirits on the physical plane.

I think that seeing the dead on the physical plane is akin to scrying and psychometry. The difference is that instead of holding something or looking onto a dark surface, you look at the scenery around you. This would be most helpful to find a spirit who could help me understand the Shadow Man.

A SPELL TO SEE THE DEAD ON THE PHYSICAL PLANE

Items Needed:
   ◆   You may perform this spell anywhere, but it is easiest at a cemetery

1.   Take a few deep breaths and place yourself into a light trance.

2.   Open your crown, brow, and heart energy centers. Be open to what you see without judgment.

3.   Know that the spirits of the dead are everywhere on the physical plane. Use your intuition and feel the presence of the dead with your heart.

4.   In your mind's eye, visualize what you think the spirit may look like. Don't worry if you are visualizing them exactly correctly. With practice, your visualization will become more accurate.

5. Superimpose your visualization of the spirit over the energy of the dead you are intuiting.

6. You may have a conversation with the spirit. You can speak to them out loud or in your mind. Always introduce yourself and speak to them like you would a person who is living.

7. When you are done speaking with them, thank them for their time and say goodbye.

I walked through Graceland Cemetery, looking for a spirit of the dead who was able to help me. From time to time, I would stop and practice seeing the dead on the physical plane. It wasn't as difficult as I thought it was going to be. I would open my energy centers and intuit when I felt the energy of the dead. Then, I could "feel" their energies, and based on that, I would visualize what they looked like in my mind. I would see their gender, age, style of hair, clothes, and how I think they spoke. I would visualize their voices, too. Then, I would superimpose that vision of the person on top of the energy. After a little while of practicing this, it became easier and easier.

I still was unsure which spirit would be able to help me. I put my attention to my heart energy center and said out loud, "I am seeking someone who can give me information about the Shadow Man."

"Hello again, mister," I heard a little girl say to me.

I turned around, and out from behind one of the tombs came Inez, the little girl who was afraid of yesterday's lightning. "Inez, how are you today?"

Inez giggled and walked toward me. "You are seeking the Shadow Man…"

"Inez, how do you know about the Shadow Man?" I found this to be very curious. "Where is your caretaker?"

"They'll be coming back for me soon," Inez answered. "The Shadow Man is here now."

"What do you know about the Shadow Man?"

"The Shadow Man likes to hide," Inez said.

"Do you know where the Shadow Man hides?" I felt odd asking a little girl about the spirit, but children often see things in the spirit realm that many adults cannot. If she was picking up on something or had even seen this spirit, she would be of use.

"The Shadow Man hides near to us," Inez said. She started running away. It seemed that she wanted to play a game, but I didn't have time for games. Perhaps she was running back to her mother. Either way, I needed to stay on task.

I needed to refocus myself and find a spirit who could help me. "Damn it," I said out loud to no one. "Where do I find a spirit who can help me?"

"You must go into the Underworld," I heard the voice of Silence in my mind say.

"The Underworld?" I thought.

"You must perform a walking journey into the spirit world."

"How do I do that?"

Then, in a flash, Silence gave me another spell. They put the instructions in my mind.

A SPELL TO WALK INTO THE SPIRIT REALM

Items Needed:
- A tomb or small mausoleum

1. Ask the spirit of the tomb or mausoleum if you may have permission to use it as a portal to the spirit realm.

2. Once you gain permission, place both hands on the doors. Connect to the energies of the spirit realm. Know that the door will transport you to the spirit realm.

3. Close your eyes. Take a deep breath, and on the exhale, visualize the whole mausoleum or tomb spinning like a wheel. Know that as the mausoleum or tomb spins, it is transporting you from this world to the spirit realm.

4. Once you feel that you are in the spirit realm, release your hands from the door and turn around. What you see is the astral counterpart of the physical world. You will see spirits, ghosts, and even gods of

the dead. You will also see physical living people, and they will see you. You are walking in two worlds at the same time.

5. Walk around and speak to the spirits you wish. As with any other spirit communication, always introduce yourself and be courteous.

6. When you are finished, find any mausoleum or tomb and repeat the spell. This time, connect to the physical plane and know that you are going back to the world of the living.

I performed the spell exactly how Silence instructed me to. It was quite easy. I let my heart connect to the spirit realm and then let the magic do the rest. When I released my hands from the mausoleum door and turned around, Graceland looked the same—except that there was a sort of twilight upon it. It's hard to describe in mere words. It wasn't as if the sun was setting. It wasn't that type of twilight. It was as if I was in a dream yet awake at the same time. I suppose you can say that about any magic or trance state.

I walked through the cemetery, and I saw many people walking about. I must admit, I could not tell if they were the living or the dead. I had taken spirit journeys to the astral plane many times, but I had never brought the astral realm to me here in the physical. When I think about it, it should be quite easy to do. The astral and spiritual planes are always here with the physical plane. The spiritual plane is the source of all things. The mental plane comes from the spiritual, the astral plane comes from the mental, the etheric plane comes from the astral, and finally, the physical plane comes from the etheric. The astral plane is always with us. I suppose Silence gave me a spell that helps us to connect better with the spirit and astral planes. I guess it's a matter of perspective and what we choose or are willing to see.

As I walked down one of the paths in the cemetery, I heard a strange sound.

Ding, ding, ding, ding, ding, ding.

I stopped and listened for the sound again.

Ding, ding, ding, ding, ding.

It seemed to be coming from a curious little mausoleum that was halfway underground. Some steps led down into a doorway. The name on the mausoleum said "Ludwig Wolff."

Ding, ding, ding, ding, ding, ding.

"Hello there!" I called out.

"You can hear the bells?" A man's voice came from inside the tomb.

"I think all of Chicago can hear those bells," I said, trying not to laugh at the nonsense that was happening.

"I seem to be trapped in here," the man called out again. "Can you open the door for me?"

Curious. In the physical plane, the doors to the little mausoleums were always locked. One wouldn't want someone to burgle a tomb. However, in the astral realm of the spirits, one could open the doors quite easily. I opened the door, and out stepped a man dressed in attire from the turn of the century.

"Thank you so much." The man was very happy to be out of that tomb.

"You must be Mr. Wolff," I said.

"Indeed, I am. I was trapped in the tomb," Mr. Wolff said. "I am very pleased that I had the foresight to have the builders put in bells and air vents in the event I was buried alive."

Curious indeed. "But you were not buried alive."

Mr. Wolff paused for a moment to think about what I had just said. "That is true. And yet, I am trapped in that mausoleum every day. Well, that is, until someone lets me out."

Even more curious. I suppose one carries one's fears into death. If we are not careful, we will be doomed to play out our fears in death. This is something I must consider before I reach my own death. What fears am I taking into death? Something to consider later, of course.

I introduced myself to Mr. Wolff, and I got down to business. "Mr. Wolff, forgive me, but I am here on business. I have been sent here by the Eternal Silence to learn more about a dark spirit called the Shadow Man. Do you know of it?"

Mr. Wolff thought for a moment. "You see, from my home in the mausoleum, I am able to see everything. Some poor saps did not build their mausoleums with holes and bells, and yet I did. Because of this, I am able to see many things."

"What have you seen?"

Mr. Wolff's face looked grim. "The Shadow Man is a spirit I have never seen before. We were peaceful here for many years, and then, one day, the Shadow Man came. But we did not know it at first. This spirit only moves within shadows and cannot move within light. It came here unbeknown to us. But we felt it. We felt the darkness slowly coming in."

"I need to find it."

"I do not know how to find it, I'm afraid." I could see that Mr. Wolff wanted to help me, but he could not assist any further.

"Do you know someone who can help me?"

Mr. Wolff paused to think again. "Oh, yes! You must speak to the Burnhams."

"The Burnhams?"

"They are very near." Mr. Wolff hurried along the path, and not too far off from his mausoleum, we came upon a large pond at the north end of Graceland. He brought me to a bridge that led to a small island in the pond. The island was surrounded by trees, and it looked as though the trees were insulating the island.

The island was small, approximately the same size as a studio apartment. As we crossed the bridge to the little island, I felt... transported. I remember hearing that ghosts cannot cross water. Over the years of working with the dead, I have found that to be incorrect. In fact, spirits of the dead use water as a portal to come to and from the physical plane. I had the feeling that the pond that contained the little island was one such portal.

"Who is the Burnham family?" I asked.

"Oh, the Burnhams are one of the oldest families in Chicago. If anyone knows anything about Graceland Cemetery, it would be the Burnhams."

When we crossed the bridge and stepped foot on the little island, I suddenly felt at peace. I felt protected, and I had a warm feeling. The kind of feeling you get when you go home after a long stay somewhere else.

Standing near the bank of the island, next to a big tree, was a gentleman wearing a brown coat, a brown hat, brown trousers, and dark brown shoes. He seemed to be lost in his own thoughts, gazing over Graceland Cemetery.

"Mr. Burnham!" Mr. Wolff called out. "Allow me to introduce you to my new friend, Kenneth Ruthan."

Mr. Burnham turned around and greeted the both of us. When I shook his hand, I looked into his eyes and felt the energy of a man who was kind and welcoming. "Welcome, Mr. Ruthan."

"Thank you. It's nice to meet you."

"What brings you to the Burnham family island?"

I hesitated for a moment. I felt odd telling Mr. Burnham that there was a dark spirit lurking about, but then I realized that Mr. Burnham himself is a spirit of the dead, and I'm sure there wasn't much that could surprise him. "There is a dark presence here that I call the Shadow Man. I'm wondering if you have seen it or can tell me anything about it?"

Mr. Burnham turned around and walked to the bank of the island again. Mr. Wolff and I followed him. He took a deep breath and took the scenery in. "From this island, I can see everything in Graceland. There is nothing in this cemetery that goes by without my notice."

"So, have you seen it?"

"There are many spirits who come and go from Graceland Cemetery," Mr. Burnham explained. "It's not just the dead who reside here. The dead are separated from the living and other spirits, but sometimes, something may come through. I have been watching this being, and it's nothing that I have ever seen before."

Upon hearing this, my heart sank to my stomach. I don't fear spirits, but I feared this. What chaos did Sandy and I release? I tried not to be fearful. Spirits can use your fears against you. That is why it's so important that you have a good foundation of magic before you work with spirits. I tried to calm myself by looking at the beauty of Graceland Cemetery. The sun shone through the leaves of the trees.

It was quite beautiful on the little island. The breeze was warm and comforting. I followed the sunlight from in between the leaves of the trees to the black soil beneath our feet. How lovely, I thought to myself. How the sunlight seems to sparkle on the ground. Then, next to the light, I noticed the shadows of the leaves. One of the larger trees took root at the bank of the island, and its leaves covered part of the pond, creating a shadow.

Shadow. I couldn't get the thought out of my mind. There was a shadow of leaves in the pond. The shadows danced in the wind. They were moving. The shadows moved and danced and moved. Then they came together. Out of the water rose the Shadow Man. It was a thin figure of darkness that looked to have long, thin arms. It had no face that I could see. It was just…shadow.

Mr. Burnham stood his ground. "You have no power on this island!"

The Shadow Man made a haunting sound. Does a shadow have fear? It crept toward the edge of the island, and Mr. Burnham stepped forward.

"You have no power on this island!" he repeated.

With its long, thin arms and faceless gaze, the Shadow Man crept toward us on the island.

"Come, my friend," a man's voice said. Off to the shore of the pond stood Mr. Young, the man that Sandy befriended and who then tricked us into releasing the Shadow Man. It looked as though he had control over it. The Shadow Man drew back from us and headed toward Mr. Young. It disappeared as quickly as it appeared to us.

"That's Mr. Young, the man who tricked us into releasing the Shadow Man," I said.

"Young man," Mr. Burnham looked gravely concerned, "his name is not Mr. Young. His name is Ira Couch. His is the last tomb left standing in Lincoln Park. It's he who controls the spirits there."

Ira Couch had a grin on his face that looked somewhat psychotic. There was more going on here than we realized. I need to tell the rest of the coven what I have discovered. Ira Couch disappeared into the shadows of the spirit realm. He was gone. I said goodbye to Mr. Wolff and Mr. Burnham and used the same spell to return to the physical plane that I used to get to the spirit realm.

On my way out of Graceland, my mind was filled with questions. Why did the spirit of Ira Couch need the Shadow Man? What was this all about? There has to be so much more to the story than we initially thought. I also wonder if this has anything to do with Margaret and the vampire Dr. Dyer. Was this all connected? I must admit, my mind is spinning.

I was deep into my thoughts as I followed the winding paths of Graceland. I wasn't giving much thought to where I was going. I couldn't stop thinking about what I saw. The Shadow Man. I noticed the air temperature drop and the clouds became gray overhead. I felt a nudge in my stomach telling me to stop and look. That's when I saw it. Encased in a glass box was a statue of Inez, the little girl who ran through the cemetery. The inscription read:

INEZ.
Daughter of J.N. & M.C. CLARKE
Born Sep. 20, 1873
Died Aug. 1, 1880

The gray storm clouds brought the rain and a flash of lightning.
CRACK!
With that, the encased statue of Inez disappeared.

DEVIL IN THE ORIENTAL THEATER

August 2, 1947
Day of Saturn. Moon in Aquarius.

It's my turn to hold this magical tome. I must admit, I have reservations about this. I've read the previous chapters in this book. What I thought was just a shared magical book, or even a diary of magic has become something more. Margaret is nowhere to be found, and the rest of us are worried. Sandy thinks all of this is her fault, but we assured her it wasn't. There's something dark in Chicago. Something is here. I think there has always been something dark in Chicago. I don't know if this land is cursed or something like that, but I've lived in Chicago my whole life, and I've always felt it. I've been a witch my whole life. When I was little, I didn't call myself a witch. I wanted to be a homemaker like my mother. But I would know things. Secret things. People would try to keep secrets, and I would know what they were hiding. Maybe it was mind-reading. Or maybe it was witchcraft.

As I got older, I started to notice things. When the cold winds of Chicago came early, I knew the spirits were out. I also knew to stay away from cemeteries because sometimes the spirits follow you home. I also knew when people were going to die. It wasn't a feeling or a psychic vision—I just knew. So, that's how I've always known there was something about Chicago. As a teenager, I ignored my gifts. I wanted to be like everyone else. A normal girl. When I turned twenty, I started to know things again. That's when I started reading books on the occult. Then, one day, I met Patricia and joined her coven, and now I'm sitting down on my couch at home writing in this book. My name is Mary Stilling, and I have a story to tell you.

We had our Lamas ritual a few nights ago, and all of us, except for Margaret, were there. There are nine of us total in the Lincoln Park Coven, and some of us cannot attend every full moon and every ritual. But Patricia called us all and insisted that we come. The ones who've already had the magical book shared more of their stories and experiences and…their fears. The spells that each person has written down are wonderful. Some of them have a lot of power. But still, there is something going on in Chicago. Something dark. I know we cast that spell so that we could learn more powerful magic, but I don't think anyone expected this. Did we do the spell wrong, or is the Devil teaching us power magic, and this is just part of the experience? Patricia says that there is nothing to fear because we have the gods and the spirits on our side as long as we work together and we are smart about our magic. I'm not so optimistic.

Last night, David Lonesdale and I went to the Oriental Theatre. There was a band playing that he wanted to see called the Ink Spots. The show was like a dream. Hell, the whole experience I had last night was like a dream. David and I took the train together downtown. When we got to the theater, it was like any other night. I hadn't gone to a theater to see anything in a long, long time. I was excited about it. I have always felt that there was magic in the theater. Maybe it was the "magic" or the illusion the performers were portraying. Or maybe there is witchcraft in music, costumes, and makeup that we don't know about.

The Oriental Theater is one of the most beautiful theaters I have ever been to. The lobby looked as if it was made out of gold. There were ornate designs on the walls, and the chandelier looked as if it was made from a star. Everyone was dressed in fine dresses and suits. Some of the dresses were so fancy that I almost felt that my dress wasn't as pretty as the others. David said not to worry about such things. He said people dressed up to show off, and once the show started, no one could see us anyway. Once we got into the theater itself, the seats were velvety red. For some reason, the red color of the seats reminded me of blood. A very morbid thought, I know.

Once we sat down, I could see the walls and the ceiling better. It was spectacular. Just like the lobby, the inside of the theater was decorated with a golden color. I think that if the gods had houses, this must be what they would look like. Off to each side of the stage were two little balconies with large red drapes behind the seats. I saw a few well-dressed people in those balcony seats, and I wondered what kind of money they had to spend to get a seat like that. Our seats were wonderful. Center-right. When I looked up at the ornamental ceiling, it looked as though it were ten stories up in the air. I kept thinking about the men who had to climb up there and create all those beautiful designs. I certainly couldn't do something like that. I was afraid of heights as it was. I couldn't imagine myself up on a platform that high up, creating art on the ceiling.

The designs of the theater were mesmerizing. You could look at them for hours and still not see all the fine details that went into it. High above the stage, there were sculptures of monsters that looked down at the audience from an angle. I think the creator of the sculptures tried to create mythological creatures, but all I kept seeing were monsters. I tried to tell myself that perhaps they were dragons. In our coven, dragons are powerful beings of the Earth and cosmos that a witch can seek out for wisdom. As much as I tried to reassure myself, I couldn't stop thinking that monsters were standing at the top of the theater, waiting to harm us. Maybe I was just being silly. Patricia teaches us that we should trust our gut instinct. That's how you develop your psychic senses. This was one of those times I didn't want to be right.

After a short while, the Ink Spots went on stage. The music they played was wonderful. The first song they played was called "Maybe." Most of their songs are about love, found and lost. I think their songs are romantic. After a few songs, I needed to go to the lady's room. I walked through the people in the seats, trying to make my way to the aisles. I hate that the seats are so close together; when a lady has to use the powder room, the entire theater knows about it. I walked back to the lobby and was looking for the restroom. During a show, a lobby is always lonely and a little haunting. For a moment, I felt like I was the only person in the world.

I found the restroom, and I could faintly hear the band playing their music. So lovely. When I left the restroom, I walked down a hallway in the theater. The hallways were darkened. Still, not a soul to be found. As I walked down the dark hall, I could still hear the band playing. I think the song I was listening to was called "Do I Worry?" Beautiful. At the end of the hall, there was a woman dressed in what looked like a gray and black dress. She wore a hat. Something that looked out of fashion. Maybe she was older. I often see old ladies on the streets of Chicago still wearing hats from twenty years ago. The woman stood next to the door that led back into the theater.

"Excuse me, did you need help getting back into the theater?" I asked the woman. She seemed to be lost or even confused.

The woman didn't say anything. She just continued to look at the door. Maybe it was locked.

As I walked closer to her, I could see that her dress was not gray and black. It was dirty. Very dirty, like she had soot all over her dress. "Would you like some help?"

Then the woman turned toward me, and I saw that her face was burnt. She had been in a horrible fire. I gasped and put my hand over my mouth so I wouldn't scream. I didn't want to draw attention to myself. She looked at me and said, "The doors are locked. We cannot get out…"

I was panicking. I didn't know what in the world was going on with this poor woman. "Let me help you. I can get some help."

The woman with the burnt face and sooty dress said nothing and walked by me. She walked slowly down the long, dark hallway. "We must find a way out."

"Let me help you!" I called out to her.

The woman kept walking, and then she vanished.

What the hell was that? The woman I saw was a ghost. But why was she burnt, and what was she doing at the Oriental Theater? I quickly walked down the hall and found one of the ushers. He saw the look of panic and dread on my face.

"Madam, what in the heavens is the matter?" the usher asked.

I couldn't very well tell him that I had seen a ghost. He wouldn't believe me anyway and probably kick me out of the theater for being crazy. "I think I gave myself a spook. These dark hallways are frightful."

"Allow me to take you to your seat."

"I can find my way, thank you."

I quickly found my seat next to David. I didn't tell him what I saw until after the show. Once we got out of the theater, I told him about the burned woman I saw. "I think maybe this ghost is meant for you. You have the coven's book now, right?"

"Well, yes," I answered, "but what does that have to do with the ghost lady I saw?"

"Well, it seems to me that whoever holds the book is the one who the spirits come and find."

I didn't say anything. Was that true? I've read all the previous entries in the book. All the dates. All the spells. Were the spirits waiting for us to have the book, or was the book opening up some kind of portal into the spirit realm?

David grinned at me as we walked down the street. "I've already had my turn. Now, I guess it's your turn."

August 3, 1947
Day of Sol. Moon in Pisces.

David was right. It is my turn to deal with the spirits. I looked back over everyone's entries last night. I was looking for a pattern. Why did those particular spirits speak to those coven members? What was the connection? I know everyone in the Lincoln Park Coven pretty well. I know their talents, strengths, and weaknesses.

So far, I couldn't draw the line between the spirits and the witch. I wondered what my connection to the Oriental Theater was. What did the spirits need of me?

A SPELL TO SPEAK WITH THE GODS

Items Needed:
- Incense of frankincense and myrrh
- Charcoal
- One white candle
- An offering

1. Decide on which god you would like to speak to. If you or your coven have a patron deity, you may use them. If not, pick a god with whom you have a connection.

2. Light your charcoal and put aside until the embers are going good and hot.

3. Light the white candle for the god you wish to speak to and say: *"(God's name), I come to you with respect and honor. I ask that you open the doors to the spirit world so that I may speak with you about (subject of conversation)."*

4. Once the charcoal is hot, place the incense of frankincense and myrrh on it. Take a deep breath and smell the magical scent. Say: *"(God's name), this incense is for you. Its sweetness is my gift to you so that I may be welcome in your presence."*

5. You may lie down or sit in a chair. Take a deep breath and close your eyes. Allow the day's distractions to flow away. Take another deep breath and allow your body to relax.

6. Once you are relaxed, state your intention again to visit the god of your choice.

7. Visualize a beam of light swirling around you in a spiral. This spiral of light transports your astral body to the part of the astral plane to the home of the god you wish to speak with.

8. Once you feel you are astrally transported to the home of the god, visualize the spiral of light going back into the ground.

9. Visualize what the god looks like to you. If it is a god you have never spoken to, introduce yourself. If this is a god you are familiar with, say hello and any pleasantries you'd like.

10. Speak with the god and ask them for their wisdom, teachings, and magic they would like to teach you.

11. When you are finished, thank the god and say goodbye. Visualize the spiral of light surrounding you and transporting you back to the physical plane and back to your body.

12. Leave the god an offering of food, water, flowers, or whatever you feel is appropriate.

I used this spell to astrally journey to Hecate. She is the Greek goddess of witchcraft. One of the things she is known for is taking care of the forgotten dead. Those souls who have no one to tend to their graves or those people who were not buried or cremated at all. Hecate is the mother of lost souls. She takes care of them. She allows them to be a part of her train. She loves those who have no one to love them.

I have often used this spell to speak with the goddess. I told her about what happened at the Oriental Theater, and she said that there was magic I needed to learn. Yes, there was a spiritual reason that I was called to work with the spirits of that theater. I'm not sure what she meant by that. Hecate—well, all gods, I think, enjoy being cryptic. They will give you enough information to get you interested in something and get you on your way, but they will not give you the answers. You have to walk the path of the witch and have experiences. Hecate often tells me that witchcraft is taught through experience and failure. When we fail, we learn. We are able to place the magic into our bodies and our spirits, where it will continue to grow.

I went back to the Oriental Theater the next night. The Ink Spots were playing again. I decided to get a cheaper seat on the upper balcony. The balcony had a different feel to it than the seats on the main floor. I could see the entire theater from these seats. This performance was far from sold out. There was a crowd on the main floor, but the upper balcony was almost empty except for a gentleman who sat a few rows down from me. I preferred it this way. This way, I could focus on the spirits in the theater and not worry so much about people wondering what I was doing.

As I sat in my seat, I took some deep breaths and put myself in a light trance. I opened my energy centers. I was ready for a spirit to appear. Nothing. The Ink Spots played the song "Address Unknown." The song was putting me deeper into a trance. It was soft and had a melody that felt like a lullaby. A few more songs played, and still, there was nothing. The intermission came, and I stayed in my seat, hoping I would feel something, but there were no spirits on that balcony.

After the intermission was over, the lights dimmed, and everyone returned to their seats. There was a gentleman who sat a few rows down and decided to get up and come sit two seats away from me. He looked like a kindly man. He was handsome and smiled as he listened to the music play. "I enjoy the theater, don't you?"

I wasn't sure if he had more on his mind than just the theater, but I wanted to be polite. "Yes, I do."

"Do you enjoy the music of the Ink Spots?" He asked softly so as to not bring attention to himself and disturb others. "Their songs can soothe the most tormented of souls."

This was an odd thing to say. "Tormented souls? What do you mean?"

The gentleman put his index finger to his mouth and said, *"Shhh…"*

The Ink Spots began to play the song "I Don't Want to Set the World on Fire." The song sounded dreamy, like the other songs the band played. But the title of the song… *"I Don't Want to Set the World on Fire."* The words sank into my heart. *"I Don't Want to Set the World on Fire…"*

The lights on the stage dimmed.

Screaming.

Another scream.

Screaming.

A shout, *"Somebody help us!"*

"Open the fucking doors!"

Screaming.

"The fucking doors are locked!"

What the hell was happening? The music of the song "I Don't Want to Set the World on Fire" echoed throughout the theater. On the stage, people were running back and forth. Screaming.

Flames were ignited on the giant red stage curtain. The flames quickly spread and engulfed the entire stage.

"I Don't Want to Set the World on Fire" faintly played as the people screamed.

A young woman's dress caught fire. Horrible, horrible screams.

I sat there watching the stage burn. I was too shocked to move. I should help them!

"Open the doors! Open the doors!"

"Somebody help them!" I screamed.

Then, like waking up from a dream, I saw that there was no fire. There were no screams. Nobody was shouting. Several people loudly shushed me. Was it all a vision?

The Ink Spots played "I Don't Want to Set the World on Fire."

Once I realized that it was a vision—or perhaps a hallucination—I sat quietly in my seat. So many questions. What was I seeing? Who were these spirits? I sat there wondering what I had just seen when the gentleman who shushed me got up from his seat and sat down beside me. "What a wonderful performance."

"Who are you?" I asked him. "What is your name?"

My intuition was telling me that this gentleman saw the same thing I saw. He saw the screaming people and the burning stage. He seemed unbothered by what he saw. He clapped his hands together. "What a wonderful performance!"

I asked him a second time but was a bit more forceful. "Who are you?"

"My name is Scratch," the gentleman said, "and you were sent here for a reason."

"Scratch." That name sounded familiar to me. "I've heard that name before. The only person with that name is the—"

"Come now," Scratch interrupted, "you don't want to keep them waiting."

"Who?" I still didn't understand what was happening. "Who are those people?"

"People who need your help," Scratch said.

"Was that a premonition?" Was I seeing a tragedy that was going to happen to this theater? "Am I seeing something horrible that is going to happen to this theater?"

Scratch looked at me with a devilish grin. "That's the thing about witchcraft. It's backward and forward. As above, so below. Topsy turvy."

I got up from my seat and walked down the magnificent staircase. The show was over, and everyone was leaving.

I had to get out of this theater and clear my head. Some fresh air would do me a world of good. I pushed on the door that led outside. It wouldn't move. I pushed again. It wouldn't move. What was happening? I pushed as hard as I could, and the door still wouldn't move. Then the lights went out.

I turned around, and all the people were gone. The theater lobby was dark, and no one was around. I was locked in the theater. There wasn't anyone around. I walked through the lobby, hoping I could find an usher or someone who worked the box office, but there was no one. I was alone. I had no idea what I was going to do.

Suddenly, a cold wind brought snow inside the lobby of the Oriental. Cold, cold snow. There couldn't be snow. It was August. Snow shouldn't be here. The snow seemed to be coming from high in the ceiling of the theater.

The doors to the main theater were open, and I could see that the stage was illuminated. I walked over a blanket of snow that covered the theater. The beautiful blood-red seats were covered in snow as well.

A man covered in black ash walked on stage. He walked to the center and then shouted, "Open the doors!"

Another man who looked like he had been badly burned walked out on stage and stood next to the man. He took off his hat and shouted, "They are locked! Someone trapped us inside!"

A woman in a charred dress came out on stage as well. Her hair was burnt off, and half of her face was burned. It was so burned you could see parts of her skull. "My children! Where are my children?!"

The three on stage took a bow.

The empty, darkened theater erupted in applause. The sound of the clapping startled me, and I quickly turned around. There they were. Thousands of people were burned. Some burned so badly you could not see their faces. Where their face once was, only charred skin that fell off the bone remained.

Applause erupted throughout the theater.

The lights suddenly flashed on.

"Madam, were you locked in?" Someone who worked in the theater had found me. "I am so sorry. I thought everyone had gone for the night."

The spirits of the dead were gone.

August 4, 1947
Day of Luna. Moon in Pisces.

I opened my eyes, and I saw only blackness. There was a terrible weight on me, and I could smell smoke. I couldn't breathe. I couldn't see anything. There was someone's leg in front of me. I couldn't move my head much. I heard moans and screams. The weight upon me was unbearable. My chest was being compressed. Smoke. I couldn't breathe. I couldn't tell if the smoke or the weight compressing my chest was keeping me from breathing. I wanted to break free. There was someone's arm next to my face. There were people pushing. Pushing and pushing and pushing. They were trying to break through. Then I saw a door that would not open. Locked from the outside. I was suffocating. I was dying.

Then I saw a match light a pipe. *Puff, puff, puff.* Smoke slowly rose from the pipe bowl.

It was Scratch. He took the match and threw it over the balcony of the theater. The whole theater was ablaze.

He puffed on his pipe again. "They are waiting for you, Mary. Will you help them, or will you join them in the dance of fire?"

I opened my eyes. It was a dream.

August 5, 1947
Day of Mars. Moon in Pisces.

Yesterday, I wanted to avoid the theater and whatever it was I was supposed to do for those spirits. The visions. The dreams. I was so overwhelmed. The spirits were trying to tell me something. I didn't know how to help them. I wanted to stay in my apartment and hide from the rest of the world for a while.

I wondered if I should give this magical book of witchcraft back to Patricia or maybe if someone else would write in it instead. Then maybe I wouldn't have these visions of death and fire and burning. Maybe I could learn magic in a different way. I wanted to quit. I sat quietly with my thoughts for a long time. The spirits were calling me. They think I can help them. Damn it.

I went back and read the chapters before me. Every single one of my coven mates experienced something like this. I wanted to just quit. I wanted to give up, but then I thought about all those spirits who needed my help. As hard and scary as this is for me, it's worse for them. I can only imagine the torment, pain, and sorrow they must be going through. Spirits trapped in a theater, reliving their pain over and over again, never being able to leave the place that killed them. I wanted someone else in the coven to do it. I wanted Patricia to do it. She was good at things like this. She taught us everything we know. But I know exactly what she would say if I asked her to do it: "The spirits spoke to you for a reason." That may be true, but what if they are speaking to the wrong witch?

I meditated on this whole thing for a long time. In reality, I was hoping I would come up with a really good excuse not to have to do this. The more I connected to the energies of the Universe and the spirits, the more my heart said that I was the one who needed to help them.

I figured if I was going to do this, maybe Scratch would be able to help me. Maybe give me some guidance.

I went back to the Oriental Theater. There was a fog that rolled in off of Lake Michigan. Interesting. All water is a portal for spirits to come through. The fog was even better. There's a reason that people see weird things on a foggy night. Fog makes a water portal all around you. I think that when you conjure spirits from a cauldron of water or even a small pond, you have some sort of boundary between you and the spirits. The cauldron creates a container, and a pond has the barrier of the land surrounding it. But with fog, It's all around you. There's no container and no barrier. It's you and the spirits. This was going to be an interesting night.

The downtown Chicago streets were emptier than they usually are. Granted, it was a weekday night. Maybe the fog was keeping people away. Or maybe the spirits were creating space for me to help them. Either way, I felt a dark presence. I felt tragedy in the air. I felt pain, and I felt the presence of death.

I walked into the theater, and the beautiful gold designs seemed more dull than they had been on the previous nights. I kept hearing a voice in my head that said something was happening. I kept thinking, "Yeah, a heart attack if I'm not careful!"

Strangely, there was no one at the box office. There was no one checking tickets. Well, I need to get into the theater. I suppose if they find me, I can pay them later. I opened the door that led from the lobby to the main theater. There stood an usher. He saw me come in, and he said, "May I show you to your seat?"

"Yes," I said.

He reached out to take my arm, and I saw that his hands were charred bones. My heart stopped for a brief moment, and I looked up at his face. Half of his face was a blackened skull. He spoke again, but this time, his voice was deep and crackly. "We have to hurry. You don't want to miss the show…"

I wanted to jerk my arm away, but I took a deep breath, centered, and decided if I was going to do this, I needed to go with it. He showed me to a seat facing center stage. I sat down and waited for the show to start. I looked around and saw that there were a few people sprinkled throughout the theater. They were all quiet, waiting for the show to start.

The curtain opened, and there stood the Ink Spots again. The music began. The name of the song was "Ev'ry Night About This Time." The music seemed like a spell of its own. I guess this is it, I told myself.

"This is my favorite song," I heard Scratch say as he sat next to me.

"Who are you?" I whispered.

"You don't want to miss the show, do you?" he said to me.

The Ink Spots played their song, and I fell deeper and deeper into a trance. I let the soft, melodic song transport me into a waking sleep. I felt like I was awake and asleep at the same time. I took more breaths, and with each breath, I let myself sink into the world of the spirits. I opened my eyes, and the Ink Spots faded away from the stage....

A man who was dressed in some sort of character costume took their place. "Ladies and Gentlemen! Do not be alarmed. We are experiencing some difficulties, but we will resume the play shortly. Please, stay calm."

From my seat, I saw smoke from behind the big red stage curtain. The smoke started to emerge, faint and small, but then more and more smoke came out from behind the curtain. All of a sudden, the curtain caught fire.

"Ladies and Gentlemen. There is no reason to panic. Our wonderful staff is taking care of everything," the actor said.

No one moved from their seats, including myself. I sat mesmerized by what was happening. Then, the entire stage caught fire. The actor on stage then said, "Ladies and Gentlemen. There is no reason to panic. You will be dead soon and be damned to this theater forever."

The audience erupted in applause. I was dumbstruck by the clapping. Why were they not evacuating? What was happening? As I looked at the audience applauding the fiery stage, I saw that each and every member of the audience had blackened skin and clothes that had been burned. I was in a waking dream. I was awake and in the spirit world at the same time.

Scratch took out his pipe and lit it with a match. "Marvelous performance! Marvelous!"

I figured out who Scratch was. I knew what he was doing, and I knew why he was taunting me. "What more do you have to show me, Scratch?"

Scratch took a puff from his pipe. "Are you ready?"

"Yes."

"Then come with me." Scratch got up from his seat. I followed him as he made his way through the audience to get to the main aisle of the theater. As we passed each person, I looked at their faces. Their burnt, charred faces... and they looked at me.

I followed Scratch out of the theater, where the fog had gotten thicker now. We walked to the alley that was next to the theater. I suddenly felt like I got punched in the gut.

A swarm of dark energy filled me up. Maybe "filled me up" isn't the right way to put it. It was more like I connected to the dark energy so strongly that I was in pain. It was overwhelming.

"What is this place?" I asked Scratch.

"Wait…"

The dark, painful energy subsided, and I gathered my strength again. I took a few deep breaths and centered and grounded myself again.

A body dropped from the sky right in front of me.

"Fuck!" I screamed. I looked down, and there was the body of a woman who had fallen and broken her neck.

Another body dropped with a hard *thud*.

Then another and another and another.

I looked up, and there they were. Hundreds of people screaming from above. There was black smoke coming from the theater. People were falling to their deaths.

Some of the victims jumped, hoping they would make it. They did not. They died as they hit the ground. There were people behind them who were so desperate to escape the burning theater that they were forcefully pushing people out of the way, and they were falling to their deaths. In just a few minutes, the bodies piled up in the alley next to the theater.

Then I saw it. There were shadows in the alley. The street lights made shadows from the bodies of people who had fallen to their deaths. For some strange reason, I became fixated on those shadows. The shadows began to dance. They moved and danced. Then, the shadows came together, forming a figure with skinny arms and hands. It looked like it was cloaked, but I could not see a face. The Shadow Man. Holy fuck! I was seeing the Shadow Man that Kenneth had written about! It was here. But what was it doing? What did it have to do with the deaths of the people from the theater fire?

My stomach sank. I felt a dark energy pull at my heart. I slowly turned to my right, and there stood a man dressed in a suit from the mid-1800s. I think it was Mr. Young. Couch. This was Ira Couch. Not Mr. Young. Ira was smoking a cigar and was looking very smug. He knew that I recognized him, and he was not concerned in the slightest. Fuck.

The Shadow Man hovered over the dead bodies in the alley that had fallen from high above. It then moved toward Ira Couch, and the two disappeared into the fog of downtown Chicago.

Then, just as suddenly as they appeared, the bodies, the smoke, and the fire had disappeared. It was all gone. All but the dread I felt in the pit of my stomach.

I raced home as fast as I could. I felt a combination of fear and anger. I was scared to know what the hell was going on but angry enough to want to stop this fucker. I was done playing games with these dark spirits. They wanted to play with a witch. Well, motherfucker, now it's time to play with a witch!

As soon as I got to my apartment, I went straight away to work.

A SPELL TO SUMMON THE DEVIL

Items Needed:
- A stag, goat, or ram skull
- A human skull (a replica is fine)
- A cauldron
- A lamp or large candle
- Incense of dragon's blood
- Charcoal and incense burner
- A staff or walking stick
- An offering of food or drink for the Devil

1. Create the magical circle to conjure the Devil. Place the stag, goat, or ram skull in the North. Place the lamp or large candle in the East. Place the human skull (replica) in the South. Place the cauldron in the West.

2. Place the incense burner and charcoal near the animal skull in the North. Place the dragon's blood incense on the charcoal and say: *"With this blood of the dragon do I call the spirits of the Old Craft and the Devil."*

3. Take the staff or walking stick, face the East, and say: *"I call the angel of light, Lucifer. He who gives us free will and free choice. He who illuminates the path of darkness and shows us the way to self-discovery. Lend me your powers of magic this night!"*

4. Face the South with the staff and say: *"I call to the Goddess of witchcraft, Hecate. She who is mother of the forgotten dead. She who keeps the keys to the three worlds. Lend me your powers of magic this night!"*

5. Face the West with the staff and say: *"I call to the witch ancestors. Those witches who came before us. Those witches who are the lineage of witchcraft unbroken. Blood of my blood. Breath of my breath. Lend me your powers of magic this night!"*

6. Face the North with the staff and say: *"I call to the Devil. Horned One. He of the cloven hoof. He who whispers the secrets of magic in our dreams and guides us through the darkest of times. Lend me your powers of magic this night!"*

7. Continue to face the North. Smell the magical scent of the dragon's blood incense. Have a deep knowing in your heart, spirit, and soul that the god of the witches, the Devil, is here. He awaits you.

8. Sit on the ground in the North and place the staff on the ground with the shaft over your third eye. Hold the staff with both hands.

9. Close your eyes and use the staff as a magical tool to astral project to the place where the Devil resides. Speak with the Devil. You may ask him for advice or wisdom or to teach you magic. When you are ready, say your thanks and goodbyes and open your eyes.

10. Leave an offering for the Devil and give thanks and farewell to the spirits you have called from the four directions.

I performed the spell exactly as written here. I astral journeyed to see the Devil. He appears to me in different ways. Tonight, he came to me as the Man in Black. He wore a black suit, like something you would find at Marshall Field's. His hat was very dapper, and he had a black cane. I think it was a blackthorn cane on account of the fact that it looked to have thorns on it. Most people fear the Devil. I certainly do not. I've never feared the Devil. Honestly, since I was a child, I knew that the

Christian Church had created propaganda against the Devil as a way to control people. The more control they have over the common person, the more money and power they have to influence people and governments around the world. The Devil, to me, is sexy. He's a spirit with unlimited power, and he will share that power with you as long as you fight the powers that be, not for chaos or for the sake of being disorderly, but because if we are to find our Divine Will, our True Will, then we need to unlearn all the things that the Church has force fed us over the years.

In my astral vision, the Devil said to me, "Why do you seek me this night?"

"I am tasked with helping the spirits at the Oriental Theater here in Chicago," I answered. "I fear I will not have the magic nor the courage to succeed in this task."

The Devil took my hand. "Mary, when your coven conjured me and asked me to help you increase your power and your magic, I selected each of you for a specific task. It was no accident that you were called to the Oriental Theater."

"You put me there?" I asked. "But why the Oriental Theater?"

The Devil said, "Your challenge is to move past your insecurities and your feelings of inferiority. You have always had magic. What you do not possess is confidence."

It seemed like there was something else that the Devil wanted me to learn. "I feel there is more than that."

"There is something more," the Devil said. "But you must discover that yourself."

I didn't expect the Devil to give me all the answers I was looking for. The gods of witchcraft are cryptic that way. I needed to figure out how to help all those spirits. "How can I succeed at my task? How can I help the spirits who are trapped in the Oriental Theater?"

"You must save them," The Devil said bluntly.

"Save them? How?"

"You must guide their spirits to the afterlife." The Devil looked into my eyes. "You must be their psychopomp and guide them out of that theater and to their ancestors. Only then will they—and you—find peace."

I have never been a psychopomp before. I have never guided the dead to the afterlife so they can find healing and peace with their ancestors. This seemed like a heavy task to me. Heavy indeed. I thanked the Devil for his insight and wisdom and left him an offering of whiskey and tobacco. I have work that needs to be done.

August 6, 1947
Day of Mercury. Moon in Aries.

I decided I couldn't wait any longer. I needed to help those spirits cross over to the spirit world and escape their harrowing ordeal of the theater. A good witch is a prepared witch, so I decided to find out everything I could about the fire at the Oriental Theater. During the day, I went to the Oriental Theater to find someone, anyone, who would talk to me and tell me what happened that night of the fire. When I got to the theater, I asked anyone who was there about the fire, but no one seemed to know a lot about it. Then I found a man, Mr. Barley, who had worked in the Theater District of Chicago his whole adult life.

Mr. Barley said that the fire didn't happen at the Oriental Theater at all. In fact, the Oriental was built after the tragedy that befell the Iroquois Theater on December 30, 1903. On that fateful day, there was a matinee of the play *Mr. Blue Beard.*

Around 3:00 p.m., an electrical light set a muslin curtain on fire. One of the main actors in the show, Eddie Foy, came out on stage to stop people from panicking.

The fire quickly spread throughout the theater. There were no fire alarms, and the theater doors were locked in an attempt to keep people from entering the theater without paying. What safety protocols they did have were either ignored or didn't work. There were no exit signs. The locks on many of the doors were unusual, and people could not open them. The theater had very poor illumination, and some of the doors were strictly ornamental. People were trapped. They panicked, and no one could escape. Audience members were crushed to death or died of smoke inhalation. Some tried to jump out of a window over the alley. The first people who jumped fell to their deaths. The dead bodies then made a cushion for others to land. Ultimately, over six hundred people died.

Those poor people. The more I heard about the Iroquois Theater tragedy, the more I understood why I had to help them. For over forty years, they have been in pain. I spoke to Patricia before I went to the Theater that night. I know she wants us to figure things out on our own, but I knew this was no ordinary haunting. Patricia told me that, sometimes, when there is a tragedy such as this, the pain and fear that is shared by everyone creates a time loop in the astral. The spirits of the dead are doomed to repeat their horrible tragedy over and over again. This explains why James saw the spirits of the Green Mill Lounge experience their deaths over and over again. Those spirits will continue to experience the Iroquois Theater until someone releases them. That someone has to be me.

Patricia helped me come up with a spell—well, a ceremony, really—that will help guide the spirits of the dead to the afterlife and release them from their torment.

It wasn't very hard to do at all. But guiding the spirits to the afterlife is not the hard part. The hard part will be convincing them to follow me. I really hope this works.

I went to the Oriental Theater just like I did the other nights. And just like the night before, no one was inside the box office. I didn't see anyone in the theater lobby, either. I guess the spirits were waiting for me. Then I heard the faint sound of music from the theater again. The Ink Spots were playing the song "I Don't Want to Set the World on Fire." The music seemed to be calling to me. An enchanting spell that was enticing me to come inside the theater.

I walked into the theater and saw the Ink Spots playing this beautiful yet haunting song. I looked around, and the seats were filled with so many people. Mostly women and children. People were sitting in the aisles. When the fire breaks out, there will be no room for people to escape. It was dark. Really dark except for the spotlights that illuminated the stage.

Then, just like the night before, the Ink Spots faded into the shadows of the stage.

From the shadows, I saw it again. The Shadow Man. The entity that lurked in the shadows and was controlled by Ira Couch. Why was it there? Was it attracted to death? Did the Shadow enjoy being around death? Then the answer came to me.

No. The Shadow was feeding on the pain and suffering of the dead who were in an astral time loop. Each night, when the ghostly fire broke out and the spirits reexperienced their deaths, the Shadow Man fed on their screams. Their deaths. Behind the stage curtain, there he was, Ira Couch. The Shadow Man returned to the shadows and followed Ira away from the stage.

THE SPELL OF THE PSYCHOPOMP
(GUIDING THE DEAD TO THE AFTERLIFE)

Items Needed: No items needed.

1. Call upon your ancestors and ask them to help you with guiding the spirits of the dead to the afterlife.

2. Call upon your patron deity or the death or psychopomp deity that you work with. In our coven, we call upon Hecate. Explain to the deity that you need their power, wisdom, and guidance to help the spirit cross over to the afterlife.

3. Call upon the spirit of the dead whom you wish to guide to the afterlife. Explain to them that it is time for them to move on to the afterlife so they may be reunited with their family and receive the healing and rest they need.

4. Listen to any concerns and fears that the spirit may have. Ask your ancestors and your deity to help you with this. They will give you wisdom and speak with the spirit as well.

5. In the event that a spirit of the dead is trapped in a time loop (repeating their death over and over), you will have to go to the astral plane and help them escape or speak to them to convince them that the loop is only astral and they can decide to leave anytime.

6. Open a portal to the afterlife either with your finger or a magical tool such as a dagger or wand.

7. Ask your ancestors and your deity to walk the spirit through the portal into the afterlife. Their own ancestors will welcome them and take them to the place they need to be.

8. Close the portal and thank the ancestors and your deity. Leave offerings for your ancestors and your deity.

A spark.

The light illuminating the stage sparked.

The spark hit the curtain.

Fire.

The curtain caught fire.

No one was leaving the theater. They think it's part of the show. They are applauding.

Smoke.

Lots of smoke.

Mr. Foy comes on stage and asks everyone to stay calm. People start getting up from their seats. They are trying to make it to the doors. The doors are all locked. They are trapped. Everyone is trapped. I'm watching the events that led to six hundred deaths. The amount of deaths puts me into a panic. I take a couple of deep breaths, and then I center and ground myself. I feel better. I have to get these spirits… these people out of here.

The curtain goes up.

The fire quickly spreads throughout the theater.

So much smoke.

So much smoke.

Screams.

Screams.

"Everyone, please remain calm." Mr. Foy tried to calm everyone down.

There were no exit signs. Where was everyone going to go?

Then I suddenly remembered. As "real" as this felt, it was not on the physical plane. It was in the astral.

I needed to call upon my ancestors, the goddess Hecate, and the ancestors of those who died in the fire. There was so much screaming and shouting I could barely concentrate. I focused on my heart and the spiritual plane and called the ancestors to help evacuate the burning theater. Many ancestors appeared, but there was so much smoke and chaos that no one paid much notice to them.

I had to get their attention. "Everyone! Everyone, listen to me!"

A few people were able to hear me, but most did not. There were so many screams. So many people were panicking. I shouted as loud as I could, "I can open the doors! I have a key!"

A man looks astounded and relieved at the same time, "You have a key! Fuck! Open the damn doors!"

"She has a key!" a woman said.

"She has a key!" another man said.

"She can open the doors!" someone else shouted.

Word quickly spread that I had a way out of the burning theater. The smoke was so black that people were coughing and having trouble breathing.

"Follow me!" I raced up the aisle to the locked doors, leading the way into the lobby and out of the theater.

I knew the doors were locked, but I tried one more time, just to be sure. Locked.

"Use your key!" a man screamed. "Hurry!"

I took my finger, and then I focused my mind on the magic of the Universe above me.

I breathed white magical energy into my crown energy center and then breathed it into my heart, down my arm, into my hand, and I used my index finger to draw a magical portal: a door. With the power of my visualization, I saw the door opening up. I told the ancestor spirits to help me guide the people through the astral doors that I had created. They began yelling into the crowd of people, "Come this way! We have a door to safety!"

The people poured themselves through the door. I quickly drew another door, then another door, and another, and another. All the panicked people raced into the lobby and followed the ancestors through the astral doors.

The theater was burning more now. I could hardly breathe with so much black smoke. I saw that the people were leaving the theater, but there were more that had gone upstairs. I had to hurry. I found a staircase to the side of the burning stage. So much smoke. I raced up to the top of the stairs. There were windows overlooking the alley down below. People were about to jump.

"Wait! I have keys to the doors!" I shouted.

I began drawing several portals that allowed the people to exit the theater and cross over to the afterlife.

The fire was burning even stronger now. I could feel the heat of the flames. The ceiling was caving in. Beams of fiery wood fell from the ceiling. One of them barely missed me.

I ran as fast as I could down the stairs. When I got to the auditorium, I saw that everyone had made it out. No one had to relive their deaths anymore. I finally got out of the auditorium, into the lobby, and out to the Chicago streets.

There they were. Six hundred spirits of light standing there.

I felt their collective gratitude for what I had done for them. They were surrounded by their ancestors. They would be taken to the afterlife, where they could find the healing that they needed.

In my heart, I heard the words, *"Thank you…"*

Then they disappeared. Six hundred spirits crossed over to the afterlife. For healing.

THE HAUNTING OF THE CONGRESS HOTEL

September 24, 1947
Day of Mercury. Moon in Taurus.

I received the Lincoln Park Coven's book a few days ago at the Fall Equinox ritual. We discussed what had happened at the Oriental Theater and all the other chapters as well. We are starting to piece things together slowly. The Shadow Man, Ira Couch, Dr. Dyer, and Margaret. I see a few of the connections, but there are still so many questions. Maybe the vampire Dr. Dyer has nothing to do with Ira Couch and the Shadow Man. Maybe he does. We still don't know. I think there has to be a connection somewhere. Chicago has always had ghosts, witches, and vampires, but not like this. Ever since we cast that spell, magical beings have been crawling out of the woodwork.

This is Richard Crompton. A little about me. Of all the coven members, I have the most experience. I'm not bragging or anything like that, but it's the truth. I have been studying witchcraft, magic, and the occult for a long time. I used to belong to a group that studied Thelema. Someone in the group got a hold of a magical book that was written by Aleister Crowley. It had a lot of information about magic, spirits, angels, etc. More so than any book that I had seen up until then. We would meet every week or so and practice magic. It was good training. Afterward, we would all go to the pub and have a drink or two. Some of us had way more than two.

One day, I met Patricia. She had heard about our magical meet-ups and joined the group for a while. We came to be good friends. Nothing romantic or anything like that. She's a kindred spirit. I believe that Patricia and I have known each other in other lives. Maybe we even practiced magic together in times gone by. I think it's funny, though, because Patricia likes to say that reincarnation and past lives are interesting, but we need to concentrate on the life we are living now. My take on it is that we should try to remember our past lives so that we can take those lessons into *this* life. Patricia has a point, though, when she says that people become distracted by their past lives too often. She says that people are often disappointed to find out that they were medieval peasants and not the Queen of France. Every time she says something like that, I chuckle.

After spending many nights drinking tea and sometimes absinthe with Patricia, she told me that she loves Ceremonial Magick, but her real passion is witchcraft. She shared with me that she was originally from Texas and that her teacher's name was Johnathan Knotbristle. Knotbristle? What an odd name. I wonder if he made it up so as not to have strangers find him when visitors are unwelcome. Still, he must be a good teacher because Patricia has the kind of talent that you don't see every day. One day, during our talks, I convinced her to start the Lincoln Park Coven. After all, that's where she and I both live. Then, like "magic," other members began joining our coven.

Now, let's get to the matter at hand. Everyone who has had possession of this book has experienced amazing and harrowing events. I have to say, as I read the chapters, I don't know that I could have done better. I believe that each and every coven member who has told their story in this book has done the best that could have been expected. Well…then there's Margaret. She cast the love spell, and we think that was part of Dr. Dyer's plan to entrap her in his magical control. But at the end of it, we all have free will. Magick or no magic, Margaret could have tried to resist. Maybe she did, and Dr. Dyer was too strong. I don't know. It pains me to think about it.

So, let's get to my story.

I've been dating this woman named Shelly Willowbrook. She's beautiful. And funny. And everything I've always wanted in a girl. I can't deny that I may be falling for this woman. All in all, she's a classy lady. The kind of woman who's kind but demands respect simply by being herself. I don't think she's afraid of anything.

Shelly and I were having a good time last night. We went out to dinner and decided that we wanted to go to a few bars. The night was young, after all. We wanted to go to someplace we had never been before, so we decided to go to the Congress Hotel on South Michigan Avenue. It just reopened after the war, and I heard that it has a great bar. The Congress is pretty old. It was built for the World's Fair in 1893. It's pretty fancy. The lobby is beautiful. Probably the fanciest lobby I had ever seen. The hotel has two towers. The north tower was built in 1893, and the additional south tower was built a little over ten years later.

The hotel bar is in the north tower, just around the corner from the lobby of the Congress. It's beautiful as well. Its decor is mostly brown wood, a style that was popular many decades ago. Some say that the bar is a bit outdated. I don't agree.

I think it carries the style and romance of a time that is no more. I loved it. I felt strangely at home in that lounge.

When we arrived at the bar, Shelly and I ordered two dry martinis. The bartender didn't say much to us as he made our drinks, but he did give me an odd look. At the time, I didn't think too much about it. He gave us our martinis, and Shelly and I enjoyed our night. I have to admit, we had far too many drinks and were feeling a bit clumsy. Well, we were drunk. Shelly succumbed to a fit of laughter from the alcohol, and I would like to think that it was something funny I said. She could not stop giggling. I suggested that we take our drinks into the magnificent lobby for some air.

We came around the corner into the lobby, both of us laughing at nothing but having a wonderful time. We sat down on one of the little couches and continued drinking our martinis. Something grabbed Shelly's attention. She noticed that several couples were doing the same thing as we were, but there were also groups of ladies without gentleman friends accompanying them. I suggested to Shelly that perhaps they were looking to meet someone. Shelly was suspicious. You see, Shelly is not a witch such as me, but she has a strong intuition. Once, when I asked her if she had an interest in learning more about her intuition, she politely declined and said that was my specialty and that she had no desire to infringe on my interests.

Shelly and I went back to giggling and having a great time, but then something else caught her eye. She became quiet and stared off into the distance.

"What are you looking at?" I asked her.

"Over there," Shelly said without dropping her gaze. "There's a gentleman charming those ladies."

I looked in the direction Shelly was fixated, and sure enough, an attractive gentleman was speaking with a couple of ladies who looked to be in their early twenties. "Charming, indeed. I think he's looking for a lady friend tonight."

Shelly continued her fixation with the gentleman. "There's something odd about him."

She was probably right. Many of the men who frequented hotel lobbies were looking to take a woman home for sex. But, I have no judgment. After all, sex in witchcraft is sacred.

The gentleman noticed us looking at him. He said a polite farewell to the ladies and walked over to us. "Hello, my name is Henry. Charming to meet you."

He took Shelly's hand and kissed it. Henry was a bit presumptuous, but I suppose he was just being polite. Shelly watched him carefully as he kissed her hand. "And what brings you out on this lovely night, Henry?"

"Beauty, my dear," Henry said. "Beauty."

Shelly was not one to fall for flattery or charming strangers. She felt in her heart that there was something, as she would say, "not correct" with this man. "Chicago's a big city. You can find beauty anywhere if you look hard enough."

"Very true, my dear," Henry said. "Are you both guests of this hotel?"

"No," I answered. "We are here enjoying the bar. Too much of the bar, if I'm being honest."

Henry laughed at my little joke. He was a charmer, indeed.

"I have a beautiful suite on the twelfth floor of this north tower," Henry said. "We should have cocktails and enjoy the stunning view."

Shelly did not trust him. Not at all. "I'm sorry, Henry, we are just about to leave for the night."

"Indeed," Henry said. "Another time."

He kissed Shelly's hand again to say farewell, and then he shook mine. When he held my hand, my stomach dropped to the floor, and in my mind, I saw the image of a dark room and walls tightly pressing against me. Very odd.

Henry walked away from us and went back to speaking with the young ladies in the hotel lounge.

"I think I've had too much to drink," Shelly said as she placed her glass on the nearby table and stood up. "We should go."

As we walked out of the lobby, I saw a man dressed in a military uniform. Strangely, the style of the uniform looked like it was over fifty years old. Maybe I was seeing things. I was drunk, after all. I turned around to get a better look at the man, and what I saw then was even stranger. The man in the old uniform had the back of his head blown out. Like he had been shot in the front of the head and the back of his skull had exploded. I turned back around and didn't say a word about it to Shelly. I took her home.

When I got home, I couldn't stop thinking about what I had seen at the hotel. I've read all the previous chapters, and every member of the coven has had something like this happen. Is this the start of my magical adventure with ghosts and monsters?

A SPELL TO REVEAL THE HIDDEN IN DREAMS

Items Needed:
- Tarot card of the Moon
- Two white candles
- Incense of lavender, jasmine, and mugwort
- Charcoal
- A small bowl of water

1. Place the Moon tarot card on a table. Place a white candle on either side of the card.

2. Light the candles and say: *"I call to the spirits of Luna. Spirits of dreams. Spirits of the astral realm. Allow me to journey into your realm so that the hidden may be revealed to me."*

3. Light the charcoal, place the incense blend on the embers, and say: *"Spirits of lavender, jasmine, and mugwort. Sacred plants of Luna. I ask that you use your powers and reveal to me what is hidden."*

4. Place the bowl of water on the table so that the flames of the candles are reflected on the surface of the water and say: *"Mighty goddess*

Hecate and the spirits of witchcraft I summon, stir, and conjure your forth. By the power of Water, do I open the portal to the realm of dreams. Reveal to me what is hidden!"

5. Place yourself into a trance. Gaze upon the bowl of water. Have a deep understanding that this is a portal to the realm of dreams. Think about your desire to have that which is hidden revealed to you.

6. At this time, you may receive a vision, a feeling, or a knowing of what is true.

7. Now, go to sleep and pay attention to your dreams. What is hidden may be revealed by symbols, colors, feelings, or knowledge, or it may be revealed through synchronicity the following day.

8. Upon waking the next day, leave an offering for the spirits.

September 25, 1947
Day of Jupiter. Moon in Pisces.

That night, when I performed the spell, I had a dream. The dream didn't tell a story. The dream was a series of images and feelings. Here's what I saw:
Dark tunnels.
Screams.
A maze.
Gunshots.
Blood. Lots and lots of blood.
A woman who can't find her way out.
Despair.
Alone. So alone.
Help.
In the afternoon, I spoke to Shelly about what I saw leaving the hotel and what the dream had revealed to me. She agreed that the spirits were telling me that I needed to help. Shelly wanted to help me as well. I didn't think that was a good idea, but I know better than anyone that a man can't tell Shelly what she can and cannot do. She is her own woman. Shelly believes in ghosts and spirits and things that I believe, but she has

no interest in being a witch. From time to time, she likes to join me in some of the witchcraft that I do. Never the coven rituals and things. No one but initiates are allowed to attend. Everything else, though, Shelly will come with me.

Shelly and I waited until after dark to go back to the Congress Hotel. The spirits of the dead are always around us, but it's harder to see and connect with them during the daytime. It can be done, but it's easier at night. During the day, the Earth is flooded with light and is filled with people coming and going. At night, it is usually calmer. People settle in, and the spirits come out.

When we got to the hotel, we walked into the lobby, trying to go unnoticed by the staff. So far, no one has seen us. As we walked through the lobby to get to the elevators, we saw Henry again. Again, he was speaking to the ladies. He must be one of those men who has a new woman every single night. When we got to the elevator, I wasn't sure which floor to go to.

"Just pick one," Shelly whispered.

Without giving it too much thought, I picked nine. The elevator doors closed, and we went up to the ninth floor. When the doors opened, I suddenly felt the presence of people…but I saw no one. Shelly and I walked through the hallway of the ninth floor.

"I'm not sure what I'm looking for," I said.

"I bet you'll know it when you see it," Shelly said. She's not wrong. If we were going to see a spirit, we would know it when we saw it.

There was no one in the halls. Good. We didn't have a room there, and we didn't want anyone asking any questions. We walked the entirety of the floor and saw nothing. We found the stairs that led up to the tenth floor, so we decided to keep going up the hotel, floor by floor. At this rate, it would take all night.

We were on the tenth floor, and again, nothing.

The hallway wound around the building in a big circle. As we turned a corner, one of the room doors was opened. Shelly and I crept slowly to the room and peeked inside. The room was occupied by a husband and wife. They didn't seem to notice us watching them. The woman had ordered room service. Two cups of tea. She then poured a powder into both cups. The husband and wife drank the tea. Moments later, they were dead. Then, like nothing had happened, the husband and wife were alive and drinking tea. The wife finally saw us and smiled. "Would you like some tea?"

My heart sank. "No, thank you."

I pulled Shelly down the hall and back to the staircase. "Let's check the next floor."

On the eleventh floor, it was much the same as the last two. Dark hallways with no one in sight. Each floor looked exactly the same. If you didn't have your wits about you, you might get vertigo or even get lost in this maze of a hotel.

Something ran by me. I looked to see what it was and saw a little boy who looked to be six years old. The boy laughed, turned down the winding hallways, and disappeared from our sight.

The boy ran by me again.

"Wait!" I called out. "What's your name?"

The boy stopped and turned around. "Karel," he said.

"Karel, it's nice to meet you," I said. "But you shouldn't be running in the hallway. You might get hurt."

Karel grinned. "I'm already hurt. We are all hurt. That's why we are here."

Shelly has a soft spot for children. "What do you mean?"

Karel came closer to us. "You shouldn't be here. You might get hurt, too."

"Karel!" A woman's voice screamed. "Karel, get over here this instant!"

Both Shelly and I turned around, and there stood a woman who… who looked as though she had her head and chest bashed in. Her face and body were contorted in a way that looked terrible. Her dress was blood-soaked. "Karel, it's time to go home. We have to meet your father back in the Old Country!"

Shelly grabbed Karel's hand, and then we saw the poor boy. His head and body were contorted, too. Shelly screamed and let go of Karel.

He looked back at us and said, "I have to go home now."

Karel walked to the woman, and she opened one of the hotel room doors. Inside was another little boy. The woman grabbed both boys and jumped out of the window.

This isn't real, I told myself. This didn't just happen. These are ghosts. Ghosts of a poor mother who lost her sanity and jumped out of the hotel window with her two young children. I took Shelly's hand as we found the elevator and went back downstairs to the lobby. We both needed a drink! At the hotel bar, we ordered two martinis and drank them as fast as we could. We ordered two more.

We took our drinks to the hotel lobby. Both of us wanted to be around the living.

"And how is your evening?"

Shelly and I turned around, and there stood Henry. He was probably a womanizer, but at least he was one of the living.

"Good," I lied.

"How are you, Henry?" Shelly said. I could tell her nerves were feeling better after the drinks.

"Splendid!" Henry said. He seemed very happy and excited. "I noticed that you were exploring the hotel."

"Yes," I said. "We enjoy Chicago's architecture."

"Oh! Then you must see the twelfth floor," Henry said. "I have a residential room that I have been renting out for quite some time. It is marvelous!"

I got the impression that Henry wanted us to visit him so that he could get his hands on Shelly. Scoundrel. "Sadly, we must be going."

We finished our drinks and left.

September 26, 1947
Day of Venus. Moon in Aquarius.

The next night, it was time to visit the south tower of the Congress Hotel.

Shelly and I walked into the lobby of the hotel, and sure enough, there was Henry. This time, he was taking a woman to the elevator. Perhaps he had convinced a young lady to go up to his hotel room. As a witch, I shouldn't make judgments about such things. But as a gentleman, I feel that he is leading women down a path they may not want to go. I have to remember that everyone has their own journey.

The hotel staff at the check-in desk didn't notice us coming into the lobby. We took a left and walked down the corridor to the south tower. The hallway leading from the north tower to the south tower was spectacular. It seemed to glisten with a magic of its own. As soon as we entered the south tower, I could feel a shift in the energy. It felt different. It didn't feel foreboding or anything of that nature. It felt—this may sound strange—but it felt as though it was in another dimension of time and space. Perhaps the south tower was built on some sort of vortex or secret portal or something like that. I remember reading occult books that talked about portals to other dimensions and realities. Maybe the south tower was one such portal.

Shelly and I got to the elevator. Even the elevator had an odd feeling to it. The doors opened, and we stepped inside.

"Where to?" Shelly asked, knowing whatever was going to happen, it was going to be…well, intense.

I took her hand and connected to her. Both of our psychic abilities complimented each other. We then, together, pressed the button. The fourth floor. When we reached the fourth floor, the doors opened. Now, it was time for a new spell.

A SPELL TO SEE THE UNSEEN

Items Needed: No items needed.

1. Take a few deep breaths and place yourself into a light trance state.

2. Calm your mind and clear your emotions.

3. Bring your consciousness to your field of sensation. Your sphere of sensation is closely related to your aura. It is the natural psychic awareness of body, mind, and spirit. It surrounds your body just as your aura does. The sphere of sensation is an extension of your psychic mind. It is often felt when someone stands too close to you, and you can feel them without seeing them. An example is when someone walks up behind you unseen, and you know they are there.

4. Visualize your sphere of sensation (I visualize it as either clear or the color of fog), and then take a breath. On the exhale, visualize the sphere of sensation expanding to fill up a room. You can also simply expand the sphere of sensation to encompass an object or person.

5. Open your brow, throat, and heart energy centers.

6. Allow the sphere of sensation to show you pictures, reveal hidden secrets, interpret psychic phenomena, and many other things.

7. When you are ready, visualize the sphere of sensation shrinking back to its normal size around your body. Mentally tell yourself to disconnect psychically from anything you have connected to.

8. Give thanks to the spirits for their aid and help.

As I performed the spell, I expanded my sphere of sensation to fill up the entire hallway. The hallways in the south tower were much wider than the ones in the north. The energy of the south tower felt much different. The north tower felt dark. Like the spirits were watching. Hiding. Waiting for just the right time to reveal themselves. The south tower felt more active. I could feel the psychic energy of movement. Things were happening.

"Do you see anything yet?" Shelly asked.

"There's a lot of spirits here," I said, "but I don't see—"

We turned the corner, and I got a strong feeling to stop. There was an energy that was pulling me…no, more like calling me. Telling me to come inside this room. Shelly and I stopped and stood at the door, which opened up into a guest room.

441.

We both stood in front of the door. It was almost as if time had stopped. We didn't breathe. We didn't move.

We walked inside together. I was hoping this room was not occupied. I didn't want to get thrown out of the hotel—or worse, arrested for breaking and entering. It was dark. Quiet. But with my sphere of sensation, I knew something was there. We lay on the bed together, side by side. I closed my eyes and took a deep breath. I connected to my sphere of sensation again. I also focused on the energy of my heart and then brought my attention to my third eye.

I told myself I wanted my sphere of sensation to go deeper into the spirit world. I told myself over and over again. Reveal the spirits. Reveal the spirits.

Something was above us.

I opened my eyes, and there was the apparition of an old woman floating over us. I gently took a breath to calm my nerves. I've seen spirits plenty of times before, but holy shit, this was nose-to-nose to me. I've never been this fucking close before.

I took another breath. The eyes of the spirit looked directly into my eyes. My heart raced. Then I knew. I just knew that she wasn't trying to hurt me or Shelly. She was attempting to understand us. To figure out what we were doing.

Shelly opened her eyes and saw the ghost. Her eyes widened as she stifled her screams. She looked at me and saw that I was trying to stay calm. I think this helped her calm herself.

I think she knew that if I was calm, then everything was going to be okay.

The spirit looked at me for a moment more then she drifted back to the foot of the bed. I sat up and sent a gentle beam of energy from my heart. I made sure that the energy from my heart was warm, pleasant, and friendly. I didn't want to scare her off. "My name is Richard Crompton. What is your name?"

The spirit looked confused. I don't think she's ever had anyone try to communicate with her before. She didn't say anything for a while. Then she said in a soft voice, "My name is Mrs. Harriet Harrison."

"Is this your room, Mrs. Harrison?" I asked.

"It is," she answered. "But this is not the place of my death. I fell from high above and into the hotel basement. I came here to this room to get away from it."

How curious. "Get away from what?"

Mrs. Harrison quickly turned toward the door and gasped.

Shelly and I both turned to see what was startling her.

"What is it?" I asked.

A shadow came from under the door. It crept behind the desk and into another shadow. I could feel the darkness. It was almost…evil. In our coven, we don't believe in evil, really. We believe in the abuse of power. But this felt…I don't know, demonic? The shadow stayed hidden.

Mrs. Harrison floated back and stared at the shadow by the wall. She looked me in the eyes again. "Leave this place or join us in spirit."

Then she was gone.

I couldn't feel the darkness of the shadow anymore. Was it gone, too, or was it hiding and…watching us?

"I think we've had enough fun for one night," Shelly said. She couldn't get out of the room fast enough. She bolted from the room and went straight for the elevator. By the time we got back to the hotel lobby, Shelly was a bit more calm.

"Are you alright?" I asked.

"I've never seen…" Shelly didn't have the words for the experience she just had. "Have you ever…?"

"Not like that, no."

"This place is like some sort of spiritual cage or something."

Or *something,* I thought. Then I saw them. Walking down the corridor between the north and south towers were Betty and Sophia Honeybourne. Our coven knew of them quite well thanks to David Lonesdale and his tale about Hull House. After David told us about the Honeybourne sisters, I met them myself. I stopped by their parlor and asked them to connect to the spirits.

I was curious to see what their magical powers were, and, indeed, they had a strong connection to the dead. Tonight, they both wore the same dress. White with tiny pink square patterns. I must say, they didn't look like they were walking—with the long dresses covering their feet, they looked as if they were floating.

I followed them down the corridor. Were they going up to room 441? I knew they had a strong connection to the dead, so I followed them. They knew I was there. In unison, they turned their heads and looked at me. They said nothing as they drifted down the hallway. Where the hell were they going? I wondered what they were going to do. I still had the Spell to See the Unseen active, so I expanded my sphere of sensation to encompass them, but I could feel a shield or a barrier of energy. They were shielded from my psychic senses. I followed them until they turned a corner. By the time I arrived at that corner, they were gone. Damn. I was hoping maybe they could help me figure all this out.

I walked back to the hotel lobby with the thought that maybe tomorrow or the following day, I would stop by their parlor again and find out what was going on. Perhaps I could convince them to help the coven solve the mystery of the Shadow Man and Ira Couch. In the lobby, I looked around for Shelly, but I didn't see her. Maybe she was at the bar. I quickly walked around the corner to the bar, but she wasn't there either. She wouldn't have gone home without me.

I was getting a bit nervous. I ran outside to the sidewalk and still couldn't find her. Damn it. I came back in and looked around the lobby. She was nowhere to be seen.

"Are you looking for that beautiful lady?" a woman's voice said.

I turned around, and a young woman holding a cocktail and smoking a cigarette held a big smile. "Yes, did you see where she went?"

"She went with that charming man," she said. "Henry."

"Henry?"

She took a puff from her cigarette. "Oh, he's a charmer, that one. He likes to take the ladies up to the twelfth floor."

What was Shelly doing with Henry? My heart sank in my chest. No. No, no, no, no, no. In my head, I must have heard one of the spirits in the hotel because I clearly heard a voice say, *"Save her!"*

I ran as fast as I could to the elevator. I mashed the button hard. I kept thinking, "I have to get her. I have to get her." The elevator ride seemed to take a long, long time. Fuck! Come one! The elevator door opened. The twelfth floor.

Directly in front of the elevator was a mirror with two lights on either side. The lights suddenly went out. The hallway was dark. Only some of the lights were on. I could barely see where I was going. Where the fuck did he take Shelly?

I couldn't see the spirits on that floor, but I could feel them. There were so many spirits. Some were filled with sorrow, while others felt dark and twisted. I could feel so many spirits there that I couldn't make out any one individual spirit. It was almost like a big soup of spiritual energy that I had to wade through.

"Where am I?" I heard a faint voice say. Shelly.

"Shelly!" I called out. "Where are you?"

Another voice came from the shadows…Henry.

"Jack and Jill went up the hill to fetch a pail of water. Jack fell down and broke his crown…and Jill came tumbling after…"

Fuck. He had her. "Henry! Let Shelly go!"

I walked down the darkened hallway, not knowing where I was going or what I was going to do. With the faint light, I could see that many of the guest room doors were opened. Odd. What the hell was Henry planning? Then, out of the darkness, Henry leaped toward me and knocked me hard into one of the opened rooms. I couldn't see him well, but I knew it was him. I could feel the energy of evil. I was winded when I hit the ground. I heard the door slam and lock from the outside.

I stood up and banged on the locked door. *BANG. BANG. BANG.* It was didn't budge. I wasn't getting out this way. There was a flickering light, and I could see that this wasn't a room at all. It was another winding hallway. The hallway was thin and had no carpet like the other hallways in the hotel. I think this was a secret hallway. Would anyone know I was even here? I was alone. So was Shelly. I had to find a way out.

I walked down the hallway that wound and twisted around. There were little rooms off the hallway as well. I looked into one of the rooms and saw that it contained chains and handcuffs. What the fuck? Another room had a cage big enough to put a person inside. The hallway wound again and again like a maze. I was getting turned around. I had no idea where I was. I started to question if I knew up from down. Then, I came to another room that had exposed pipes running through the ceiling.

Hissssss.

Gas.

I could smell poison gas coming from the ceiling. I pulled my shirt over my nose and mouth. I had to get out of there. I tried to make my way back through the hallway maze, and then…

Thud!

I must have fallen through a trapdoor. God dammit, that fucking hurt! I slammed down on the floor below. Wherever I was, it was dark. I couldn't see anything. I kept thinking that I was going to die. This is how I die. Alone in the dark. I didn't know what to do. Then something came over me. I don't know if it was a spirit, an angel, a god, or what, but something came over me.

A SPELL FOR THE WISDOM OF THE GODS

Items Needed: No items needed.

1. Take a few deep breaths. Ground and center yourself.

2. Focus on your heart, third eye, and crown energy centers.

3. Call out to your patron god with your heart.

4. Visualize the god in front of you. Send a beam of energy from your heart to their heart. Send a beam of energy from your third eye to their third eye. Send a beam of energy from your crown to their crown.

5. Visualize the god stepping into your body. See them joining with your legs, torso, arms, chest, and head.

6. Allow your mind to gently join with the mind of the god.

7. Ask the god to give you the wisdom you need. You may ask them questions. You can also use this technique when you are doing a psychic reading for someone.

8. When you are ready, disconnect your mind from the god. Visualize the god disconnecting from your body and your energy centers.

9. Give thanks and offerings.

The spell just came to me. I don't know from where. Maybe it was Hecate herself who gave me the spell. However it came to me, I am grateful. I used the spell to connect with Hecate.

In my mind, I could see her as clear as day. She was dark, beautiful, and powerful. The great Titan who keeps the keys that unlock the above world, this world, and the below world.

The voice of Hecate was strong and sweet. "I am here, Richard. What do you ask of me?"

Connecting with her in my mind gave me strength, confidence, and a kind of healing. "I am trapped somewhere in the Congress Hotel. I need help escaping. I need to save Shelly from Henry."

Hecate filled my body with her love and energy. "'Henry' has been dead for many years. Most know him by the name H. H. Holmes, the nefarious murderer from decades past. Henry Howard Holmes took the lives of many women in his life. He is a spirit who haunts this hotel."

A spirit? "But he's physical? How can he achieve physical form if he's a ghost?"

"Spirits can have a strong influence on the mind," Hecate said. "When a spirit is strong, they can convince your consciousness that you are not seeing a spirit but someone in physical form."

Oh my god. I had never known this.

Hecate continued, "The mind has the power to convince you that you are seeing the spirit in physical form. Much like when a person who is mentally ill believes that their illusions are real."

"So, Henry is a ghost," I said.

"You must banish him just as you would any other spirit," Hecate explained. "But be warned. He is powerful and no easy spirit to banish."

"How can I fight him?" I asked.

In my mind, Hecate touched my head and sent my mind a new spell.

"Thank you, goddess." I was so grateful that she was able to help me.

"Be well," Hecate said, and then she was gone.

A SPELL TO DISPEL MAGIC SET AGAINST YOU

Items Needed: No items needed.

1. Witches and spirits can manipulate energy to confuse you, influence your mind, or place a glamour on you so that you fall under their enchantments. This spell will help you create a boundary between you and the magic that is being sent to manipulate you.

2. Take a few deep breaths. Center and ground yourself.

3. Become aware of your physical body. Feel your heartbeat. Become aware of your breath. Feel the pressure of your feet on the ground.

4. Inhale energy from the Earth, then exhale the Earth energy all around your body, creating an energy shield.

5. Become aware of the energy inside and around your body. This is your reality. You are whole, and you are balanced. This is you.

6. Allow your consciousness to be aware of the energy beyond your Earth energy shield. Know that this energy beyond your shield is magic that is attempting to manipulate you. Allow your senses to feel the difference between your energy and the energy outside of your Earth energy shield. Feel the two energies as separate forces.

7. Take a deep breath, and on the exhale, send the energies outside of your shield into the ground.

8. Know that the energy has no further power over you. You are free from its influence.

I performed the spell that Hecate had given me. During the spell, I allowed my mind to connect to the energy of the hotel and the twelfth floor. I connected to the energy of the mazes and strange rooms. I was shielded with Earth energy. It protected me from Holmes' influence. While focusing on my center, I grounded the energy that was trying to confuse and influence me. Then it was gone. The magical illusion was no more. The glamour of the horrors of the twelfth floor faded, and the halls looked like any other hall of the hotel. It was all an illusion built by H. H. Holmes.

"Richard!" I heard Shelly scream from one of the guest rooms.

I quickly ran to the room and opened the door. There, Shelly was lying on the bed. She seemed to be okay. She was safe. I was never going to let her out of my sight again. "Are you alright?"

"Yes, I think so," Shelly said, trying to understand what had happened. She was under the illusion as well. "It was the strangest thing. One minute, Henry was saying hello to me, and the next, I was up here in this hotel room."

"There's no time to explain, but that's no ordinary man. That's the spirit of a killer. We need to get out of here," I said firmly. "Before he comes back!"

"Too late!" Holmes appeared right in front of us. "I'm here. There's no escape from me."

Fuck him. I was no longer scared of him. He was a lost soul. A hungry ghost that fed on the fears and life forces of other people. He was a murderer in life, and now he was a parasite in death. I had the power of Hecate with me, and I was powerful. I stared into his eyes and simply said, "Hecate."

The goddess Hecate joined me in my body and mind instantly. I was her, and she was me. We shared the same thoughts. The same heart. The same spirit. I placed both of my palms facing up, and the mighty torches of Hecate appeared in my hands. Without hesitation, I crossed the two torches, forming an "X." I took a deep breath and forced my magical breath upon the astral flames of those two torches. With the power of my breath and Hecate's torches, I sent a powerful astral fire toward Holmes. His ghostly astral body disintegrated. Only his eternal spirit remained as a small white sphere.

Hecate spoke to my mind, "I will take him where he needs to go."

I thanked Hecate for her assistance. I was so relieved that she was able to use her divine powers to help me stop Holmes. I could not thank her enough. She stepped out of my body and took the spirit of Holmes with her back to the Underworld.

Tomorrow, I will give this magical book to Patricia. She'll write the final entry of the Lincoln Park Coven's book of witchcraft.

THE DANCE OF THE DEAD

October 30, 1947
Day of Jupiter. Moon in Taurus.

The time has come for my own entry into this book of witchcraft. When I decided to begin this book, it was an exercise in magic. I wanted the Lincoln Park Coven to grow magically and become more powerful. I have read each chapter of this book carefully. I see where each member of the coven succeeded and where each one struggled. I don't like to think of a struggle as a failure. I think that if we want to become more powerful witches, then we will see the lessons in our "failures." Challenges and struggles are meant to be a learning opportunity. I think many of the coven members saw this opportunity. Some did not.

As the leader of this coven, it pains me to watch members struggle with magic and the spirits. But they must learn on their own. Too many times, I have seen students of witchcraft fail to grow on their own because they are either too dependent on their teachers and leaders or they choose to remain stagnant in their practices. A good teacher and magical leader must let their students struggle and learn on their own. Even if it means being the villain in their eyes. This is a role I will accept.

When our coven began writing this book, I was told that a darkness was coming. Well, if we are ready or not, that no longer matters. The darkness is here. I think the darkness has always been here, but it's coming for us. Perhaps there is an alignment of the stars that is opening an astral gate that will let the spirits out. Or perhaps the spirits and the hauntings have always been here, and it wasn't until now that we noticed them. The tide of Samhain is here, and this is the time when the spirits can be better seen. The dead will have more power over the land. More power than they do any other time of year. I fear that now that the portals of the dead are wide open, the spirits will come after us. We must be ready.

My visions tell me that a great battle approaches. For those of us who are ready, we will face it with strength and grace. For those who are not…I don't know.

Allow me to help you understand who I am. I am Patricia Glasspool, and I am the leader of the Lincoln Park Coven. I have lived in Chicago for many years. I was born and raised in southern Texas. My magical teacher is Johnathan Knotbristle. He is a kind soul and a good man. In his old age, he doesn't travel much around the countryside like he used to. I think he enjoys time at home with his rocking chair and his tobacco pipe. He's fine with only the spirits keeping him company now. He had dreams of spreading his witchcraft all around the country, but I think that will never be. Instead, he asked me where I wanted to go, and wherever I ended up, he asked me to teach witchcraft.

I came to Chicago many years ago. I grew restless with the country, and I yearned to learn more about magic, not just the Southern brand of witchcraft I learned from Johnathan. His magic is powerful, yes, but his magic is that of the land and the spirits, and I wanted to learn more. I came to Chicago in hopes I would meet other like-minded people from around the world. I joined a Thelema group many years ago, and I learned a lot. It wasn't my brand of magic, but it does have value. I am grateful for the lessons I had learned from those spirits.

I started the Lincoln Park Coven many years ago with the hopes that whoever the spirits bring to us, we will learn magic together with an open heart and an open mind. Each person in the coven brings much value to the others. I am grateful for each one of them. As I teach them, they teach me. This is how the circle of magic must be. Even skillful leaders of witchcraft must continue to learn, and the best way to learn is through the skills of the young. Sometimes, I am surprised by their skills and talents.

But now, it is time to face the darkness together.

Halloween is tomorrow night. Chicago's children will roam the neighborhoods, asking strangers for candy. This will be the first

Halloween since the beginning of the war that the country will have trick-or-treating. During the war, there was a sugar shortage, so families had to celebrate Halloween indoors at parties instead of going door to door.

I believe that the events in each chapter of this book of witchcraft, written by each coven member, are somehow connected. I'm not sure how they are all connected, but it is my intention to find out. I needed to do a little investigating of my own.

I started at the beginning with the Couch Mausoleum in Lincoln Park. I went to the tomb at night. Lincoln Park is busy during the day, and I didn't want to bring a lot of attention to myself.

A SPELL OF MENTAL PROJECTION

Items Needed: No items needed.

1.   This spell is similar to astral projection, but instead of traveling into the astral plane, you travel to the mental plane. Your mind is connected to the mental plane with your thoughts and ideas. This allows you to speak with spirits and gods mentally, but it is contained in your mind. The experienced witch knows that this is a powerful magical practice and not an imagined scenario.

2.   Take some deep breaths. Center and ground yourself. Place yourself into a light trance.

3.   Focus on your thoughts. Allow any unwanted thoughts or feelings to fade away with each breath.

4.   Allow the image of where you want to be or what entity you wish to speak with to enter your mind. Know that what you see is real and that you are using your psychic powers of telepathy, psychometry, visualization, scrying, and intuition.

5.   Allow the images to unfold as they will. Speak with the entities present. Pay attention to any energies you see or feel. Intuit the meanings of these energies.

6. When you are ready, say goodbye to the spirit. Take a breath and bring your awareness to your physical body.

7. Give thanks and offerings to the spirits.

At the Couch tomb, I was able to see that upon the death of Ira Couch, a coven of witches trapped the Shadow Man in the tomb. The mausoleum was turned into a large spirit trap. The spirit of Ira Couch stayed near. He chose not to move on to the afterlife. He had a reason. My mental magic was powerful, but I could feel that something was blocking or protecting the secrets of Ira Couch. Although much was revealed to me, so many more questions came to mind. What was Ira Couch's purpose with the spirit, and what did it have to do with the hauntings in Chicago?

The next place I went to was Hull House. The house was still occupied by residents, and it was getting late. I did not want to disturb them or stir their attention. My spirit guides and helpers are telling me that there are more magical beings in Chicago than we think.

Our coven has known many of the local witches and Ceremonial Magicians, but there are more than we believe. I like to think that our coven is one of healing, wisdom, and magic, but I would be fooling myself if I didn't think that there were magical people, and perhaps covens, out there who did not have the best intentions. Many people seek out the mysteries of magic for power.

Hull House has a certain magic of its own. I walked the perimeter of the house, and I could feel that there were many spirits inside. I expanded my sphere of sensation, and I could feel the psychic reminiscence of the people who came to the house for help. Most were immigrants, but along with them were single mothers and the poor who came here with the hope of making their lives better. I also sensed that there were people who despised this place. I felt the hate from those people who thought that this house brought in "riffraff" and the "undesirables" to Chicago. So much hate projected on this place. I could sense that someone was watching me. I looked up to the window on the second floor, and I saw someone quickly close the curtains and step away from the window.

Next, I went across town to the Oriental Theater. Mary did well by being a psychopomp and leading all those poor souls to the afterlife so they may find healing with their beloved ancestors. There was a show going on when I arrived. I went around the side and into the alleyway where so many people had died. Again, I used my mental magic to understand more about this place.

Before the spirits were released, it was a ghostly time loop. The spirits were doomed to repeat their tragedy over and over until they found their way back home.

Again, more questions were raised. Why were my witches led to these places? Who were these men who seemed to show up and guide them? Were these guides spirits who wished us to help the dead, or were they leading us down a dark path?

I took the train back north and went to the Green Mill Lounge. The lounge is but a shadow of the glory it once was. Instead of glamor and beautiful people enjoying the night, it was full of drunks and drug addicts who wanted to stay out of the sight of people who may judge their addictions.

Here, too, the spirits were released to the afterlife. But there are other spirits too; not those who were murdered here, but those spirits of the people who either died of an overdose or who, after death, still yearn for their next drink. The energies in places like this often attract the Hungry Ghost. Ghosts who yearn for something to cover up their trauma. Many shadows lurk here, but I do not see the Shadow Man.

I took a cab further north to Rosehill Cemetery. This cemetery is by far my favorite in Chicago. Graceland is nice, and there are many spirits there, but Rosehill is an enigma to me. It's a little further north than Graceland, and there is a dark quality that attracts me. Not the kind of dark that most people fear, but the kind of dark that leads you down the road of mystery and witchery. The kind of dark that leads you to the dark parts of yourself, and once revealed, will lead you to Hecate herself.

I entered Rosehill Cemetery in the cloak of night. The cemetery felt peaceful and calm. As close to Samhain as it was, I thought the dead would be more active, but they were not. I could feel their presence, but they stood mostly silent. This gave me pause.

With my psychic vision, I could see the spirits standing near their graves in silence. They were watching me. I could feel that they were waiting for me to do something, but I did not know what. "Are you coming with me, or am I doing this alone?"

A SPELL TO READ THE SPIRIT WINDS

Items Needed: No items needed.

1. This spell is to read the energies of time and space. This allows you to understand the more subtle energies of what has been placed in motion.

2. Close your eyes and take a few deep breaths. Place yourself into a light trance.

3. Feel the air and wind on your skin. Open your heart and brow energy centers.

4. Face each of the four directions and connect to the psychic energies that are flowing toward you. Imagine the currents of energy rushing by you as if they were waves or currents of water.

5. Allow your consciousness to go into the currents of energy as if you were looking into the deep water. Allow your heart and third eye to connect to the energies.

6. What do you feel? What do you see? What do you intuit? What do you suddenly know?

7. Thank the spirits for their guidance.

This spell allowed me to feel more deeply what was going on not only in Rosehill Cemetery but in all of Chicago. The spirits were restless, yet they were waiting for something. They were waiting for some great event. But it was not quite time yet. Things were put in motion. Positioned just in the right place at the right time. Then it came to me. Everything that my coven members had experienced was part of the great game. Like pieces of a chessboard.

Every spirit and every witch in the coven was placed just in the right position to wait for this great event. Whatever was happening was a mystery, but my intuition told me it was powerful. I also received the guidance that the Lincoln Park Coven needed to act. If we did not, there would be lives lost. However, just as the spirits were placed on the chessboard, so were we. What game are we playing, and what is that that we are fighting?

A SPELL TO SUMMON THE POWERS OF WITCHERY

Items Needed:
- One white candle
- A suitable grave
- A talisman of witchery

1. This spell is intended to connect you to the current of magical power we call witchcraft. This power is the ebb and flow of the stars, the land, and the afterlife. It is the power that connects the living to the dead. The power that connects the past, present, and future. The power that connects the mystery and the fate of us all.

2. Use your intuition to find a suitable grave. This is the grave of a spirit who was either magical in life or the grave of a spirit who is connected to both the spirit world and the living world. This is your conduit of witchery.

3. Place your talisman around your neck. This is not a talisman to protect you from the spirits, but any talisman of your choice that helps you connect deeper to the spirits of witchcraft and the dead.

4. Take a few deep breaths and place yourself into a light trance.

5. Place your white candle at the center of the grave. Call to the spirit and energies of the grave. You may use your own words or say: *"(Name of spirit), I come to you this night to ask that you aid me in my conjuration of witchery. Guide me to the magic and mystery I seek. Open the portals of witchcraft and the unknown."*

6. Open your heart and connect with the spirit. If the spirit appears before you, introduce yourself and ask them for their aid. If they do not appear, know that the spirit is working to open the gates of witchcraft.

7. Visualize the spirits of witches long dead around you, creating a magical circle. These spirits are here to guide you and offer you wisdom. You may also ask them to add their magic to your own for even greater power.

8. When you are ready, thank the spirits for their attendance and give them offerings.

I summoned the spirits of the witches long dead with my spell. They appeared all around me. I could see by their clothing that they were there from all different periods of time. Some looked to be from the 1600s or older, while others looked to be a bit more modern. I do not believe it is wise to question the witches who appear. The witches who have come to help me are those who heard my call in the Otherworlds. I am grateful that they are here.

One of the spirits spoke. "Patricia, leader of the Lincoln Park Coven, why have you summoned us?"

"I have summoned you because I need your aid," I said to them. "My coven is in danger, and I fear we do not have the power to stop the coming darkness."

Another one of the spirit witches responded. "We have been watching the coming darkness."

"What insight can you give me?" I asked. I was desperate for any information they had. The witch ancestors could see the inner mystery workings that living witches cannot. They are not bound by time and space like those of us in the flesh.

One of the witches dressed from the 1600s said, "You are right to fear what you call 'the Shadow Man.' He is an ancient being. He does not belong in the earthly realm. He should not be here."

"Who is he?" I asked. "Where does he come from?"

A witch spirit who looked to be from the 1800s spoke this time.

"This being is from another dimension in space and time. He is from a world that is vastly different from our own. A world where shadow is common and light cannot be found."

"How did it get here?" If I was going to lead the fight against this being, then I needed to know everything I could.

"This being crept through a door that was created by the common man," a witch ancestor said. "No witch did this. It was mankind that allowed the Shadow Man into this world."

How could men with no magical power open a portal into another dimension?

"Rivers are the blood source of the land," the witch spirit continued. "As you know, water is energy that has manifested as liquid. All bodies of water are magical, but rivers take the energies of the Earth into different regions. As the moon controls the tides, the rivers control the flow of energy and water throughout the land."

Another witch ancestor spoke up. "Men polluted the river, and the river spilled into Lake Michigan. Men then reversed the flow of the river. Instead of flowing into Lake Michigan, the river was made to flow from Lake Michigan into the river. The pollutants would eventually be sent to the Mississippi River. This caused the energies of the land to go against the natural flow. This caused a crack in our dimension, in our reality. This crack created a door into our world from an unknown place."

Another witch ancestor responded, "The spirit of Ira Couch watched the comings and goings of Chicago for many years. He saw what the men were doing. He saw the Shadow Man coming into this world and saw an opportunity."

Another witch ancestor continued, "As the Shadow Man searched for its way back to its own world, it came by the Couch tomb. Ira Couch enticed the being to come into the tomb to rest. Once there, Ira Couch imprisoned it inside the mausoleum, only to wait for the right time. The right witch to release them both."

"What is his goal? To what end is he playing his games?" I asked them.

Another witch ancestor responded, "This is unseen to us."

Damn it. This was disappointing. The spirits of the witches were very helpful, and now I had more to go on than previously. I thanked the witch spirits for their insight and wisdom. I left an offering of bread, honey, and wine.

Now, it is time to summon everyone from the coven.

Halloween is coming.

October 31, 1947
Day of Venus. Moon in Gemini.

The day of Halloween has come. The tide of Samhain has been upon us for several days now. Beginning in the last week of October, the gates to the spirit world slowly begin to open. Things become stranger than usual. Spirits begin to come out, and the air is much cooler than before. The life of the land is withdrawing, allowing the spirits of the dead to manifest more clearly.

Once the sun goes down on Halloween, the gates to the spirit world are cracked wide open. For the next few days, the topsy-turvy energies of the land, the spirits, and the dead wreak havoc upon the land and on us. My psychic senses were telling me that Ira Couch was going to make his move tonight.

I summoned everyone from the Lincoln Park Coven. Even Margaret was summoned. I called her, but she did not answer her telephone. I did not expect her to, but my heart was hoping something had changed in her and she would want to mend what was broken between her and the rest of the coven. My heart is broken. I cannot think of that right now. I must focus on the matter at hand.

The following were in attendance:

Mary Stilling.
Linda Winfield.
Sandy Dorey.
James Bower.
Richard Crompton.
David Lonesdale.
Kenneth Ruthan.
…and myself, Patricia Glasspool.

We met at noon. Everyone usually took the day off work for Halloween. It was a witch's sacred festival, after all. But tonight, we would not be celebrating the tides. We would gather our magic together and defend the people and spirits of Chicago. We all sat in a circle of chairs that I had set up before everyone had arrived.

I started the meeting. "Thank you, everyone, for being here today. What was supposed to be a day of celebration and honoring the dead has become a time to use our magic to defend ourselves and our community."

Richard was the first to speak. "We've all read each chapter of the book of witchcraft that each of us has written in. What is it that we need to do?"

"Yes," Mary said, "What is it that we are to do?"

I took a deep breath. I told them everything that the witch ancestors had told me last night when I had summoned them. Ira Couch needed to be stopped.

James looked gravely concerned. "We've learned a lot of magic, yes, but how do we stop him?"

"By joining our magic together," I said. "By taking everything we have learned and connecting to each other. We must share our magic with each other."

David looked nervous. I could tell he had his doubts. "Is it really up to us? Each of us has had to deal with a spirit who was…evil. I think we are making things much worse. Isn't there another coven who can do this?"

"My roommate is dead," Linda said. "An innocent man is in jail because Margaret, our own coven member, possessed him because she chose to become a vampire." She began to tear up. "People are dead, and spirits are out to get us. We are not ready."

I understood the coven's concerns, but the spirits summoned us for a reason. "If we do not fight Ira Couch and the Shadow Man, then who will? The spirits guided us on this path. It must be us. Whatever Ira Couch is planning, it's going to happen tonight. If we do not do everything we can, all will be lost."

"I think this is all my fault," Sandy said. "I was the one who released the Shadow Man. I was the one who fell for Ira Couch's trap."

Poor Sandy. It was not her fault. Any one of us could have released the Shadow Man.

I needed to reassure her that it was not her fault at all. "Oh, Sandy. No. It's not your fault. You and Kenneth may have released the spirit, but I think the release of the spirit was something that had to happen. It is not your fault."

"From reading all of your entries in the book of witchcraft," Kenneth said, "it's clear that we have each learned more about magic and the spirits. Patricia is right. It's up to us."

I could see that what Kenneth was saying was reassuring the coven. I can always count on Kenneth to rally the troops when they are struggling with something.

Mary sat up in her chair. "Okay, so what do we need to do?"

"Let's meet at sundown. Then we will all go to the Congress Hotel together," I said. I have a plan.

James looked around the circle. He could see everyone's doubts and concerns. "Well, let's hope it's a good plan."

Before everyone left my apartment, I gave each coven member a bag that contained a ritual tool for Halloween that we would need tonight. Hopefully, this tool would help us manifest the power we needed to stop Ira Couch and the Shadow Man.

As the sun was setting, people began coming out of their homes to take their children trick-or-treating. Halloween night was upon us, and there was much excitement in the air. I could feel the energies of Samhain all around me. The children were especially excited because this was the first time since before the war that trick-or-treating was happening. Tonight would be very special for many of the children. Adults, too, I would think.

Before I met the coven for our work tonight, I needed to do something important. There is a special magical tree in Chicago that I call "the Faery Tree."

This is a magical place. This tree is one of the nearby forest areas. One of the reasons I love Chicago so much is that along with the metropolitan city are nearby wooded areas. These are great for a witch who wants a quick journey to a wooded area to do witchcraft and speak with the spirits.

The Faery Tree is in one of these magical wooded areas. The Faery Tree is not hidden or kept secret. It's in plain sight.

People might pass by this tree from time to time and never know what it's for. A witch can easily find this magical tree. It doesn't look like any of the others.

It grows differently from the rest, and it's a bit gnarled. In spring, its leaves seem to bloom greener than others. This tree is a portal to the Otherworld.

SPELL OF THE FAERY TREE

Items Needed:

◆ A tree that is magical

1. This spell creates a portal into the Otherworld, a place of witches, faeries, elves, and other magical beings.

2. Find a tree that feels magical to you. It can be in a wooded area, a park, or your own yard. It does not have to be any certain kind of tree. The most important thing is that it feels magical to you.

3. Close your eyes and take a few deep breaths. Place yourself into a light trance.

4. Place your hands upon the tree. Open your heart and have a deep longing to be in the Otherworld. Think about the spirits who dwell in the Otherworld. Allow your mind to paint a picture of how the Otherworld will look.

5. Take a few more deep breaths. Connect your energies to the energies of the tree. Connect your energies to the roots and feel the energies of the below world. Connect your energies to the branches and feel the energies of the above world.

6. Know with all of your beings that this tree is a doorway into the Otherworld.

7. Once you are connected to the energies of the tree, visualize it turning clockwise. See how the tree rotates you from the physical world to the Otherworld.

8. You are now astral projecting to the Otherworld. You can visualize yourself letting go of the tree and exploring the Otherworld. You can meet faeries, elves, and other witches who are in the Otherworld. Remember to be polite to any spirit that you meet here.

9. When you are ready to return to the physical plane, return to the tree and place your hands upon it once again. Visualize the tree turning counter-clockwise. See it rotate from the Otherworld to the physical world.

10. Leave offerings for any of the spirits that you spoke with.

The Spell of the Faery Tree took me into the Otherworld. I wasn't here to see faeries or elves tonight. I needed to see a witch, a very particular witch, who could not help but be "un-particular." The Otherworld seemed dark and shadowy tonight. I could see that the spirits of the Otherworld were prepared for Samhain. The doors between the worlds were open. It would be difficult to distinguish between the physical world and the Otherworld. There was a spirit wind that was blowing the branches of the trees. The leaves seemed to dance in the wind. Maybe dancing was not the right word. They were almost singing.

Out of the shadows from behind the Faery Tree stepped Johnathan Knotbristle, my old teacher from Texas. "A good Samhain tide to you!" he said.

"A good Samhain tide to you as well," I said. I was so glad to see him. Johnathan was my teacher who taught me everything I needed to know about witchcraft. I studied with him for many years. Then I moved to Chicago. I miss him and have thought of him often throughout the years.

When I met Johnathan, he was in his 60s. Even back then, as old as he was, he still traveled on his little horse-pulled wagon and visited witches throughout the area in Texas. He was magister of the south of Texas, after all. He has a charm to him that you cannot find anywhere else. He is truly a kind and unique man. Now he is in his 90s and not as spry as he used to be. He no longer travels throughout the land teaching witchcraft. He says that he's too old to be going here and there, and if someone wanted to learn witchcraft, then they needed to come to him. In his later years, he's become a bit ornery. He put up a hand-painted sign above his front door that says, "A Witch Lives Here. I'm Old, Knock Loudly." He no longer cares what the town folk say, and he simply lives his life how he wants to.

It was good to see my teacher and friend. "Johnathan, how have you been?"

"As good as old gets, I 'spose," Johnathan said.

"How's your health?" I asked. Johnathan is a powerful witch and healer but he never grasped the idea of taking care of himself. Before I left for Chicago, I made some of the local witches promise to check in on him from time to time.

"I'm as healthy as any man half ma'age," he said. "You ain't be need'n to worry about that!"

Johnathan always had a way of making me smile. "Johnathan, I called you here tonight because I need your help."

"I been see'n what's been go'n on," he said. "Been peak'n in ma'cauldron and been see'n all kinds of bullshit here in Chicago. I been see'n what ya'll call'n 'the Shadow Man.' I'll tell ya, ya'll got ya'll's work cut out for ya t'night."

I needed a big favor from him. I've never asked Johnathan for anything. My pride, I guess. Tonight is too important for pride. I needed his help.

"Johnathan, can you help us? Can you send magic to us so we can stop Ira Couch and the Shadow Man?"

Johnathan didn't say anything for a while. I could see he was in his thoughts. I also knew him well enough to know that he had something to say.

"I wish I could, Patricia. I really do. But you need to be known'n that this is your coven's fight. I can't be get'n involved any. I got me my own troubles to deal with t'night. Got me some real big spirits out there, too."

Shit. I really could use his help. A part of me wondered if he was teaching me something with this. A kind of "you are a coven leader, so clean up your own problems." Maybe. My experience of Johnathan is that if that were the case, he would just come out and say it. I understood, though. He was a nintey-something-year-old witch, and his strength wasn't what it used to be.

"I understand, Johnathan."

Johnathan felt something. He turned his head slightly so he could focus on the psychic impressions he was feeling. "I got to go, Patricia. Someth'n big is come'n ta'old south Texas. I gotta get it gone!"

I smiled at my dear old teacher. "Be well, my friend."

"Good luck, Patricia." Johnathan faded from view. "Get it gone!"

Johnathan was gone, and I was alone with the Faery Tree in the Otherworld. I took a deep breath, centered, and grounded myself. "Time to get it gone…"

The Congress Hotel…

The coven all met at a nearby diner that was only a few blocks away from the Congress Hotel. The sun had set, and the magic of Halloween was afoot. The Chicago streets were filled with people going to Halloween parties and bars and parents taking their children trick-or-treating. Many people were dressed in costumes, not just the children. There would be many parties, much drinking, and other shenanigans happening tonight. This was a good night to battle the Shadow Man. This was the one night of the year that wearing our ritual robes and looking like a witch would be overlooked.

We sat in a large booth in the diner. Each of us brought the bags that I had given everyone. At the same time, we opened our bags and took out the Halloween gift I had placed in each. The sacred tool that would be needed for tonight. Masks of the gods. I designed and enchanted each mask to be able to invoke the powers of the gods.

Mary received the mask of Eris.
Linda received the mask of Cerridwen.
Sandy received the mask of Artemis.
James received the mask of Thor.
Richard received the mask of Odin.
David received the mask of Horus.
Kenneth received the mask of Hades.
…and I received the mask of Hecate.

THE SPELL OF THE GOD MASKS

Items Needed:
- A mask of your choice
- A candle dedicated to the god of your choice
- Incense favored by the god
- Essential oil favored by the god
- Offerings to the god

1. This spell is to imbue the mask with the energies and essences of the god of your choice. When the mask is worn by the witch, you will be able to invoke the power, wisdom, and magic of the god.

2. The mask may be simple or designed to resemble the god of your choosing.

3. Place the mask on the table or altar. Light a candle that is specifically dedicated to the god that you wish to enchant the mask. You may use your own words or say: *"I call upon (god's name). I ask that you imbue your powers upon this sacred mask."*

4. Light the incense that is dedicated to the god and say: *"(God's name), please accept this offering of incense. May the sweet smell please you."*

5. Hold the god mask in your hands. Have a deep longing to connect to the god. Close your eyes. Take a deep breath and visualize your astral body journeying to the home of the god.

6. When you are in the presence of the god, ask them to imbue their godly powers into the mask. Explain to them that when you put on the mask and call their name, you wish to invoke them into your body. Once inside your body, you wish to have access to their wisdom, power, and magic.

7. If the god agrees to this, astrally return to your body. Maintain your connection to the god. Take a deep breath, and on the inhale, visualize the god sending its divine energy into the mask. Once you feel the mask has the power of the god, take the essential oil and anoint the brow of the mask. This will seal the energy in the mask.

8. If the god says no, you must find another god that will agree to this magic.

9. When you are ready to invoke the god, place the mask over your face and call to the god. As you call to the god, visualize them coming into your body and joining with your mind, your heart, and your physical body.

10. When finished, thank them for their magic and remove the mask. When the mask is removed, the god will leave your body.

11. Leave offerings for the god.

We arrived at the Congress Hotel. There was a large sign in the lobby that said:

HALLOWEEN GALA
MASQUERADE BALL
GOLD ROOM

This is where we needed to be. The Gold Room was one of the ballrooms on the second floor. My senses told me that this gala is where Ira Couch will release the Shadow Man.

We entered the ballroom, and everyone was wearing their finest clothes. They all also wore their finely decorated masquerade masks. The masks were beautiful. Some had jewels and beads, while others had strings of ornaments hanging from them. Some masks had bands that went around the head. Other masks were held to the face by a stick.

The Gold Room was adorned with the most elegant of Halloween decorations. Somehow, the decorators turned a day of ghosts and goblins into an extravagant delight for the rich.

The band came out on a little stage. It was the Ink Spots. They began to play their song "It's All Over but the Crying." The haunting melody caused everyone to get up from their seats and dance.

A voice came over the microphone. "Ladies and Gentlemen, welcome to the Congress Hotel Halloween Gala." It was Ira Couch. "We hope you will enjoy yourselves. Happy Halloween!"

It was time to put this to an end. I said to the coven, "Let's spread out. We need to be ready for anything."

The coven disbursed into the crowd.

Once in the crowd, Mary felt someone grab her arm. It was Scratch from the Oriental Theater. "Ever dance with the Devil?"

"You!" Mary wondered what Scratch was up to. "Let me go."

"One dance, my dear," Scratch said. "Then it will all be over."

Mary tried to pull away, but Scratch had incredible strength. He pulled her close to his chest, and they danced a dark dance.

Scratch pulled her closer and whispered in her ear, "Happy Halloween."

Mary felt a darkness from within the crowd. The lights dimmed, and there were shadows everywhere. The shadows danced and then came together. The Shadow Man.

David saw Mary with Scratch and tried to make his way through the dancing crowd to help her, but before he got to her, the crowd parted, and there stood Mr. Talbott.

David was taken off guard. This was a man he thought he could love one day, but he revealed himself to be a devil. Mr. Talbott put his arm around David's waist, pulling him close. "You didn't forget about me, did you, David?"

"I'm not surprised that you are part of this," David said. He admitted to himself that he didn't know if he was happy to see him or if he was disgusted. "Let me go, or people will see us together."

Mr. Talbott dipped David down and then back up again. He whispered into his ear, "Let them look. They'll be dead soon anyway."

The ballroom became more crowded. More and more masked people drifted into the Gold Room to celebrate Halloween. Sandy lost her nerve. She wanted to leave but knew she couldn't abandon us. She looked for me. She looked for any sign of where I might be, but she couldn't see me through the dense crowd. The partiers danced and swayed and swirled to the music of the Ink Spot. Then, a masked man slipped himself into Mary's arms. He twirled her around and pulled her close to him. She began to lose all sense of herself. She was falling under a spell. Her mind began swirling as if she had been drugged. The man was masked, so she could not see his face. She managed to focus enough to look into his eyes. Ira Couch.

Sandy wanted to pull away, but she was falling deeper and deeper into his trance.

"It's no use," Ira said. "You are mine now…just like Margaret."

A spotlight turned on, shining on a couple in the middle of the dance floor. Two people danced and danced. It was Margaret and Dr. Dyer, the vampire. Their dance seemed to mock us. They laughed and danced. They knew all of us in the coven could see them. They wanted us to see them dancing together. They danced and swirled through the crowd. The crowd was under their spell as well. The magic that they were conjuring with their dance was powerful. They danced and swirled some more. They both swirled at the same time, and each of them turned into the crowd. Margaret turned into Kenneth and began dancing, and Dr. Dyer turned into Linda and began dancing. Kenneth and Linda couldn't help but dance with them. Their magic was too strong.

James saw Kenneth and Linda dancing with the vampires and rushed through the crowd to help them. Beth Willows, the spirit from the Green Mill, appeared before him. She began dancing with him, too.

"Don't go trying to stop him," Beth said. "It's not your time to die."

James was happy to see her, but he desperately wanted to help his friends. "I have to. I can't let them die."

"Then you will die with them," Beth said. "Don't go. Dance with me."

James wanted nothing more but to see Beth one more time. They danced and swirled together.

Kenneth felt himself falling deeper and deeper into Margaret's spell. He knew that vampires had the ability to fascinate someone and take control of them. "Margaret, come back to us. Come back to the coven."

Kenneth and Margaret danced and danced. Margaret reached into his mind. She wanted to possess him like she possessed that poor man. "Your witchcraft is weak. Vampire magic, now that's some powerful shit."

Kenneth and Margaret danced and danced.

Margaret spun Kenneth around. "Ever feel the power flowing through you as someone bled to death?"

"Margaret…" Kenneth was losing himself in the dance. All he could do was dance. He searched the dance floor for Linda. He couldn't see her. But then he saw Dr. Dyer kissing her. Linda was under his fascination. She was his.

As everyone danced, I could see that they were in trouble. I could help them, but the Shadow Man gathered himself from the dancing shadows. I had to trust that my coven could take care of each other. I had to focus on why we were here. The cloaked figure with long, thin arms took shape. I watched him as he looked around the room at all the people. No, not at the people dancing, but their shadows. He was attached to their shadows. I sent a beam of my sphere of sensation to him. I had to find out what the Shadow Man was doing. The beam of energy I sent from my sphere of sensation told me that the Shadow Man was using their shadows to tap into their subconscious. By attaching to their secret fears and desires, he could control them.

I suddenly felt an energy shift in the ballroom. It felt as if an enormous spiritual portal had opened up a door to the spirit world. No, that wasn't right. The ballroom *was* the portal into the spirit world. I felt them appear. I looked around the ballroom, and the spirits of the hotel appeared in visible form. Standing off to the side of the dance floor was a woman and her husband drinking tea. Then, the mother appeared, who had jumped out of the hotel window with her two young boys. Many more spirits appeared.

I quickly pushed through the crowd to get to the Shadow Man. I pushed and elbowed my way through. The crowd didn't seem to notice me at all. They danced and danced and twirled. They were under the spell of Ira Couch and the Shadow Man. I was just about to reach the dark spirit when Ira Couch pulled me back and began dancing with me.

"Can I tell you a secret?" Ira had a smug look on his face. "I don't give a fuck about these people. They are simply an energy source."

"An energy source for what?" I knew that whatever his plan was, it was evil.

Ira placed his index finger over my third eye, "Look…"

Ira placed a vision in my head. In the vision, the Shadow Man used his attachment to the crowd to drain their life force and gather power for himself. The power of life, of human life force, was then directed by Ira Couch to the Chicago River. There rested the spirits of the Eastland ship disaster. On July 24, 1915, the SS Eastland was chartered to take employees from the Western Electric Company on a picnic in Indiana. Because of the recent tragedy of the Titanic, extra lifeboats were ordered to be placed on top of the Eastland. The ship became top-heavy and unstable. As a result, the Eastland toppled over and trapped people below deck. Eight hundred forty-four people lost their lives that day.

It was Ira's plan to send human life force to the Eastland spirits and give them energy, resurrecting them from the river. Along with the backward flow of the river, which caused a backward energy surge, the spirits of the Eastland would help Ira create a permanent portal from the spirit world to the physical world. This would create a hell world on earth. A world where the physical world was no more and would be overrun with the dead.

"You see, dear Patricia, it is a marvelous plan," Ira said. "I just had to wait for the right witch to set me and the Shadow Man free."

I could feel myself falling deeper into a trance. Ira was using his fascination to take control of my senses. No. This would not be so. I quickly brought my awareness to my heart. This is where my witchcraft lies. This is who I am. I am Patricia Glasspool, magister of the Lincoln Park Coven. I will not be defeated!

I summoned the power of self from my heart, and I shot a powerful magical beam of light through my arms and into my hands. I shot the beam to Ira's heart and shouted, *"NO!"*

Ira fell back on the dance floor.

I pushed my way through the people as fast as I could to the Shadow Man.

"You are not going anywhere!" Margaret pushed me hard to the ground. Damn, her vampire strength was overpowering.

"Margaret, stop this nonsense," I pleaded with her. "Come back to us. Come back to the coven."

Margaret laughed. "You are such a stupid bitch. Do you really think that I would fall for that? Convince me to give up my vampire ways so that you will win? It's too late for me. You would never welcome me back."

"Margaret…"

Margaret punched me hard in the face. My nose was bleeding. She took her finger and wiped the blood off my face. She put her finger in her mouth to show her dominance over me.

As everyone danced, they began to slowly lose consciousness. Their life force was being drained by the Shadow Man. The dark being was filling up with power. So much power. Ira got himself off the floor. He flew off the ground and hovered over the Shadow Man. Ira summoned the life force from the Shadow Man into himself and then sent it to the Chicago River. In my mind, I saw the energy going into the river. Then, slowly, the 844 spirits of the Eastland accident rose from their watery graves. They walked the streets of Chicago on Halloween night.

THE SPELL OF ASTRAL CONNECTION

Items Needed: No items needed.

1. This spell is to link yourself to another person or your magical group in the astral realm.

2. Close your eyes and bring your awareness to your heart and your third eye.

3. Call out to the person or people you wish to connect with in the astral with your heart. Say their names out loud.

4. Visualize yourself with the person or persons in a safe astral temple, grove, or other setting that is protected from outside spirits or influences.

5. In your mind, speak with them with your astral senses.

6. When you are ready, disconnect from them and return to your everyday awareness.

I could feel that all members of our coven were disconnected. I closed my eyes and called out to them in the astral. Our connection has always been strong, so I knew it wouldn't be too difficult to summon them. In the astral, we were all standing in a circle. We held hands.

I took a breath and summoned power from the goddess Hecate into my body. I exhaled and sent the energy of the mother goddess into everyone in the coven. The energy of Hecate, our patron mother, bolted through our hands and into our hearts, bringing everyone back to themselves. We then reconnected as the Lincoln Park Coven.

The spirits and devils who were dancing with everyone in the coven no longer had power over us. We all woke up from our trance. We were ourselves again. We remembered who we were. Powerful witches!

We all placed our masks over our faces.

Mary put her mask on and called to the goddess. "I invoke you, Eris, Goddess of Chaos."

Linda put her mask on and called to the goddess. "I invoke you, Cerridwen, Sacred Crone, shapeshifter."

Sandy put her mask on and called to the goddess. "I invoke you, Artemis, Goddess of the Wild Hunt."

James put his mask on and called to the god. "I invoke you, Thor, God of Justice."

Richard put his mask on and called to the god. "I invoke you, Odin, trickster, Shaman of the Runes."

David put his mask on and called the god. "I invoke you, Horus, warrior God of the Sun."

Kenneth put his mask on and called the god. "I invoke you, Hades, God of the Dead."

...and I put on my mask and called the goddess of our coven. "I invoke you, Hecate, Mother of Witchcraft."

The power of the gods flowed through us. We could see with their eyes, hear with their ears, and speak with their voices. We had just enough of the power of the gods to use their abilities while maintaining control of ourselves. We needed to use our human faculties to stop Ira Couch.

Mary felt the surge of the goddess Eris flowing through her. Eris is the goddess of chaos who often causes havoc with the other Olympian gods. She released herself from Scratch's grip. In her hands, she held a golden apple.

Scratch could see the power of the goddess through Mary.

"You understand, I was only trying to help you and the spirits in the theater. They needed your help," he said.

Mary was no longer interested in what Scratch had to say. "And now you are here bringing the phantom world to Earth. It was part of your plan. Get me to use my magic so you can connect with me. So you can get into my mind easier."

Scratch said, "Your magic can control the phantoms. Leave the ancestors to the afterlife and live in a world of phantoms with us."

Mary took the apple in both hands. She blew on the golden apple, and its energy was forced into Scratch's heart. His astral body disintegrated, and he disappeared.

David knew that Mr. Talbott no longer had power over him, but he didn't want to stop dancing with him. This was the famed Devil of Hull House. Mr. Talbott seemed human enough to him. David wondered how he was caught up in all this. He hoped there was a good reason Mr. Talbott was here, but he knew in his heart that whatever the reason was, it was diabolical. "I could have loved you."

Mr. Talbott placed his cheek against David's cheek. They danced, but David knew it was a dance of endings. A dance to end dances.

"By the power of Horus," David conjured the power of the hawk-headed god, "by the power of the sacred sun—"

Mr. Talbot backed away from David. "If you love me, you won't hurt me…"

"—I conjure the spear of light." David knew what he had to do but didn't want to harm Mr. Talbott. He knew he had to protect the coven. "May the spear of the gods strike you down!"

David sent a solar energy blast into Mr. Talbott. He fell to the ground. He didn't disappear like a spirit would. So he *was* flesh and blood, after all. "Your powers are stripped from you. By the powers of Horus, you are stripped of your magic!"

Linda became aware that Dr. Dyer was draining her of her life force. She could feel herself leaving her body, her spirit sinking deeper and deeper into him. She hated him and was drawn to him at the same time. She called out to the goddess Cerridwen. "Mother goddess, crone, shapeshifter, help me."

The power of the crone filled her body. She was connected to the astral realm. The astral realm was fluid, commanded by the planets and stars and by the power of the gods.

Linda astrally shapeshifted into a lion. Filled with the power of the sun, Linda knew that solar power weakened vampires. She let out a roar! The energy of her growl disconnected Dr. Dyer's attachment to her. He was no longer a frightening vampire, he was a parasite that needed to be destroyed.

Dr. Dyer became angry that his power over Linda was lost. "You fucking—"

Linda took her astral claws and swiped at him, leaving a bloody scratch on his face. She roared again. She jumped on him, pushing him down to the ground. With her lion claws, she ripped out his heart. The vampire, Dr. Dyer, vanished into nothing.

Margaret flew out of the crowd of dancers and knocked Kenneth to the ground. She punched and scratched him as hard as she could. His mask of Hades had fallen off his head, and someone kicked it deeper into the crowd of dancing people. Kenneth, on his hands and knees, went after it. Margaret grabbed his legs and pulled him away. With her great strength pulling him, he slid further away from the mask. She jumped on top of him. Straddling him, she took a deep breath and pulled his life force out of his body.

Kenneth felt himself becoming weaker. He could feel himself coming closer and closer to death. His life was fading.

"You cannot give up…" A strange voice said in his mind. "You must fight to stay alive." The Silence. The Silence from Graceland Cemetery was reaching out from the graveyard to help Kenneth.

Kenneth could feel the presence of the Silence, the helpful spirit from the Eternal Silence statue. "Fight!"

Kenneth gathered what little strength he had left. He managed to knock Margaret off of him and leaped toward the mask of Hades. He quickly put it on him and simply said, "Hades…"

The power of the Lord of the Dead poured into his body. Kenneth now had control over the dead. He got to his feet and was ready for Margaret. He used his hands and pushed the powerful magic of the Underworld at her, causing her to fall to the ground. "Margaret, had you studied more witchcraft, you would have known that vampires steal life force because it feeds the part of them that is dead. And now I control the dead!"

Kenneth used his power to bind Margaret. She could no longer harm anyone. He then summoned several spirits of the dead to bind her. The spirit of the dead took her voice, her sight, and her mind. She would harm no one else.

James saw that the coven was taking back their power and destroying the dark spirits that wanted to kill us. He kissed Beth one last time. "I have to go…" he said sadly.

Beth faded away into the spirit world.

The Shadow Man was still draining the life force of the dancers and feeding them to Ira Couch. I could see in my visions the spirits of the Eastland roaming the Chicago streets were becoming even more powerful. The life force of the dancers fed them even more power to influence the Earth plane. I sent out a telepathic message to the coven. *It's time!*

By virtue of his mask, Richard wielded the power of Odin. Odin is the father of the Nordic gods and the keeper of the sacred runes of magic. The runes hold all the mysteries of the Universe: life, death, and rebirth. There is no magic that the runes do not contain. Richard used the power of Odin to send the runes to the Shadow Man. The runes contained the power of the Universe itself. The runes surrounded the Shadow Man, creating a magical circle around him that prevented him from moving. The Shadow Man could no longer harm anyone.

Sandy had the power of Artemis, the goddess of the hunt and the moon. She summoned an astral bow and arrow. She drew the arrow back and invoked the power of the goddess and the Moon. Sandy released the arrow, and it shot directly into the heart of the Shadow Man. The dark spirit fell and was powerless.

"Open up a portal to the abyss," James said. James summoned the power of Thor, who held the sacred hammer *Mjolnir*.

Kenneth used his power of the Underworld to open up a portal that led to the Abyss, a void in the Universe where dark spirits were often found. When the portal opened, we could all hear great winds of power and the sounds of creatures I cannot begin to describe.

James took the hammer of Thor and swung it as hard as he could, throwing the Shadow Man deep into the Abyss. Kenneth sealed the portal so that nothing could escape back into our world.

The Shadow Man was gone forever. Ira Couch knew that he did not have the power to defeat us. Over the past few months, he had led the coven to various hauntings across Chicago. Ira had tricked some of us into inadvertently releasing spirits. These spirits would become his allies, and the whole time he was watching us. He was watching so that he might understand our strengths and weaknesses. But Ira is no witch. Ira didn't know that as he was watching us and collecting his army of dark spirits, we were becoming more and more powerful.

Ira tried to vanish and escape, but the hand of Hecate prevented him from doing so. Hecate spoke through me. "You will not escape the mother of lost souls."

"You cannot contain me!" Ira screamed. "I have been here for so long. Chicago will wither away without me!"

Hecate kept the balance of the realms. She is the great Titan, the keeper of the keys, and the goddess of witchcraft. Ira had caused the spirits of the Eastland disaster to be raised from their grave to walk aimlessly through the city. Things must be put back into balance. In almost all Pagan cosmologies, if the dead roam the Earth freely, then the Universe will be thrown off balance, and chaos will reign. Hecate spoke through me. "The balance must be restored."

The Lincoln Park Coven gathered at my side. We formed a circle around Ira Couch. We held hands and connected to each other. We connected as a circle so deeply that a sphere of light formed around us. This sphere contained the spirit of Ira Couch. Then, the witch ancestors appeared around us. The spirits of the witches gave us more power. We had the power of the gods, the witch ancestors, and each other. Hecate left my body and took the spirit of Ira Couch away, off to the afterlife. What his fate is now, I do not know.

With the Shadow Man and Ira Couch gone, the spirits of the Eastland disaster had no more power to sustain them in this world. Hecate, the mother of lost souls, escorted them to the gates of the afterlife, where they were met by their ancestors.

All is well...

Epilogue

⌐ ONE DAY... ¬

October 31, 1984
Day of Luna. Moon in Aquarius.

My name is Stephanie Brenkman. I discovered this book in my mother's attic. She died a few months ago, and I wanted us to go through her old things. There are a few things we want to keep of hers, but most of it, we'll most likely throw away.

I found a box in the very back of the attic. It had some weird things in it: half-burned candles, jars of herbs, little bags filled with who-knows-what, and a mask. Weird.

I read through this book, and I see that it's a book of witchcraft. Was my mother, the queen of oatmeal cookies, a witch? She never talked about it before.

I've read this book cover to cover and...I don't know...I think I'm a witch, too. I found a spell to summon the power of the Devil and...guess what! I did it. Maybe I'm crazy, maybe I'm making things up, but I was initiated by the Devil to become a witch!

I can't wait to cast the spells in this book.

Tonight is Halloween, and the spirits of the dead will be out tonight. I'll write what happens in this book. After all, it's mine now. No one knows I have it. Now that I think about it, I remember when I was very young, someone came to our house and handed my mother a book. Was it this book?

Oh my God! I remember what the person said to my mother when they gave her the book. They said, "Keep it safe until we need it again."

November 1, 1984
Day of Mars. Moon in Aquarius.

Last night, after I called the spirits of the dead, there was a knock on the door. Three people shrouded in black cloaks were at the door. I should have been frightened, but I wasn't. I was now a witch, and I think they were, too. I invited them in. I made coffee and brought out chocolate chip cookies. Apparently, witches don't eat babies. We like our coffee and cookies. My little joke.

As we sat eating the cookies, they told me that the Devil had come to them and said that they needed to find me. They said I was the last of the Lincoln Park Coven. I wasn't initiated into a coven, but maybe because I'm the blood of my mother, I belong to the coven somehow. I was hoping they were here to teach me witchcraft, but they said they were here for a very important reason. The reason the Devil sent them to me is because...

...the darkness is coming, and I have to be ready...

BIBLIOGRAPHY

"11 of Chicago's Most Haunted Places." *Choose Chicago*, Sept. 21, 2022, www.choosechicago.com/blog/tours-attractions/chicago-most-haunted-places/. Accessed 27 Dec. 2023.

Alexander, Kathy. "H.H. Holmes and the Murder Castle of Chicago." *Legends of America*, Oct. 2023, www.legendsofamerica.com/h-h-holmes/. Accessed 27 Dec. 2023.

Allaun, Chris. *The Black Book of Johnathan Knotbristle: A Devil's Parable and Guide for Witches*. Crossed Crow Books, 2023.

Bielski, Ursula. "The King of Haunted Chicago: Ghosts of the Congress Plaza Hotel." *American Ghost Walks*, www.americanghostwalks.com/articles/the-king-of-haunted-chicago-ghosts-of-the-congress. Accessed 27 Dec. 2023.

DeGrechie, Eric. "Ghosts Of Graceland: Chicago Cemetery Filled With Haunting Tales." *Patch,* 15 Oct. 2020, patch.com/illinois/chicago/ghosts-graceland-chicago-cemetery-filled-haunting-tales. Accessed 27 Dec. 2023.

Guy, Fiona. "William Heirens: The 1946 Lipstick Killer." *Crime Traveler,* July 12, 2015, www.crimetraveller.org/2015/07/william-heirens-the-lipstick-killer/. Accessed 27 Dec. 2023.

Harrington, Adam. "Chicago Hauntings: The Congress Hotel, The Home Of Presidents…And Ghosts." *CBS News,* November 1, 2021, www.cbsnews.com/chicago/news/chicago-hauntings-the-congress-hotel/. Accessed 27 Dec. 2023.

_. "Chicago Hauntings: The Mysteries Of The Couch Mausoleum In Lincoln Park And Who, If Anyone, Is Entombed There." *CBS News,* October 27, 2021, www.cbsnews.com/chicago/news/chicago-hauntings-the-mysteries-of-the-couch-mausoleum-in-lincoln-park-and-who-if-anyone-is-entombed-there/. Accessed 27 Dec. 2023.

Lindberg, Richard. *Return to the Scene of the Crime: A Guide to Infamous Places in Chicago*. Cumberland House Publishing, 1999.

Maragha, Nadia. "'Finding Folklore': Jane Addams and Hull-House's Supernatural History." *Jane Addams Hull-House Museum,* September

19, 2022, www.hullhousemuseum.org/hullhouse-blog/2022/9/14/findingfolklore. Accessed 27 Dec. 2023.

Ogden, Tom. *Haunted Chicago: Famous Phantoms, Sinister Sites, and Lingering Legends.* Globe Pequot Press, 2014.

"Room 411—Chicago's Most Haunted?" *Demented Mitten Tours,* dementedmittentours.com/blog/room-441-chicagos-most-haunted/. Accessed 27 Dec. 2023.

Seltzer, Adam. *Mysterious Chicago: History At Its Coolest.* Skyhorse Publishing, 2016.

_. "The Strange History of 'Eternal Silence,' Graceland's 'Statue of Death.'" *Mysterious Chicago,* Dec. 10, 2015, mysteriouschicago.com/the-strange-history-of-eternal-silence-gracelands-statue-of-death/. Accessed 27 Dec. 2023.

_. "Vampirism in Chicago." *Mysterious Chicago,* October 18, 2012, mysteriouschicago.com/vampirism-in-chicago/. Accessed 27 Dec. 2023.

Sisson, Patrick. "An Oral History of the Green Mill." *Reader,* Mar. 20, 2014, chicagoreader.com/music/an-oral-history-of-the-green-mill/. Accessed 27 Dec. 2023.

Stranahan, Susan Q. "The Eastland Disaster Killed More Passengers Than the Titanic and the Lusitania. Why Has it Been Forgotten?" *Smithsonian Magazine,* Oct. 24, 2014, www.smithsonianmag.com/history/eastland-disaster-killed-more-passengers-titanic-and-lusitania-why-has-it-been-forgotten-180953146/. Accessed 27 Dec. 2023.

Uenuma, Francine. "The Iroquois Theater Disaster Killed Hundreds and Changed Fire Safety Forever." *Smithsonian Magazine,* Jun. 12, 2018, www.smithsonianmag.com/history/how-theater-blaze-killed-hundreds-forever-changed-way-we-approach-fire-safety-180969315/. Accessed 27 Dec. 2023.